A Hunter's Moon:
Winged Guardians

A HUNTER'S MOON:

WINGED GUARDIANS

ALEXIS D. CRAIG

Book Cover Design by Rebecca Poole of Dreams2Media
Edited by

First Edition
First Edition: April 2020
ASIN: B084NYL745
ISBN: 978-1-7339018-9-5

Published by
Three Fortnights Press
P. O. Box 168401
Irving, TX 75016
Submissions.34Press@gmail.com

For Crowe, for reasons.

"Absence doth sharpen love, presence strengthens it; the one brings fuel, the other blows it till it burns clear."

- Sir Thomas Overbury

TABLE OF CONTENTS

SPOTIFY PLAYLIST

Alexis is an avid music lover and has curated a playlist to accompany your reading of *A Hunter's Moon.*

You can listen at https://tinyurl.com/A-Hunters-Moon-Spotify and immerse yourself in the world she's created.

WINGED GUARDIANS

Prologue

VASILY-*then*

Nobody went to Moe's for the food. It certainly wasn't as flashy as some of the in-town options, no dance music or strippers, just a bar. With a worn-out jukebox and windows stained yellow and almost opaque from nicotine, it was a postcard from the edge of the world, a tiny speck of normal life he allowed himself off base, off duty, and away from the real world. Cold beer, some darts, maybe a baseball game on the big TV mounted to the wall. He wasn't Gunnery Sergeant Bretcu here. Here he was just Vasi, as the waitresses called him.

Well, one waitress in particular, with her smooth dark skin, long, long legs, and sexy riot of curls the color of fine whiskey. In a sleeveless shirt knotted under a rack so spectacular it deserved a shrine and miniskirt brief enough to constitute a pause, Cherry Belmont had the eye of every single Marine and sailor in the joint, and she knew it. Sexy bit of sass, something about her drew him in, more than her looks.

Maybe it was the offhand conversations she'd have dropping off beers at his table, or the way she'd pause when the Mariners were on to catch an inning or two with him. One night close to closing, he found himself learning about the sexy waitress, whose daytime disguise was being a girl from Anchorage getting her journalism degree from Pepperdine.

It was a long way from Anchorage to the Stumps, and while nowhere near as long, Twentynine Palms, California, was a far cry from the Ivy League in Malibu.

The eponymous Moe was Morris 'Moe' Garza, the owner of the bar and father of Cherry's college roommate and bestie, Pacey. He was a short man with a boxer's build that had gone to seed, whose short order cooking skills ran to 'burnt and crispy'. He was also the man who loved his little girl so much he gave her a job and one for her college roommate whose scholarship paid for school, books, and food, but not a trip back home for the summer and back.

What started as an occasional dip into the bar outside the base gates became a regular situation, with him showing up off duty and casually making time with the most beautiful woman in the world. And considering they were just outside LA, that was saying something.

They'd met in the summer between her junior and senior years, where she was branching out into the world and he was out doing his best to save it. She didn't ask much about what he did. The haircut and the Jeep he drove gave it away, according to her. She also said she didn't date Marines, but maybe she'd make an exception kissing him senseless one night long after closing when he drove her back to her little apartment she'd shared with Pacey on the other side of town.

The first time he'd held her in his arms, he knew. Her lips were soft, perfect, and the sounds she made... gods, they haunted his dreams for weeks afterward. He didn't know it then, but she'd owned his heart from that moment on, given without reservation and, as he was occasionally reminded, foolishly. Eagle-owls mated for life, and he happened to be mated to a wolverine from Anchorage.

It wasn't something he planned, for damn sure. But the fall

was hard, fast, and well beyond anything he'd seen coming. Some tactician he was.

Summer bled quickly into autumn, and he found himself spending a good deal of his time off duty either in Malibu or texting with her when either his job or her schooling intervened. It wasn't quite a long-distance relationship, but they made it work. At least, until her graduation.

"It's a good job, Sweets. Exactly what you wanted." His soft words were almost drowned out by the ocean below them as they sat in the open Jeep watching the fade of red to purple overtake the sky at sunset. "You should take it."

Cherry took his hand, forcing him to look at her. Her dark eyes were glittering in the gathering twilight, unshed tears collecting in her lashes. "I don't want to leave you."

"And I don't want you to go," he admitted with a shrug before disengaging his hand from hers. The job in question was a gig at the *Savannah Morning News*. It wasn't glamorous, but it was a place to start and he couldn't let her pass that up. "But you can't put your life on hold for me."

"That's not what this is," she protested, her tone sharp, defensive.

"That's *exactly* what this is." Staring out at the ocean, he raked his upper lip with his teeth as he chose his words. "I could be gone tomorrow. Hell, I *will* be gone tomorrow, for god knows how long, and you're left here with what? Hope that I'll come back? That's not the life I want for you. And you shouldn't want that for yourself."

"You don't get to make decisions for me, Feathers."

"And more's the pity. You're worth more than waiting for me." He shrugged, his eyes never leaving his lap. Just saying the words hurt and feeling her recoil like he'd slapped her carved slashes into his tender heart. "I can't give you the life you deserve right now. And I will be damned if you settle. You've worked too hard for that."

Her tears as he drove her back to her apartment that night were the memory that he'd live with for the rest of his life. Breaking up before a deployment was, by far, one of his worst ideas at that point, and yet... he knew he was right. He didn't have the right to tell her how to live her life, but he wasn't above maneuvering her that way.

Saying goodbye for the last time ripped at him. Watching his mate walk away, knowing it was likely for the last time... well, in his line of work, he wouldn't have to worry about it too long. The life expectancy wasn't that high, anyway.

CHERRY – *now*

Women went missing in these woods. That part was an undisputed fact since time immemorial. More to the point, shifter women went missing. Which was how she ended up out there in the first place.

Five women in the last year had vanished in and around Black Moon Creek, a tiny speck of a town southeast of Anchorage surrounded by Chugach State Park. The most recent, according to the newspaper, was five days ago when Bernadette Bonilla went to meet a guy she'd only spoken to online and that was the last she'd been seen. Up to this point, the cops hadn't had anything to go on for any of the girls, so Cherry had no problem going to hunt for the latest girl herself.

A reporter for the online investigative media outlet, *Third Eye News*, she was damn good at tracking people and finding those who did not want to be found. In this case, she went to the family and asked some questions. She didn't make promises, but the family appreciated her willingness to help when the cops had seemingly had no leads.

Black Moon Creek was the kind of town where everyone knew everyone a few generations back and were all intermingled in one way or another. An outsider like Bernadette, tall, dark-skinned, and built like a runway model in the off season, she grabbed attention in the city, much less a small town of fewer than a thousand people.

Cherry wheeled her beat-up turtle green Jeep Wrangler onto Eagle River Road. She was thankful the heater worked, even though it was April. Springtime was relative this far north, and only for a few days in, like May or June.

Even though it wasn't exactly in the park, the road was near enough to the glacier and the river that there wasn't a whole lot out this way but impenetrable forest, occasional campgrounds, and maybe a moose or two. Remote would involve more people, and the people she did see out here were, as her dad liked to say, *real serious* about being left alone. People didn't come out here this time of year, and especially not to just get lost.

According to both the map of the park and the young woman's GPS tags, she simply had to follow the road to the Eagle River Nature Center, and she should be there. There hadn't been any snow in the last few days, so that wasn't the reason she'd stayed away, and Cherry knew something was wrong when she parked next to the deep blue Rav4 she'd been looking for with melted snow still on the windshield and around the tires. It hadn't snowed in a couple days and the way powder was built up around the tires, she knew the vehicle hadn't been moved in quite some time.

The radio died as she killed the engine, head down as she pondered her next step. This wasn't an outcome she'd anticipated, and she didn't have a handle on how to proceed. Cherry's instincts said she needed to get into the SUV, though, thus she figured that was as good a place to start as any.

According to her mother, Bernadette kept a spare key hidden inside the back bumper because the last thing you wanted in an Alaskan winter was to be locked out of your ride. Once inside, Cherry found the usual odds and ends in the front, some gum wrappers, a receipt from a gas station not far from her apartment from two weeks ago, and a mostly frozen insulated cup half full of water. The back seat yielded more interesting results. On the passenger side of the back-bench seat, she found a set of clothes, the last set Bernie's family remembered seeing her in, a pink cardigan, white turtleneck, jeans and boots, all folded neatly, with her cell phone hidden underneath wedged between the seat cushions. Basically, everything to indicate that the young woman had come here, shifted into her moose form, and was off in the woods somewhere.

The fact she hadn't returned home yet was especially

worrisome, considering all the things that could happen to a shifter in their animal form, especially in the woods. Hunters weren't terribly particular, and the laws could be quite murky as to what was murder, involuntary homicide, versus merely a hunting accident or an act of poaching. That gray area was why Cherry made up her mind right then and there and stripped out of her clothes.

After stowing her clothes, she looked around the empty parking lot one more time before locking up her car and letting the heat of the shift wash over her. She wasn't flashy like an eagle, or hard to miss like Bernie's moose, but her wolverine was uniquely suited to the terrain with reddish brown fur that blended in nicely with the carpet of dead leaves and pine needles.

Her animal had the advantage of size, much larger than a conventional wolverine, and was capable of taking down larger prey if she wanted to. It had been a long time since she'd really gone out to hunt for things, but fortunately, her family had trained her enough as a child that it was like riding a bike. More or less. Only with fur, and a bite that can break a femur and take down a caribou.

She'd no sooner dropped down to all fours and disappeared into the underbrush than she caught a brief whiff of the trail. Following the faint traces of the young woman's scent through the dense warp and weft of trees, underbrush, and growing shadows of fading daylight, she found herself following the wood line along the river, leading in the direction of some of the larger houses in the area.

The scent was an oddly pungent mix of moose and Burberry Body, which would have been amusing under other circumstances. Bernie was probably the best-smelling moose in history, and considering how funky they generally were, that was saying something. Tenuous tendrils of fragrance moved past her. She judged it at a few days old, but definitely still there, pooling in some places like she stopped to rest before continuing on to... wherever the hell she was.

Cherry stopped, coming up on two legs to look around. Most of the wildlife stayed out of her way, thus the forest in her immediate vicinity was very, very quiet. In the immediate distance, across a clearing on either side of the river that would leave her exposed as she crossed it, was a brightly lit, absolutely enormous multi-story mansion with a wall of windows that looked out over the valley. Since the scent seemed to emanate from that direction, she figured it was as good a lead as any.

With streaks of green and gold blooming in the night sky overhead and reflecting off the river, she felt a chill pass through her as she heard her grandmother's voice in her head reminding her that the streaks of green and gold in the sky were more than just a pretty atmospheric phenomenon, they were an omen of a coming battle.

I'm here to look around. Nothing more, she reminded herself as she neared the outbuilding closest to the house and slipped into the concealing darkness of a shadow. The scent was closer, but more muddled now. So many different scents, it was hard to discern one from another. She was peering in an apparently blacked-out window when she heard the leaves shift beside her and felt a pinch behind her shoulder like a mosquito bite.

Her head whipped around as the stars and night crept in on her. "What the..." The words left her as she slumped to the ground.

The roil of her stomach woke her right before she puked all over the concrete floor. Whatever she'd been dosed with definitely didn't agree with her system. She supposed she should feel lucky she didn't vomit all over herself, but the pain in her stomach was intense and she couldn't focus on much beyond that and the overwhelming stench. All manner of animals, with a tang of human sweat and blood and fear... a fuck lot of fear. Quickly, the acrid stink overcame her again and she retched but nothing came out.

In the darkened room, three things became clear. First, she was chained to the floor by the neck, a hand, and opposite foot. Second, she was, for whatever reason, unable to shift back from her animal form, and third; she was not alone.

She couldn't make out anything visually, but her nose told her there were five other animals in the room besides herself, two moose, a caribou, a Kodiak—Christ almighty—and ... a sheep of some kind? It would be easier if she could call out, but shifted, she was left with her low growls and snarls which, while menacing, weren't much in the way of helpful communication.

There was no way to tell the time of day or how long she'd been down. The room had no windows and was stiflingly warm even as it was otherwise featureless. Cherry pulled her paw up to her mouth, to see if she could bite her way through the restraints and found them to be maddeningly out of reach, forget about trying to get her foot. Her claws dug into the cement, and she figured she may be able to climb out, provided she got free somehow.

Pulling at her neck, she ran the pads of her paws over the collar, finding it to be leather and metal, with some kind of box of "'nope'" attached to it. Tracker, Taser, she had no idea, but that wasn't something she particularly wanted to find out.

The quiet was odd, though. She could hear breathing, deep huffs and occasional whimpers, but there was no other sound to be heard. She'd think a group of animals together, predator and prey, would have a lot more to say to one another. The quiet made the wrenching of heavy, old hinges on a metal door swinging wide and slamming hard against the wall seem that much louder.

The cool breeze carried with it strange smells of leather and industrial cleaners, as well as gunpowder and deer piss. Her concerns about her situation grew by leaps and bounds even as the stifling room smell dissipated slightly.

"Rise and shine, ladies!" It was hard to tell much about the guy, though the voice was high enough she couldn't sign off on that entirely. Plus, he was obscured by all the bright light flooding into the room from the doorway and seemingly dying just inside the room. It was enough for Cherry to see that all the animals were chained to the walls and the floor, leaving a vast space in the middle empty except for the odd stain or tuft of fur.

Chucklefuck Number One, as she decided to call him, was a big white guy, on the heavier side of six feet tall, wearing a heavy, insulated canvas snow suit and boots that had clearly only ever seen mud. His weak chin and encroaching brow ridge spoke of both entitlement and likely inbreeding, while the oily black mop he claimed as hair and wore slicked back to cover his advancing bald spot shrieked of his vanity. He strutted through there with a sneer on his greasy, pasty face, pausing and looking over each animal before turning his nose up with a sniff. Only she and the Kodiak didn't cower away from him, and Cherry figured it was because of the six, they were the two most likely to take his arm off if he got close enough.

He knelt in front of her, just out of reach. "You're a pretty one," he sneered with a smirk that made her feel like she needed a bath. "I haven't seen one like you before."

'Come closer and see me, then,' she wanted to reply, but all that came out was a guttural snarl that made the caribou in the next paddock over whine in fear and a show of teeth that should give every creature in the room pause. She'd never wanted to bite a human being in anger so much in her whole damn life… at least, not since kindergarten.

"Oh, you're a feisty one, aren't you, sweetheart?" His accompanying laugh was full of glee as he pushed to his feet. "You're going to be *lots* of fun to play with. I'll keep you for next time."

Cherry had no idea what he meant by "'play,'" but the bleating whine when he took the caribou by the collar and yanked her to her feet said she didn't want to stick around to find out. He slapped the deer's ass in the doorway as he dragged her from the room, and the bellow that followed was cut short with a painful-sounding electrical zap. Whatever happened was strong enough to take out her legs and send her to the concrete floor in a heap.

"Get up, you raggedy bitch. Let's go," the asshole snarled, and she did, slowly, and not without a fair bit of wobbling. He handed her off to someone waiting outside the door,

Wherever Chucklefuck was taking her, Cherry knew they wouldn't see her again. Before he left for the night, he looked around the room one more time, finally settling on her eyes. "Remember, keep quiet or you'll get it worse than she did. Nighty night, ladies."

If she hadn't been resolved before, she sure as hell was now. She was gonna kill that man or die trying.

Time was a relative construct on a good day, and this was not a good day. With the four other animals in the room, she felt the exhaustion tugging at her bones. She was long past the time she should have shifted back, resumed her human form, and between the feel of her body fighting to shift back and the eternal wariness of the dour surroundings, the urge to give in to sleep was strong, but the desire to stay alive was stronger.

Maybe that was the plan, to keep them hungry and tired so the animals would be more pliable for whatever it was their captors had planned. Whenever her time came, though, her plan was to chew a hole through whoever was unlucky enough to take her.

Across the room, a gasp drew her attention as one of the moose shifters slowly came back to her human form. Even though they couldn't see her, her pained whimpers and choked-off sobs filled a silence that was quickly torn by the door slamming opening. The bright light and nauseating scent of food tumbled in, followed by their captor, Chucklefuck Number One, again.

"Dinner time—oh, shit! Junior!" he yelled over his shoulder as he turned quickly.

Cherry felt something wet hit her fur as he flung the food bowl aside and lunged for the recently de-shifted woman who cowered against the wall. A lumbering shadow filled the doorway as Chucklefuck Number Two came to aid the first one as they fought with the feral woman who screamed and clawed the moment, they got close enough to touch her. Too bad it was with human nails instead of lethal hooves.

The screaming was heart-wrenching and terrifying, but Cherry figured this might be the best chance she'd get at an escape. Folding her paw up slowly, carefully, she tugged until the chain attached to the cuff went taut. The same mechanism that let her spread her paws wide enough to stride over snow and not fall through allowed her to come out of the cuff with some yanking, some blood, and likely some bare spots where fur used to be. No matter. One paw free was all she needed as she quickly slipped from the rest and darted out of the darkened room and down the corridor.

The hall was weirdly lit, like the fluorescent lights had some kind of greenish cast that rendered everything a weird mint color. There were no signs on the doors, no directions to the exit, and she found her claws scrabbling against the slippery polished concrete floor. She heard male voices behind her and knew she needed to find a hole, and quickly.

Fortunately, her nose led the way, via the aggressive citrus scent of some industrial floor cleaner. A utility closet door was ajar at the end of the hallway far enough for her to see the mop and bucket, and definitely big enough to hide in while she planned her next move. She darted inside just in time for the heavy scents of testosterone, sweat, fur, and fear to waft past her through the open slats in the door. Two shadows paused right outside the door, and it was all she could do to keep her panting breaths silent as she prepared to attack if they discovered her.

"Jesus, man, you didn't have to hit her that hard!"

"The fuck was I s'posed to do? She *bit* me! I have to get fucking shots now, dammit!"

"*Her* bite isn't the one you should be concerned about. We gotta find the client another fucking moose."

Annoyance, sweat, frustration all washed over her as they spoke but, she noticed, they were all alone. She didn't know where they had taken the girl, or what they'd done with her, but that also wasn't her concern as the voices faded down the hallway. If she was going to make a break for it, she might not get another chance. Especially if they discovered she was gone before she was out the door.

Following the trail of their scents, Cherry tracked them until she found a door to the outside world, and from there, she was gone. The chill in the night air was liberating after being stuck in that stifling room. *First thing's first, though*, she thought as she clawed her collar off, abandoning it under a bush along the path leading away from the warehouse.

She had no idea what direction she was running or where she was; the new moon overhead was doing her no favors. Pausing at a stream to take a much-needed drink of fresh water, she looked up at the sky through the dense tree canopy. This wasn't the first time she lamented her shitty sense of direction, but it was definitely the most dire.

By sunup, she found a ranger station for Chugach, and as fucked-up as showing up naked on their doorstep was, at least she could shift back into her human form, such as it was. She had some abrasions on her arms, legs, and neck, but nothing that would truly speak to the horror she'd endured. Or what the other women were still enduring.

She'd terrified the poor park ranger on duty by showing up in her animal form initially. Apparently, wolverines were even more fearsome when they were un-caffeinated. He'd fed her coffee by the pot and loaned her a shirt and a pair of shorts from the gift shop while she'd waited for the cops to arrive.

The Black Moon Creek Town Marshals, all two of them, came out to speak to her, for all the good it did. Without an exact location, or really anything resembling proof, they weren't interested in her fairy story about a house she couldn't even point out on a map. Hell, the only thing useful she'd gotten out of them had been a ride back to the visitor's center where she could pick up her Jeep and her clothes. She was in no shape to go back out there and follow her own scent back to the scene of the crime, her hours of wakefulness and time between shifting forms had left her exhausted almost to the point of delirium, and it was all she could do to convince the cops not to take her to the nearest hospital instead of allowing her to go home.

Pacey, bless her, while attentive and highly concerned over her time missing and the apparently fantastical story she had to tell about it, had not been a lot of help, either. Her roommate wanted to bring the Anchorage cops in, specifically Daniel, Pace's adorable oaf of a boyfriend. He also happened to be an aggravated assault and robbery detective for the Municipality of Anchorage PD.

Cherry wasn't sure how he made it to being a detective considering she found him more useful moving a sofa than having an in-depth, thoughtful conversation. Still, that wasn't the topic. Bringing him in wouldn't matter if she had less than nothing to offer in the way of corroborating proof that something happened, beyond her word and a vague idea of where she'd been held.

As much as the idea of going back there scared her, she couldn't get the faces of the other women out of her mind. Her being free meant nothing if they weren't free also.

"You're going to go out and find her yourself?" Pacey watched as she put her dishes in the sink and turned on the water to rinse them. She'd been packing her life away as she prepared to move in with Daniel.

"Don't look so shocked," Cherry snarked over her shoulder. She'd spent every hour that insomnia would grant her running down information on the missing girls, everything that could be pulled from the paper, their social media, all of it. There had to be something, somewhere. "I'm an investigative reporter. It's right there on the tin. So, I'm gonna go out and investigate."

"And what happens if they catch you again? Huh? How do you see that going?"

A vicious smile curled her lips as she imagined the bloodshed and screaming as she took off Chucklefuck Number One's hand at the wrist. "Then they better hope the gods are feeling merciful, because I won't be."

The blonde hummed in irritation before stomping back down the hall to get more of her belongings. It wasn't like Cherry had a death wish, exactly, but she certainly had no problem going all in when it came to finding the truth, and her bestie knew it. "I don't like this. Like not at all."

"I don't have a lot in the way of other options, Pace," she called after her. "The cops won't do anything without more evidence. Ergo, I need to get more evidence."

The blonde came back down the hall with an armload of bath towels and a ferocious frown. "And get yourself killed in the process?"

Cherry dried her hands and returned to the living room, flopping down onto the couch while snatching up the remote to the television. "It's not gonna come to that."

Pacey's bottle glass green eyes considered her for a moment before taking up her packing tape and permanent marker. "I really hope you're right."

"Truthfully? Me too."

Flipping through the channels rather than argue with her best friend of way too damn long, she paused when she saw King Niall giving a press conference outside of what appeared to be Mass General. His collapse had happened right after she'd gotten back from captivity and been covered breathlessly by the press, shifter and otherwise.

The monarchy had never been much of an interest for her, though she could see its exceptionally limited usefulness. Being a member of a nation within a nation made for strange politics sometimes but being far and away from both the contiguous US and the greater purview of the Therantian kingdom, life was a little different in Alaska.

She almost changed the channel when the fireworks went off. The King announced a change to the line of succession, punches were thrown, and in the thick of it all, a familiar face.

Vasily Brețcu was number one with a bullet on Cherry's Big List of Regrets. Not for anything either of them did, exactly. Just how they left things. She'd gone off to Georgia and he--she sighed deeply as she flexed her hands, so she didn't dig her nails into her palm--he had recently re-upped to the Corps. They'd parted with tears and the knowledge that when it came to life, she would always be second in his heart. He was her first love and she... It was an ache that never really left. She just learned to live with it.

"Is that...?" Pacey asked over her shoulder, both of them clearly caught up in the drama unfolding on the screen.

"Yeah." She nodded absently. His dark chocolate hair was longer, much longer, but there was no mistaking that build, that jawline sharp enough to cut glass, and those eyes. Standing between a feral wolf and the new crown prince like he could take them both on and wouldn't even wrinkle his suit, Vasily was the definition of dashing.

"My, my. Who'd'a thought he'd stay that pretty? And all that hair..."

Cherry glanced over her shoulder at her roommate's lascivious little smirk and snorted. "Pace."

She rolled a shoulder before heading back down the hallway. "Hey, he may be the asshole who left you, but it wasn't 'cuz he was ugly. And besides," her head popped out of the hallway to stare her down, "you could do better."

CHAPTER 1

CORA

She woke up with her eyes swollen, gritty, mouth parched like she hadn't seen water in years, and she was alone. That last part didn't surprise her. None of it really surprised her. Everything had happened all at once the night before. Finding out she was truly pregnant with Finn's child, the death of the King, Finn's new role as the Crown Prince Regent. There was a lot to sort through and come to terms with very quickly.

Not the least of which was the coronation, which would be moved up to accommodate the new timeline. Instead of a month from now, with the wedding out another two weeks beyond that. The coronation would take place the week after the funeral. Sometime the week after next. Thankfully, the wedding was still six weeks out. There was, apparently, a threshold beyond which catering and sartorial miracles were simply not possible.

As it stood now, the King's autopsy was top priority. And that, she had advocated, and Finn had fought. He may not be speaking to her still, but she maintained her certainty. Her suspicions were strong and the King's death too sudden to be a mere accident.

Everything about this was wrong. Her heart was broken. For the family, for Finn. Especially for Finn, as he couldn't even appropriately mourn, at least not publicly. But they'd arrived back at the palace the night before, and he'd dissolved into her arms in tears the moment the antechamber doors closed. She'd held him, the bastion of strength for him to cling to in a storm. She'd be that for him no matter what happened.

Father gone, brother a traitor to the crown and their people, the man he considered as close as a brother shot protecting him, his aunt a hateful bit of dried-out pith best discarded. The people who had his back had gone through a major overhaul, the direct result of the assassination they'd foiled and the death of his father. In her heart, she knew it was the one assassination they'd been unable to prevent.

Finn had understood her reasoning and appreciated her concerns, her attention to detail, but the idea of the autopsying a King, his father, did not sit well with him. It was an indignity that a man as great as his father should not have to bear, even in death. Of course, so was murder, but that argument had been a little too pointed for Finn's appreciation, and he hadn't been shy about telling her that.

Cora assumed that might make it too real for him, too far past the point of no return for him to rest comfortably in the denial stage of grief.

She wanted coffee, so much coffee, and every single pancake in existence, but there was no food to be had. No cart—nothing— only faint wisps of daylight streaming in from the splits between the panels of the heavy brocade curtains. He was gone, she had no idea where, leaving her well and truly alone in his room. Their room now, she supposed. Sighing, she swung her legs over the side of the bed and headed to the shower.

When she finished with her morning rituals and came out of the bathroom, he was seated in an armchair by the table, a cart of food next to him, including blessed, blessed coffee. Her normal caffeine intake was cut by more than half, thanks to a worrywart with a crown, so she poured her demitasse and savored it as best she could.

Finn was dressed, not in his normal shirt, waistcoat, and trousers, but a soft-looking denim blue cashmere sweater, and a pair of jeans with frayed ends trailing over his bare feet. Gods, she loved the laid-back look on him, maybe because it was so rare, but he tended to favor shirts that were a shade too tight and had an ass built for worship when he wore jeans. She was shameless in her adoration of his body, in addition to his absolutely brilliant mind and beyond compassionate and empathetic personality.

He didn't appear to hear her when she emerged from the bathroom dressed for the day in a warm, chenille sweater and a soft, stretchy skirt, everything about her crafted to be inviting and snuggly for him. Her goal was to provide him as much physical comfort as he needed, a warm, safe haven he could cling to even if he couldn't act on it as he wished.

"What's your title?" he asked as she made her way to the table and picked up her cup of coffee, already steaming.

"My title?" She perched on the couch cushion next to him, unsure as to where his mind was going with that question. It wasn't something she'd given much thought to after her family abandoned her. One last vestige of her life before that had simply ceased.

"Yes." He looked up with the barest smirk painted across his lips. "You're the daughter of the Marquise. Surely, you have a title."

"I did," she averred, snagging up a piece of bacon from his plate and crunching on it rather than acknowledge the heat of shame that washed over her face, even if her skin tone didn't let it show. Even after all this time, knowing damn well that none of what happened was her fault, she still felt guilty somehow. Like she'd driven her father to his cruelty. "Past tense. It was taken from me when he cast me out." She sipped her coffee thoughtfully. "Given to one of my sisters, I assume. I don't know."

Finn's normally warm and affectionate blue eyes were hardened chips of ice as his jaw set. "He...took it from you."

"It was his to do with as he pleased," she reasoned, the words coming easily to her after having years to make her own peace with it. "I mean, I guess, *technically*, it's a title from my mother's side, but whatever. It's no longer mine. Why?"

"Do you want it back?"

The softness of his voice as he posed the question did not disguise the razor-sharp intent behind it. All the tension and angst of the last few days appeared to have coalesced into a solid state. He needed a war to fight, a target for his aggressions, and so he would fight for her. If she would let him.

"That's not necessary," she murmured. "I don't need anything from them. Nothing at all."

"Not even what's rightfully yours?" he growled, but even as angry as he sounded, he still reached for her and tangled their fingers together.

She shook her head with a sad little smile. "No. Not even that. I'm done with them."

He held their joined hands to his lips and kissed each of her fingertips. "You'll be their queen."

Not that she'd needed the reminder; other than the pregnancy, her mind had been occupied with little else. "Then…" She sipped her coffee as she tried to quell the smug smirk, she felt brewing behind the rim of her cup. "I guess they'll have to deal with that when the time comes."

Finn gave her a saucy wink as he grinned, and she took that to mean their fight was over. Snuggling into his side, they both reclined on the couch with their coffee mugs and his plate of bacon and toast in his lap for them to share. As much as Cora was unused to it, she enjoyed Finn's protective side, though she was still unsure if she'd ever admit to that out loud.

"You'll be the Queen of Therantia." His lips brushed her temple as he spoke.

"I will," she agreed, snagging a small triangle of toast with strawberry jam and popping it into her mouth.

"I could make you the Duchess of Corbeau," he offered. The Duchy had been vacant since her father's uncle had passed when she was six and had left no heirs. It covered Eastern France, Switzerland, and Northern Italy down to Florence.

"You could, but it's not necessary. I'll always be the queen, right?"

He nodded. "True enough. But for our children..." His voice trailed off as he laced his fingers with hers and placed them over her belly. The heat and warmth of the possessive gesture sank through the layers of fabric and gave her a calmness and tranquility she'd never known until him. "He or she will need a title."

"Prince or Princess isn't enough?"

"That's not how this works, and you know it." He sighed deeply, the motion moving through both of them as they lounged there together. "My full title right now is Crown Prince Regent Finnegan mac Néill Ó Cathasaigh, The Vigilant, Prince of Therantia, Archduke of the Chernyvolk, Prince of the Obake, Protector of the Boto and Encantado, Champion of the Kanima." When he paused to take a breath, he must have noticed her big eyes, because he chuckled. "Well, you get the picture. Long story short, our child will have a title from both sides of the family. At least one."

That was certainly a mouthful. As a side note, the children would need better middle names, but she wasn't planning to say that out loud. Still, this was more of a thought exercise than anything else. "Then I suppose they'll be whatever you decide."

"We decide together." He punctuated the declaration with another kiss on her forehead, and she let her eyes drift closed as he held her. For a moment, it was so peaceful between them.

"I still can't believe it," he whispered.

"I certainly did not intend for this."

"I know," he assured her with a light squeeze. "I know." He fell silent again for a moment before muttering, "And yet I can't help but be so happy."

"Really?" Cora braced a hand on his chest as she sat up, turning to face him, so she could see him, judge the veracity of the words as they matched his body language. "Really. You're all right with this? Me, being pregnant. Carrying our child."

His brows drew down in confusion. "Of course! I love you. Why wouldn't I be happy?"

It was not often that Cora was caught flat-footed, but his casual and honest admission of love definitely left her a bit flummoxed. "I—" The room was suddenly very warm, uncomfortably so, and the air appeared to be going out of her lungs as well. She opened her mouth a few more times, but words had apparently abandoned her for greener pastures.

"It's all right if you don't say it back," he rushed to assure her, though the slight downturn to his mouth as he spoke said otherwise. "I understand. This has all been very rushed, and a great deal has been put upon you…" His words died as his eyes widened and the color rapidly drained from his head. "What do you want to do?"

"I beg your pardon?"

"I just realized…" The color that had left returned in concentrated splotches on his cheeks above his beard and his ears. "No one even asked you what you wanted to do about this. I'm so sorry." His hand covered his mouth as he sighed and pulled at his bottom lip in thought. "What is it *you* want from this? Do you even want to keep the baby?"

She could tell he was trying desperately to keep his voice devoid of any emotion, but the tentative softness with which he spoke said far more than his practiced indifference could possibly camouflage. "I honestly don't know." She sighed, resuming her spot with her head on his shoulder. "It had honestly never occurred to me. The life I lived didn't allow for it. I had no reason to expect that this was even an option for me."

"And now?"

"And now…" She huffed a small, ironic chuckle. "I'm pregnant with the heir to the throne of my people. That's not the kind of thing you can just walk away from."

"I won't force you to keep it. You know that, right?" He shifted around until he could meet her gaze, his face a mask of utter seriousness. "I mean, I couldn't if I wanted to, but I don't. And I won't."

"I know." Cora's lips curled as her eyes fell shut in exhaustion.

Whatever else was going on between them, that part of him she'd never doubted for a moment. "I'm still trying to wrap my head around it."

"I know! I am, too!" he agreed eagerly as he snuggled back down with her in his arms. The silence that filled the room for the next few minutes was fraught but wasn't nearly as smothering as it could have been. She took that as a good sign.

"Are we really getting married?" she asked softly.

His first answer was silence, then a great sigh that moved through his whole body. "Yes, if you'd like."

She rolled her eyes at his quick acquiescence. "I mean, the child should be legitimate if it were to ascend to the throne."

His dry chuckle came with a swift brush of his lips across her forehead. "Well, yes, but there are ways around that." Tentatively, he took her left hand, his fingers going to the ring on her third finger. Twenty-eight tiny, but significant, pearls surrounding an oval amethyst so deep in its purple it may as well have been black, set in gold. His grandmother's ring. Licking his lips, he drew her hand to his face and brushed his lips across her knuckles. "I screwed this up initially," he whispered against her skin.

With a deep breath, he looked in her eyes. They were a blue so dark and fathomless, it reminded her of the ocean at night. "I'm sorry I screwed this up the first time, but I adore you. And I've never known joy like you've brought into my life. Even in the darkest times, you've made them bearable. I can only imagine in the joyful times. You'll make them incandescent. I love you. Probably should have opened with that. And I would hope that you find me worthy enough to do me the honor and privilege of being my wife. Even if you don't wish to be queen, you don't have to. I ask nothing of you but your love. Everything else, we can work out."

As proposals went, it was pretty flooring. Hearing him say the words was nothing she ever expected and everything she had secretly ever wanted. And maybe it was the hormones, but the tears running down her face were unabated and copious. She scraped the back of a shaking hand across her cheeks for what felt like the millionth time, her lips quivering too hard to answer. Choking back a sob, she finally whispered, "Yes. Yes, I will marry you, Finn. Yes, I love you." She closed her eyes on a watery chuckle. "Just yes."

He pulled her to him then, tilting her chin up as he took her mouth in a deep kiss. His lips were soft, salty from his own tears as his tongue licked into her mouth. She tasted coffee, warmth, home. In her soul, she knew she could not ask for more.

"I'm sorry I'm an idiot," he murmured as he nuzzled his nose against hers when he pulled back. "Please don't cry, I'm sorry I'm an idiot."

Cora sniffled, her chuckle quiet and more than a little waterlogged. "Yeah, but you're my idiot. It'll be all right."

VASILY

"We need to tell him." Even if he didn't open his eyes, he could pick out that definitive snip of a voice as none other than Cora Westgate, his best friend's girl and the future queen.

The best friend in question was having none of her suggestion, though. "We do not."

"We *need* to tell him," she insisted, and Vasi could almost see the face she was making solely from her voice.

"And do what, give him a heart attack?" Ah, the sarcasm was strong with this one.

"Even better, he's already in the hospital. It's a great place for them." Listening to the snark-on-snark violence almost made him laugh, though the pain from a deep breath told him that was a terrible idea.

"I can't just drop this on him. That's not okay," Finn grumbled.

"It was his idea!"

"Not to get actually pregnant." The silence that followed had a lethal point to it, and he could actually hear Finn cringe. "I didn't mean it like that. I'm sorry. I'm just...I'm overwhelmed."

"Who's pregnant?" Vasi asked from the bed, his voice rough, and his throat felt like he'd been gargling with glass. He didn't open his eyes, but he was tired of listening to them bitch at each other. *"Ce naiba mi s-a întâmplat?* What's going on? How long have I been here?"

Finn rolled a shoulder, looking stiff and exhausted in his soul from his bedside seat. "Eh..." he hedged. "It's been a day or so, a little bit more."

That wasn't right. That didn't make any sense. "What the hell happened? I feel like I've been hit by a truck."

"You kinda were," Cora's overly cheerful voice replied from her spot by the door. "Driscoll shot you."

"That doesn't make any sense. Why the fuck would he do that?" Belatedly, he remembered he was swearing at the future queen, but then he also remembered it was Cora, and so he let it go.

Her nose wrinkled as she grimaced. "That's a bit of a long story."

"I'mma fuckin' kill him," he slurred. The memories were there in bits and pieces floating in the morphine-coated ether of his mind but he kinda sorta remembered that part.

"Um... well..." She drew in a sharp breath. "Finn took care of that."

That got his attention, and he opened his eyes and tried to sit up all at once. "I'm sorry, what?" The room was ridiculously bright, the pain from the too-intense lights coupling with this pain in his chest and shoulder to make him wither back into the hospital bed. It was almost enough to distract him from the fact that his notoriously gentle best friend, the future King, had killed the man who tried to murder him. It felt like the world was upside down, and not entirely because of the narcotics. "What happened to me?" he asked as he noted the lights slowly dimming from behind his eyelids.

"You got shot saving the prince."

"Huh." Well, in terms of all possible outcomes of that statement, just having shoulder pain and maybe some new scarring was a distinct plus. "You're alive, so I take it I was successful. Yay, me!" he cheered weakly.

Finn laughed as he squeezed his best friend's hand. "You're such an asshole."

"Hey, be nice to me!" he whined. "I've been shot."

"Yeah, yeah." He dismissed him and moved from the side of his bed for Cora to take his place.

"So, who's pregnant?" Vasi asked again as he hit the button on the bed to make it sit up more. He watched Cora's eyes dart to Finn and the prince's pointed look back in her direction and then at him. All of a sudden, the anesthesia-induced clouds cleared, and the sun burst forth and horror followed. "*No*. No, no, no. You're what, now?" He addressed the interrogation to Cora, as she seemed the least mortified of the two of them.

She had the decency to swallow hard before she answered. "Pregnant with the heir to the throne?"

"*Is that a question?*" The throb in his shoulder intensified as his pulse and blood pressure kicked up at the news.

"No. No, it's really not."

All too quickly, the thoughts and memories of that night came rushing back in double time. Losing Cora to an attempted kidnapping, losing Finn and then Cora to actual kidnapping...he took the future queen out on an op. The *pregnant* future queen, holy fuck. And his traitorous protégé enacting his plot under his very nose? Letting go of Finn's hand, he hit the button for his pain meds. This was not his first rodeo.

"Huh." It was then all the pain meds converged and he checked back out. He figured that was probably for the best.

FINN

Finn left Cora in the capable hands of Shayla, the assistant wedding planner. Regardless of the amusing and occasionally profane epithets his fiancée had for the woman, he at least knew her name. They had some sort of dress fitting or something today, and from Cora's reaction to the news of the appointment, he could tell she'd rather shave her head and set herself on fire.

A fond smile curled his lips as he scratched at his healing wrists. He couldn't tell an A-line from an A-shirt, and figured it was better he stayed out of it, though he was more than happy to be her sounding board as she vented. His appreciation for her attention to detail knew no bounds as she went into her reasoning for seeking out certain designers and certain elements. Truly, though, he was glad all he had to do was wear his royal uniform and show up shaven and sober.

Reading the latest quarterly financial report for the Society of Angels on his phone, the prince sipped his coffee while he waited for his friend to return from la-la land. That was one thing he appreciated about this weird time in mental and emotional limbo, orphaned prince, not quite a king, sorting through the sordid details of a plot against his life. People were giving him a bit of much-needed space. He'd had more moments to himself to think than he had in years, and it was honestly magnificent.

Vasi stirred in the hospital bed next to him, where he'd been stationed since he passed out again. There were Guards outside, of course, but Finn felt better being there to look after him just in case.

"You alive?" he asked unnecessarily. His sensitive ears could pick up the shift in his breathing as he came back to consciousness, and the answering grunt and middle finger made him smile. "Here, drink." He held the cup with the bendable straw up to Vasily's chapped lips and left it there for him to drain it dry. "Better?" he asked as he refilled it.

"Much." His best friend nodded and inclined the bed to sit up. Finn waited. He knew Vasi had to be the one to start the conversation, and there were several to be had, but whatever he was up for, his best friend was right there. "I failed you."

That was not how Finn saw this starting at all. "I'm not sure what you mean."

"Man..." He ran both hands through his long hair, frowning

when one caught on the rubber band. "I let you get kidnapped. I led Cora straight into a trap. I took the *pregnant future queen* on an op. I mean, fuck me. I apparently ran out of rookie moves and started creating them on the fly."

Halfway through the diatribe, Finn was shaking his head. "No. Don't do that."

"Do what?"

"Take responsibility for shit you could not have possibly known about. Hell, we found out about the pregnancy while you were in surgery a couple days ago. We never suspected Driscoll, and I sure as hell never expected shit to go both sideways *and* pear-shaped."

"I *know* you didn't expect those things. It's *my job* to expect those things!"

The vehemence in his voice, coupled with the slight wheeze and surreptitious rub of his injured shoulder, concerned Finn enough to move to perch on the bedside. "Cora missed it, too," he reasoned, doing his best to bolster his friend's obviously shot self-esteem. "It was as much her job as yours, and she didn't see it coming either."

"What happened to Brendan?"

The Crown Prince rolled a shoulder as he cringed. "Unconscious, still, under guard just in case. There's a really good chance he might not wake up at all."

"Good," the owl replied with a vicious grin that matched his murderous glare.

"Probably for the best," he agreed. "Cora fucked up his face pretty bad and..." He sighed. It was still too soon to talk about the Lunacy. He still had no idea what to make of it, but the burns on his wrists were healing as a daily reminder of his trip out of his mind. "If, and this is a generous 'if,' he does wake up, it'll be to a whole new world for him, and most of it will be excruciating."

Vasi's lip curled into a sneer that would make Billy Idol proud as he looked away. At least he wasn't arguing about it. "What about the King? Did they make a move on your father while we were tied up dealing with that fuckery?"

Merely hearing the question stole all of the air from Finn. His jaw locked even as the pain burned behind his eyes and in his nose so fiercely, he feared they'd bleed. He knew he could let go in front of his best friend, but if anyone else walked in...He couldn't allow himself that respite, so he focused on taking slow, even breaths until the desire to curl into a ball and weep, or flip tables over and set the world on fire, subsided.

The warm hand on his arm startled him. "I'm so sorry, Finnegan." Vasi's blue-gray eyes were bright with unshed tears of his own.

"It's not your fault."

"Not so sure about that. Was it...?" The owl blew out a deep breath as he obviously sought a more delicate phrasing than his level of upset and pain medication would allow.

"No, no. At least, right now, we don't think so."

"Good." He grabbed a tissue from the box on the rolling table next to him and blew his nose as he regained his composure. "Autopsy, then?"

Finn swallowed hard. "Cora insisted."

Vasi nodded decisively, though he blinked a few times after, like his brain might still be rattling. "Good. We don't need any more surprises."

"Like the pregnancy?" he joked, grateful for the opportunity to change the subject.

Vasi threw his head back and laughed outright. When he reached up to play in his hair again, he seemed to remember the issue from last time. "Grab me a comb, would you?" Finn went to the bag he'd packed himself of his friend's belongings and did as he asked, watching as the owl tended to his surprisingly long mane. "So, you're gonna be a dad, huh?" he asked with the comb between his teeth as he braided his hair from touch alone.

Every time he thought about it, he couldn't help beaming. "Yeah, looks like."

"You'll be good at it." Vasily nodded decisively as he wrapped the braid into a bun at the base of his skull. "Is Cora as happy about it as you are?"

"I think she's still getting used to the idea," he answered honestly. This wasn't a conversation he could have with anyone else, but he knew the Commander would keep his counsel.

"It's quite the leap from spy to monarchy to motherhood." He cocked his head to the side as he snared Finn with a surprisingly sharp gaze.

"It is," he agreed readily. "I don't know of anyone better suited, though." In truth, she was proof of divine perfection in the universe, and he could not imagine anything better than being with her for eternity. Or longer, if possible.

"You still gonna marry her?"

'Oh, hell yes,' was the phrase that came to his mind first, but he kept it back. "Actually, now that you mention it, I kinda need your help."

WINGED GUARDIANS

CHAPTER 2

VASILY

Time off was for the weak, or so he told himself, but he only took a week off his post with the Guard before returning to light duty status. There was a shit-ton of things to do, even without running a shift, since Driscoll's defection to the dark side had left a lot of troubling questions in its wake.

When Cora came, she'd vetted his staff, and Driscoll's record had come up incomplete, but clean. Though Vasi had been pissed at her high-handedness at the time, now he saw it for the necessity it was. His first goal was to do his own staff audit and deep dive and make sure to root out any other infections before they become a problem for the organization and the crown.

It wasn't like he had any more pressing matters or a lack of time.

"Commander?"

He had no idea how much time had passed since he'd started,

but his tired eyes immediately snapped from the laptop screen to the voice in his doorway. A younger man, pale and thin, familiar... "Fielding, right? From the kitchen? Bedelia's brother Francis?"

The young goat in all black entered his office with a tentative nod and wide eyes, carrying a zipped leather portfolio of some sort a little bit larger than a legal pad in size. "Commander Brețcu, I was told you were the one I'd need to speak to."

He sat back in the chair slowly and tried to appear as nonthreatening as possible., The kid was the sibling to a murder victim, so he was predisposed to help as best he could, provided he was able. "About?"

The Hircine took a seat across the desk from him and pushed the portfolio in his direction. It was newer, black pleather with the zippered edge threatening to give way to whatever was almost bursting inside.

Vasi picked up the book and examined the exterior carefully before setting it back down. "What am I looking at?"

"It came in the mail about a week after..." His voice faded as his gaze dropped to closely examine the corner of the desk closest to him and not look the Commander in the face. "We...didn't see it? Had...other stuff..."

"Of course, you did," Vasi reassured him. Their family had been through the absolute wringer since Bedelia died and the media circus surrounding her murder and Prince Brendan's ultimate implication in her death. Four weeks out, and they were still piecing things together. "So, this came in the mail? Do you know from whom?"

"Delia."

Silence spread out through the room like ink dropped on tissue paper as the Commander regarded the kitchen steward. The young man had no reason to lie, and it was an intriguing thought, but how? And more importantly, who?

He closed the door and grabbed a bottle of water from the mini fridge he kept hidden behind his desk. Holding it up for Francis, he grabbed the young man one as well. "Start from the beginning, and I'll be recording, okay?"

The goat nodded and exhaled a shaky breath. "Yes, sir."

XANDER

Since taking over for Vasily on Night Watch, in addition to his emotional equilibrium, he found his sleep schedule trashed as well. Getting used to day-sleeping was not the kind of thing a hawk enjoyed, even if he overlooked the fact he didn't see nearly as well at night.

He was sleepwalking past Vasi's office door in search of fresh coffee when it popped open, and the man himself, the one who was supposed to be off on convalescent leave, emerged with a look of haunted incredulity. Blue eyes wide and glassy, his wrinkled shirt and slightly sallow complexion said he'd been there for quite a while.

"Exactly who I wanted," he pronounced before Xander got dragged in the door.

"I'm...sorry?" His body could ambulate or speak, but not both before caffeine, and he found himself both taciturn and seated at Vasily's desk in front of an open diary. "What's this?"

Thankfully, his friend placed a steaming mug of awake-and-functional by his hand as he turned back a few pages in the book, pointing out a section. "Drink. Read. I'll wait."

Very much aware of the agitated owl pacing in front of the desk, Xander started with the open page in front of him. The writing was quick, but feminine, written with a light hand and a penchant for flourishes.

Page after page, notes, pictures, actual physical receipts, even. This book was a trove of treasures absolutely no one wanted to claim. "Holy shit."

"Right?" The Commander's eyes took on a kind of manic cast to them as he nodded.

Poleaxed, he sat back in the chair with his coveted cup of wakefulness. This was a—if not *the*—smoking gun that tied Brendan to all the mayhem that had been thrust onto the kingdom. "We need to tell the prince, like, yesterday." He slammed the book closed and zipped it before scrambling to his feet.

"No." His friend and colleague shook his head vehemently, leaning down to hold the book to the table. "We absolutely do not."

Xander knew he was tired, but there was no way Vasily Breţcu, the beacon of rectitude and justice, was suggesting they keep this quiet. "We can't sit on this."

The tall man cringed as he raised a shoulder and took his seat across the desk. "You're right, but we can't go to him until we know more. He has enough on his plate to deal with right now, without adding this kind of incomplete information. We need to run down every detail and witness before we even think of interrupting Finn's coronation plans with this."

As much as he didn't like that answer, the reasoning was solid. "Agreed."

CHERRY

She gathered her long blonde-tipped mahogany curls into a ponytail as she checked her laptop for signs of life one more time. Having changed out of her pajamas into some concert t-shirt from long ago and some jeans that were likely even older, she laced her boots with the intent to go out.

She hadn't heard from Vasi. She'd debated reaching out to him, for a lot of reasons. Time, distance, the way they left things. But in her heart, she knew she needed help if she was going to crack this case, and that help wasn't coming from anywhere nearby.

Pacey had offered to bring her boyfriend into the situation more than once, even though she said she understood why Cherry was hesitant. She wasn't sure how she'd react to not being believed again, and by someone she knew, too.

The rage at that simmered just under her skin. There was so much wrong with the situation. Two more girls had gone missing in the time since she'd been back, from the same area, with no witnesses and no further information to be had. It seemed like the world was content to keep its eyes closed until bodies started dropping from the sky. And even then, they were shifter women, so that might not generate as much public outcry as others.

That part was especially galling. She wasn't a delicate, sweet, innocent shifter woman who couldn't fend for herself. She was a fucking *wolverine,* and they'd managed to kidnap her like they'd done to those other women. Somehow, she'd find information and break this open because this kind of festering rot only healed when exposed to light and cleansed.

In the Jeep on her way to Chugach again, she thought of her short stint in captivity. Wondered what had happened to those women. If there were more. If they were the only ones. What made her crazy, though, was that no one believed her about them.

It wasn't even that no one believed her, not really. It was that the people who could fix the situation—the *horror*—that was still going on seemed disinclined to do so. Her mind wandered briefly back to Vasily.

He was a cop, of sorts. And he would be invested in looking for missing shifter women. Still, she fought with herself about making the call. She wasn't even really sure why. He'd answer if she called; Cherry knew that in her heart. He wouldn't turn her away, regardless of their time apart, but maybe...there was a part of her that worried that there was a first time for everything.

She pulled into the park and left her Jeep by the visitor's center again. Nightfall added a layer of chill to the ever-present frigid temps that tormented her as she abandoned her clothes and assumed her animal form. At least as a wolverine she was better suited for the weather, or at least unbothered by the cold. She'd search again tonight, and then tomorrow, she'd bite the bullet and call him.

GWEN

News of King Niall's death and subsequent autopsy spread like wildfire, in the shifter and non-shifter media alike. If there was one thing her family did well, it was gossip and intrigue. It was only a matter of time now.

Gwen knew from the moment the news alert came across her phone in the exquisitely appointed penthouse suite of the Lapa Palace Hotel in Lisbon that she was on a clock and had to be ready to move, and soon.

Which was how she ended up in a private sleeper with a private bathroom on the night train from Lisbon to some podunk little town in the southwest of France where she could catch a TGV to Paris. Anonymity was easier to preserve traveling overland, but even then, she still had to be mindful since cameras were everywhere.

Her little Lacertine helper had outlived the majority of his usefulness about three days into the hotel stay. It was fortunate he was still tasty after such a long trip for them. Conveniently, all the European sightings of Brendan ceased right before he made his move on Finnegan and his whore. Just the thought of the bloodline being so polluted by a Corvid, of all things, made her blood boil. She'd worked far too hard to mold and shape those boys into the men they were now for them to throw it away on something as paltry as love. As a wise man once said to her, '*Liubov' dlia durakov,*' love is for fools.

Speaking of...Gwen powered on the burner phone she'd purchased with cash in Lisbon to check her messages. She'd reached out to a longtime associate uniquely skilled in the ways of helping her disappear. There had always been a backup plan, she was not a stupid woman, but now she needed to make use of it.

Though it was a little past nine at night somewhere in the Spanish countryside, her phone chirped with a new message from an unlisted number. *"Ya soskuchal'sia po nashim razgovoram, dorogaya. Skol'ko let, skol'ko zim."*

Dimitri always did have such a damn flair for language. Even when chastising her about her lack of correspondence outside of business dealings, he still made it sound beautiful. *"Mnogo,"* she typed back before deciding that since he was awake, though it was midnight in Moscow, she would call instead. The personal touch always went a long way, in her experiences. *"Dima, droog moy. Da,* it has been far, far too long since I've enjoyed the pleasure of your company."

WINGED GUARDIANS

CHAPTER 3

CORA

Mos knew she was coming. When everyone else of his rank in the governmental diplomatic 'East Wing' of the palace, as it was referred to, had an individual meeting with her today as the incoming consort of the monarch, it was the spy equivalent of lining up targets to shoot at the range. Not that she minded, because she had the advantage of directing the agenda, and he had to deal with both the anticipation and dread of her visit. Win-win.

Ordinarily, she'd meet with him in some out-of-the-way place where they could ensure neutral ground for the two of them, or someplace public to enforce civility on both sides. This new life out in public as the regent's fiancée meant she had to get creative with her cover stories. Fortunately, that had never been a problem for her.

Her brother's assistant smiled politely at her as she approached her meticulously organized desk. Another cousin, Cora noted. To be expected.

"Miss Westgate." The woman smiled as she rose from her

chair like an elegant shadow. She was tall like Mos was, effortlessly ethereal in her sleeveless black sheath dress, delicate in ways Cora could only imitate, never internalize. "This way, please. May I get you some coffee?"

She allowed herself to be herded to a waiting room with boring, overstuffed furniture and smoked glass coffee tables. As much as she wanted to avail herself of the offer, she knew she couldn't. "No thank you, but water, if you could."

"Of course, ma'am. The Deputy Minister will be with you momentarily." The woman nodded and backed out of the room. That was a strange thing, she noted. People no longer turning their backs to her. There were good reasons for that kind of thing, relative health and safety being chief among them, but the royalty thing…

"I hope you haven't been waiting long." Her brother's all-business voice interrupted her musings, and the smile he gave her was a frail and sickly imitation of actual joy.

"No, you've asserted your dominance just fine." Cora glanced at her watch. "Two minutes." That was how long he'd made her wait. It was a subtle technique, a way to show his time was more important than hers. They'd both learned that at their father's knee. "Just long enough to annoy but not anger outright. Unless you're me."

"Unless you're you," he agreed. "Though, to be fair, I'm pretty sure you were born angry." Nicodemos blinked, otherwise expressionless in his cloudy gray suit and black tie that made his dark skin look like smooth silk. His clothes said he was every bit the well-dressed government functionary, but his eyes…well, they had that in common, the two of them. He turned his back on her and headed to his office, holding the door for her in a mocking display of politeness. "After you." It was only the potential for witnesses that kept her from snarling as she stalked past him into his office.

"Your water, ma'am."

He plucked the ice chip studded bottle from his assistant's hand before Cora could even speak. "Thank you, Sylvia. Hold my calls."

She railed on him as soon as he closed the door, hissing, "The fuck is wrong with you, asshole?" as she followed him to his desk.

Nicodemos set the bottle on a preplaced coaster on the desk in front of her before throwing open the buttons of his suit coat and flouncing into the leather seat behind his ultramodern cherrywood and frosted glass desk. "Why are you here, Coretta?"

Like she had many times before in her life, she truly desired to smack the shit out of him. With a chair. "No pleasantries?" She perched in the chair directly across the vast expanse of glass and wood from him, the space between them broken up by a collection of office supplies, files, and a dock for his laptop. Cora channeled all her focus into keeping her posture as ramrod straight and regal as possible. Fuck him if he thought he can goad her into a brawl.

"No point. We both know you want something. What is it?"

He wanted to be that way? Fine with her. "You owe me."

"I beg your pardon?"

"You heard me. I didn't stutter. You. Fucking. Owe. Me. Nicodemos." She enunciated each word slowly before taking up her bottle of water and sipping from it, content to let the weight of the silence squeeze a reply from him.

"Do tell," he purred as he sat back in his chair with a snotty little smirk staining his lips.

Holding up a finger, she listed her complaints. "I got shot at because of you. Someone attempted to poison me because of you. Scored, marked up, and the proud owner of additional scars *because of you*. Are you sensing a theme yet?"

Mos sniffed and picked up one of his pens—something expensive and Italian, if she had to guess—to twirl it between his fingers. "I would argue those things happened because of Finn, and, let's be fair here, you came out of those all right." His glance slipped over her as much as he could from his seated position, making sure to stop on some of the more expensively attired bits of her, ending with a pointed look at her engagement ring. "So, tell me, really, how is it you think I owe you?"

An ache settled in her jaw just below her ear as he perused her, like she was an experiment he found lacking. "How long have you known?" she asked quietly.

His eyes widened at her query, and it was like all other ambient noise in the room died as he focused on her. "How long have I known what?" he growled, his eyes fully gold now as he glared balefully at her. "That you were sleeping with the prince? Early on."

His attempt at deflection was laughably weak. "How *long* have you *known*?" Her patience with his little dances and prevarications was quickly coming to an end. Cora planned to sit there, drink her water, and out-wait him until she got what she came for.

The standoff lasted five whole, solid, excruciatingly awkward minutes and half a bottle of water until finally Mos caved, looking away with a sneer. "Pretty much since you were recruited."

In her mind, she heard the screech of sparking brakes and the impact of all her trains of thought crashing into one another resulting in a flaming mess. "I'm sorry, what?"

It was a reflexive response. She heard him fine, understood him even, but processed? Accepted? The very idea of it confounded her. And the pit of rage she reserved solely for her blood family opened a bit more inside her. "You've known this whole time." She could not control the octave drop in her voice, nor its increase in volume, as she felt the heat of her shift fight its way to the forefront.

He nodded, gaze falling to the pen in his hand. "I got worried. Your birthday came around and, well...everyone was treating it like it was just another day."

"*Quelle surprise.*" It shouldn't hurt, after all this time. The rejection happened long enough ago that it didn't carry the weight in her heart that it used to but talking about it still stung. Especially with someone who had a front row seat.

His cheek began to tic as a ghost of a smile crossed his lips. "I missed the cupcakes and the terrible action flicks at the movies. I missed *you*."

Now she was the one with the crossed arms and closed body language. "Not enough to call, though, I see."

His head snapped up at her sarcasm. "I looked for you. I had to be careful since there are rules against that kind of thing, you know. Imagine my surprise to find you not only out of law school but on assignment in the Special Protectorate Division."

Just hearing the words brought the rage to a boil within her. This was probably not healthy for the baby, but it also wasn't something she could help. "I was assured my whereabouts would be kept from my family. Guess I know what government promises are worth. And that's garbage, by the way. You had fucking years! *Years!* And you said nothing! If you missed me so damn much, why didn't you reach out?"

"I couldn't!"

"Bullshit!" Cora slapped the desk hard enough to jostle a nearby cup of pens. "Do you have any decency at all? You would lie to my face like that…the fuck is wrong with you? You could have said something, but you didn't want to. Don't lie. It's a helluva lot easier to be the favored child when you don't rock the boat. All of you could pretend I was never there at all."

"What would you have had me do?" he bit out.

"Speak up for once!" she roared. The only thing keeping her seated was her grip on the chair's armrests. "Just once, you could do what's right and not what is most beneficial to you."

She inhaled sharply, drawing back her talons and her feathers. "I'm not sure why I'm surprised. It's been more than clear that I have always meant less than nothing to your family. You let him tear this family apart and, rather than say anything, you sucked up to him so you could keep your barony and your cushy little government gig. Clearly, your priorities were in order."

He blinked at her outburst, his desk phone beeping with the intercom. Eyes never leaving hers, he answered, cradling the handset between his jaw and shoulder. "I'm fine, Sylvia. Thank you for checking."

"Does Father know?" she demanded, working diligently at reining in her rage, as soon as he hung up. She couldn't imagine the old bastard wouldn't, given his high placement in the King's court and their Ministry of State. He was the equivalent of the Secretary of State and Minister of Therantian Interior, keeping track of such things like the security services. Was this all a game for their old man? A sick form of amusement to him? She wouldn't put it past him. Either of them, really.

After a moment, the feeling in the room shifted as her brother sighed slightly and crossed his arms. "No."

The how's and why's that followed that answer were overcome by another more pressing question. "Are you the one who sent me to the prince?"

"I am." He nodded slowly.

"'Family Discard' is too good to be claimed in the bloodline but fine to whore out to royalty, huh?" The jibe felt too good to keep inside. At least he had the decency to wince. "Was this your idea?"

"No."

"Who're you working for, then?"

"I'm not at liberty to say."

From anyone else in his position, that would have been a fine enough answer. From her brother, it made her want to rip his teeth out until he gave up the name and then take the rest as a warning not to do it again. "So, you've known I was a spy this whole time."

He nodded once, his eyes darting to the large file cabinets across the room. "Read your case reports every time they came in the door."

"And when I was discharged?"

"You were requested for this job specifically."

"By someone who knew me?" She pointed to herself. "Or someone who knew *me*?" and she gestured to the rest of the room.

The corner of his mouth kicked up for a hot second. "Is there a difference?"

"There is now," she was quick to remind him. "My whole life is different now."

Mos dipped his chin, conceding her point. "You weren't supposed to get quite that close." He chuckled.

"Yeah, well, you send me after my childhood crush, weird shit happens." She rolled a shoulder and drained the rest of her water. "Surprisingly poor planning on your part."

He snorted, his lips almost smiling. "True enough." He held out his hand and tossed her empty bottle in the recycling bin under his desk. "Suppose I do owe you. What do you want?"

Cora was sure that, under other circumstances, Mos would try to politely cajole the information out of her. Finesse it in his way. Anyone but her may have entertained that foolishness. As it was, the only thing keeping them from coming to blows was the very large desk between them and the fact she was pregnant. And really it was more the desk than the pregnancy. She didn't want to ruin her outfit by leaping over the vast expanse and ripping a seam. Bad form, and expensive.

"I need you to come on a mission." It was as good an opening as any, and even mostly true.

Her brother's dark eyes narrowed. "Since when do you hand out missions?"

"Since I've been in the employ of people who shouldn't know I'm here to do things for them that they cannot do themselves," she snapped. "Why didn't you look after him?"

"I couldn't get that close."

Cora didn't even disguise her scoff of incredulity. "Liar."

"Not without raising extensive suspicion."

"So, you brought in an outside agent...?"

"Because my benefactor knew you could get the job done."

She hummed in annoyance, torn between disbelief and grudging acceptance. Either way, there were objectives to meet, and she needed to get on with those. "Regardless, eight o'clock, night after tomorrow. Be there. Nice suit."

Cora dipped into her purse and produced a calling card that

she slid across the desk in his direction. On it was the address for the most luxurious boutique hotel in New England, The Beacon Hill Abbey. It was out of the way and catered exclusively to upscale shifters and other high-end clientele.

"What's the job?" her brother asked as he looked the card over on both sides before slipping it into his breast pocket behind his pocket square.

"Observation, mostly. You shouldn't need any weapons, but you know how it is."

He nodded slowly and stacked his hands on the desk in front of him. "And this makes us square?"

Cora favored her older sibling with her sweetest, most unfelt smile. "Oh, no, good sir. Nowhere close." If he thought he could buy her forgiveness through acts of service, Nicodemos LeStrange had another thing coming.

"At least you're honest." He pulled a notebook from his desk and uncapped his pen. "Let's talk details."

FINN

His phone had been a steady stream of condolences since his father passed. In a way, being at work was a kind of reprieve from the never-ending parade of grieving and associated well-wishers. Goddamn, if everything didn't fall apart...

Finn sighed, shaking his head. That train of thought only led to a downward spiral. *Here there be monsters.* He didn't have time for that. In addition to the upcoming state funeral, for which he needed to write his eulogy, then the coronation, and then the wedding, and then, a while after that, impending fatherhood, he also had a child homelessness and hunger initiative he was spearheading and a shifter health and wellness seminar he was putting together with Boston Children's Hospital. It was like his whole life had suddenly gone from a dead stop to light speed.

"Your Highness, your eleven o'clock is here." Finn's assistant

Henry was a good kid, Vulpine, solid, good at his job and keeping him on task, if only there weren't so damn many tasks….

"Thank you, Henry. Please show the Marquise in," the prince responded as he rose from his desk and buttoned his suit jacket.

Outside of being his fiancée's father, Marius LeStrange had been his father's friend and confidante for decades, so when he reached out to Finn regarding some of the King's unfinished personal business, the prince felt obliged to at least hear him out, if not take up the cause outright.

The dark-skinned, older man in the very nice suit had mastered the art of being forthright-but-deferential and entered his office with a confident stride. The small army of dark-suited Guards he left in the lobby were hard to miss as well. Odd, but given the King's recent death and his own attack, not terribly abnormal. "Your Highness, thank you so much for seeing me on such short notice."

"Of course, Lord LeStrange." He held out a hand to direct him to the leather couches in his seating area. "Please, call me Finn. May I have my assistant get you something to drink?" His eyes caught on the large attaché case the Minster was carrying as he set it by his foot. Hard-sided, with a complicated locking mechanism, it seemed an odd accessory to bring to this meeting.

"Tea, Your Highness, would be lovely." He smiled, and for a moment, Finn could see shades of Cora in his mischievous grin and regal bearing.

The click of heels and the closing of the door told him his assistant was on the job. "We'll have it to you momentarily, My Lord. Now, what brings you by?"

Dark eyes that shimmered to yellow and black took him in, also not at all unlike his fiancée. The subtle similarities were spooky and more than a little unsettling. "My family and yours go back a long time. Centuries, even."

He nodded once, eyes narrowing slightly. "I know, and your faithful and diligent service has been above reproach, as always." Already, the meeting was off to an unusual start, and Finn couldn't help but hope Henry returned soon with refreshments to break up the strangeness.

"Your father was a good man, a good friend. I loved working for him, and I plan to serve you just as well, if you'll have me." It was unorthodox, to say the least, to pitch a job interview under these circumstances, but he hadn't been regent long enough to know if this was truly bizarre. It sure as hell felt like it.

In the silence that followed this proclamation, Finn was unsure how to respond, but fortunately, Marius rushed to fill the void. "I'm not here to discuss that. We can discuss that later. What I need you to understand is, as the de facto putative head of the Corvids, you marrying a Corvid girl makes me so happy. In my soul. It's clear she makes you happy. Your father saw that, too."

He felt the smile freeze on his lips. "I'm glad you think so. She's amazing, and it's wonderful that you and he have seen her as I do." Finn truly hoped his growing horror didn't show on his face. Marius was sharing this profoundly emotional moment that would have never happened if he knew who she truly was. His personal level of discomfort was approaching 'secured to a chair via silver cuffs' levels, and for the love of the gods, where was his assistant?

"My family has, as I'm sure you're aware, some vacancies within the hierarchy."

The room was suddenly far too warm. "I'm sorry?" he inquired warily.

The old raven waved a hand dismissively. "Well, we have an open duchy here, an open baronet there, and your father, when you became the regent after announcing your wedding and impending fatherhood..." His eyes grew misty as he smiled fondly. "Your father and I discussed it, and we know she doesn't have to have a title. She can marry you and become the Queen Consort without any issue at all. However, having a title would make her Queen, full stop."

Finn's eyebrows shot up as his eyes widened. Securing a title from Marius to replace the one he'd taken from Cora had been at the top of his list of things to do. Yes, she told him she didn't want anything from the old man, but the prince knew it wasn't fair and wanted to restore that to her. Only he hadn't really thought of a way to bring it up that wasn't a more refined version of a shakedown.

Could it really be that simple? Clarification became imperative. "I don't understand."

Marius took up the briefcase by his feet and deftly worked through both of the side locks, as well as the thumb scan on top. All of them popped at once, and the lid lifted slightly. He withdrew an ancient, oxblood leather case, strangely shaped as though it housed an instrument of some sort with a tall central bridge not unlike a violin, and certainly similar in size. He placed it on the coffee table in front of the prince.

"Go ahead and look," he encouraged.

Finn picked up the case, turning it over in his hands, even going so far as to shake it. It made no noise and gave no clues as to its contents and felt a little like a jewelry box as the stiff hinge creaked when he lifted the lid.

"Holy shit," he whispered with his hand over his mouth in shock. Glittering light burst forth in front of him, shimmering facets of diamonds in all shapes and sizes. Spread out across a bed of fine black velvet, he counted two bracelets of fine platinum mesh with diamond-haloed ruby findings, a string of oval diamonds the size of butter beans that formed a necklace that dropped into a blood-red ruby pendant the size of a plump fig, earrings with stones so large they may be painful to wear, somewhere in the neighborhood of fifteen diamond-and-ruby hair pins—he stopped counting at ten—a heavy, glittering cuff, a broach that appeared to bear a coat of arms in addition to three more diamond-and-ruby butter bean-sized pendants, all leading up to a tiara on the raised center so breathtaking in its perfection, he didn't realize he'd reached for it until it was in his hands. Interlinking loops and whorls composed of round stones of graduated and decreasing size, each surrounding a ruby the size of a nickel, leading to a pinnacle in the front the size of a walnut, all resting on three rows of smaller diamonds, woven together with the platinum in almost a lace-like pattern.

"There are almost seven thousand diamonds and thirty-five pigeon-blood rubies in this case, the total carat weight of which is an obscenity best committed only to paper, all going back to at least 1562, when the set was gifted to the Duc du Corbeau, Robert LeStrange, by Elizabeth of Austria to spite her ex-husband, Charles

IX." Well, that explained the small platoon of Guards in his waiting room. He'd be worried about traveling with something like this, and he was the damn head of state.

"One of the last of the Valois kings." Finn knew of them due to the history with his family and why they'd fled Brittany all those centuries ago. You 'didn't forget the people who delighted in hunting your family for sport.

Marius nodded. "She didn't like him, and she *really* didn't like his mother. Spite is an interesting motivator. In any case, the Duchess of Corbeau has a parure fit for a queen. How appropriate."

The air around him stilled as he appreciated the older man's statement. "The Duchess of Corbeau..."

He grinned broadly as he plucked the tiara from the prince's hands and placed it back in the case, closing it just before the soft knock at the door signaled the return of Henry with the tea and snacks. Finn waved him over as Marius removed some paperwork from his briefcase, waiting until his assistant left to set it in front of Finn, next to his tea.

"Allow me to present my wedding present, and your father's dying wish."

CORA

"I'm not going."

"It's a command performance. You don't get to *not* go."

"I'm not going," Mos reiterated, shaking his head.

Cora rose from her chair and planted her hands on the desk as she leaned into his face. "He's your fucking King." She left off the part about being his fucking sister, as she knew that held less than no sway where he was concerned.

Not to be outdone, Mos, too, got to his feet to square off against his sister. Again. "Not yet, he's not."

The standoff resolved a moment later when they both pushed

away from the desk in annoyance, neither of them having patience for the other.

"You can't make me go."

"Oh, but I can, in fact." She chuckled darkly. "This marriage needs a government official in attendance in order to be considered 'legitimate.'"

"Which would happen if you were having it *legally*."

"It would be legal if you were there."

"I would be lending legitimacy to an act of treason."

"It's not treason if he's the King." She felt her blood pressure rise as her eyes began to throb.

"He's not the King yet," he spat, yellow eyes on fire and showing absolutely no give in his thought process.

"Details, asshole. Details. And…at the risk of repeating myself, you owe me." She gathered her purse and turned to leave.

"The fuck are you going? Don't walk away from me! We're not finished!" He stalked after her, slamming a palm against the door as she attempted to open it. He knew enough to understand touching her would be at his own peril.

Her smile was a mouthful of razors. "Oh, but we *are*. We really are. I have an obstetrician appointment, and you have shit to do to prepare for the night after tomorrow. It's not a request, and I only asked you as a courtesy. Consider yourself volun-told."

Cora yanked the door open the moment she felt the slightest give in his position, stomping out past his assistant. "I'll see you in two days, LeStrange."

VASILY

He'd taken part in more than a couple hostage situations over the years, first as a Marine with the 1st Reconnaissance Battalion out of Camp Pendleton, and then again as a member of the Royal

Guard of Therantia. And still, he'd never seen anyone look as put-upon or under-duress as Mos did, slinking in through a side door to the private dining room right before the festivities were to begin.

Dressed in his customary black on black on black, the Baron put the 'fun' in funereal. Honestly, he looked like he hoped one of the shadows of the room would swallow him whole and remove him from this mortal coil. Pinched face, squinting in the low light of all the candelabra and wall sconces, he looked like his tie was too tight or the hold on his temper was a little too loose. Either way, Vasi doubted very much that the raven's sister gave a damn. He was here, and that meant Vasily didn't have to commit any capital crimes on a day that was, for the most part, celebratory.

The whole reason they were in the Abbey's private dining room was because the owl knew a guy who knew a guy, in this case, his sister's husband, Alfonse, the Strigine hotel manager with enough sense to appreciate both the historical significance and eventual social cache of hosting a clandestine royal fete. His brother-in-law was the only person Vasi could think of who could pull this off. For an event of this magnitude, the level of secrecy and planning that had gone into making all this possible in less than three weeks was impressive. The private dining room looked out onto a stone patio, gardens just coming into their greenery. Everything was fresh and the world felt like it was beginning anew. It was restorative, more or less.

The guest list was sparse, which, given the very nature of the event, was not that surprising. Xander was on duty as Finn's personal Guard, and Dev "'just happened to stop by" ' on his day off. Vasi was sad that Finn had no other family but was more than happy to step up and look after his friend on such a joyous occasion.

On Cora's side, though…'that was where things got *hinky.* Her curvy little Saurian assistant was there to stand with her, much as he was there for Finn, but her other two guests were, for lack of a better phrase, sketchy as fuck. Bedecked in sketch, as it were, even if they were both in khakis and button-down shirts. The taller of the two looked like he'd spent the last couple past lives subbing as a drawbridge or load-bearing wall. Perhaps a gargoyle, given both his size and his glower. He was enormous, with darkly tanned skin, salt-

and-pepper gray hair just shy of being bristly, and wearing a navy-blue dress shirt that looked like the last time it had been out of the closet was his parole hearing. Vasi had scented a cat in the room as soon as he'd walked in the door, and he'd bet money it was this guy.

The cat's husband was a different story entirely. He was almost equally tall, but more lithe, longer, shaggy blond hair tied back loosely with a ribbon and lighter all over in both demeanor and attire. Something about his eyes, though, greenish gold and hard, gave the impression that the Canid knew more than he showed and was a lot tougher than he looked. They were an odd pair, but Vasi sensed any questions he may have had were better left unanswered.

Two tables were placed in the room, one for the happy couple and each 'side of the aisle' as it were, and one for the cake. They were beautifully appointed with black tablecloths and place settings, and over-the-top centerpiece floral arrangements of black roses, black calla lilies, and bright red poppies tied with ribbons of deep gray silk. The effect was elegant and understated, but still quite striking.

A wrought iron archway adorned with black and red flowers stood by the windows, with a row of chairs on each side. This was the most pared-down setup Vasily had ever seen, and yet it worked on a fundamental level. Exactly like the couple in question.

From the corner of his eye, he watched as Finn absently fingered the poppy and lily boutonniere on the lapel of his black bespoke Italian tux as he stared out the window. "You're gonna mess it up. Leave it alone."

The prince winced as his hands dropped away, one getting stuffed into the pocket of his trousers, the other to his mouth as he nipped at his cuticle. "But what if she changed her mind? What if this isn't perfect?"

Vasi looked pointedly around the room, with the candlelit glow, and their excruciating formal attire, right down to the frock coats, ascots, cufflinks, tie bars, and tie pins for Finn, Xander, Dev, and himself. Even the sling for his arm matched. "Yeah, if this isn't her idea of perfect, then nothing is." He smiled as he gently shoulder checked his anxious friend. "Besides, she's already got perfect. She's got you. This is just paperwork and a formality."

Finn blinked at him; eyes narrowed as the corner of his mouth curled into a wry grin. "I thought you were a monk. Who knew you were a closet romantic?"

The owl snorted. "I've been known to have my moments."

The sound of tinkling crystal by the main entrance drew the attention of everyone in the room. The pastor of the Salem Unitarian Congregation of Shifters, Bishop Zion Rook, the person his brother-in-law had listed as the on-call officiant, stood in their white vestments, grinning broadly, a vision in tattoos, gold, and glitter.

"It's about to begin, if you'll take your places."

Vasily stood by his friend, his best friend since he'd been assigned as a Marine Gunnery Sergeant special liaison to the Palace Guard who shadowed Finn getting his International Relations degree at Tufts. Finn had been his housemate, his friend, his confidant, and very soon, his King, and the honor of being by his side for this momentous occasion was not lost on him at all. "You good?" he muttered as the prince shifted from foot to foot when the music began.

The main doors to the private dining room swept open during the stringed intro to '*My First Love*', revealing Venus, Cora's assistant in a black, off-the-shoulder dress that could have doubled for a skin graft, carrying a bouquet of black lilies and red poppies. She was the quintessential pinup girl, with her black hair in a chignon, dress that lovingly caressed all her generous curves before stopping at her knees, and a red lipstick strong enough to negotiate treaties.

Dipping her head deferentially as she passed the prince, she took her place across the aisle from him with a broad grin.

It was something she and his best friend shared.

"Could not be better."

CORA

The doors swept open, and it felt like everything in her life had been leading to this moment. Every decision, every success, every failure, every choice right down to her slinky gray dress and Louboutin t-straps that made her look like a 1940's femme fatale, had brought her to this place, and she could not be more elated. Following Venus up the aisle, she took in the lovey-dovey grins on Mookie's and Sam's faces and couldn't help but return them. Absent her blood family, besides Mos, who was holding up the wall at the back of the room like she wouldn't see him, these were the only people in her life who mattered.

Walking down the aisle to Finn felt like some kind of fever dream. She was too happy, too warm, too ready to swoon for the bearded fairytale prince with his big blue eyes and strong arms and smile that took her breath away every time she saw him. And it felt glorious. No, her life didn't start out like this, or even hint that this was a possibility, but standing next to him in his black frock coat tux, well. Consider her inner romantic tweaked.

The blood rushing in her ears blotted out the officiant's first words, but when Finn whispered, "You ready?" she nodded once. Never been more ready.

"I never imagined you," Finn whispered as he gazed at their joined hands. After clearing his throat, his cheek ticked with a bit of a smile. "You came blazing into my life, blasting color where there had been none, bringing life to feelings I'd thought were long dead. You're my angel, my lover, my protector, and my friend. Soon to be the mother of my child," he chuckled softly, "and I could not be more privileged. I promise to stand behind you in faith and trust, beside you as your honored partner, and in front of you as your greatest defender. I give you myself, and all that I am, until I no longer draw breath. This is my vow."

Cora felt the carefully banked emotions dissolve and start running silently down her cheeks somewhere around him mentioning her being the mother of his child. Lips pursed against a sob, she quickly swiped at the tears and silently thanked the gods for waterproof makeup. With a watery grin, she sniffed. "I should have gone first." Snickers and giggles rippled throughout the room, and Finn smiled broadly as he brushed her knuckles with his lips.

"I'm not sorry."

She shook her head, feeling all the humor of the situation draining away. "You shouldn't be. You're an amazing man, my Finnegan, and I am absolutely unworthy. You make me happier than I deserve, honestly. This," she gestured vaguely around them, "is not the life I'd planned or even knew was possible, and yet now I can't imagine anything better. I will be your partner in all things, even if we disagree. I will defend you, always, no matter what. I will love you the same. I do not take the privilege of your love and devotion lightly, and I won't. You have me, all of me, as I am, a collection of jagged and unvarnished pieces you somehow make whole, and I will treasure you for my life, until there is no breath in my body. This is my vow."

The rest of the ceremony itself was a whirlwind, stripped down to its essence. It was just about the two of them. Their declarations of love were already on the record for each of them, so this was really a more joyful form of paperwork. One thing she will never forget, though, was the surge of elation at hearing the words, "Mrs. Cora O'Casey." She was pretty sure that would never get old.

Finn held up a glass as they were seated with their families. "I know it's traditional to let the best man speak right now, but there's very little traditional about this day. So, if you'll indulge me," Vasi chuckled and nodded at his best friend, "thank you. The official wedding in a few weeks, that's the public ceremony that will fulfill all the state obligations and whatever else. This, right here, is just for us, and our families." His loving gaze felt like a hug as he smiled down at her. "I love you, Angel. Having you in my life has been the singular most bizarre, wildest, best adventure possible, and I could not be more grateful. You've made me so damn happy I could burst, and you deserve the same happiness."

Xander, who'd been sitting next to Vasi silently observing like he did, grinned then and reached under his chair to pull out a box and slide it down the fine linen tablecloth to Finn. A wicked little grin unfurled across her husband's lips.

"What did you do?" she demanded warily as she took in Vasi's and Dev's matching grins.

"Me?" He was the wide-eyed paragon of innocence and virtue as he pushed the box the size of a viola case in front of her. "I didn't do this."

"Uh huh. And yet, here it is." It was large, enrobed in cracked, blood-red leather and looked a lot like the parure box her mother had in the back of the closet and only removed for special occasions. Only this was bigger, by quite a bit. To be honest, she was kinda afraid to touch it, her childhood memories kicking in hard for the whoopin' she'd received for trying on her mother's 'princess crown'.

Finn sat down next to her, turning in his chair to take her hand. "Hey." He waited until her eyes slid from the offending item to him. "This wasn't me. My father's dying wish was to give you this. He wanted you to have it. I'm just the messenger."

Honestly, the idea that the King had wanted this for her terrified her even more. "I...I can't—"

"You can," he assured her, inching the box closer. "Please."

Cora felt all the eyes in the room on her keenly. Willing her hands not to shake, she touched the box, the velvet smoothness of the leather soothing to her fingertips. The creaking hinge of the lid as she cautiously lifted it seemed inordinately loud to her ears, and then her eyes attempted to leave of their own volition.

"Fuck me, Boss," she heard Sam mutter next to her as Venus gasped farther down the table, and honestly, she agreed. Diamonds--she'd never seen so many diamonds--in platinum settings and in all configurations. And rubies, the smallest of which was the size of a cherry pit, like drops of blood in a sea of glass, enough to make her palms sweat. Bracelets, a necklace, a broach, hair pins, earrings, a ring, and of course, a tiara that gave her neck strain simply from looking at it.

For a minute, all she could do was look, hand over her mouth and eyes unblinking, blinded by the enormity of it, both the present and the gesture. It wasn't every day someone gifted several million— capital M—dollars in jewelry to anyone, much less her. And all at once, her sense caught up to her, and she slammed the lid down and turned to the man she loved more than life.

"Finnegan, a word." She didn't let him respond, instead sweeping straight from the table across the room to the windows overlooking the garden. The air at the table had been too thin, and no amount of chilled tonic water helped her regain the composure that had clearly fled for safer climes.

He was at her side in an instant. "Angel. Talk to me."

"I can't take that. I can't accept something like that. I'm not…" She found her mind whirling, groping in the sea of all the things she wasn't, trying to seize on one that would make him understand why this was a terrible idea.

Strong arms folded around her as he tucked her head under his chin against his neck, his warmth and spicy scent immediately easing her tension. His deep voice was pitched lower, for her ears only, and she calmed down even further. "Cora. You are the love of my life, and you are my queen in every sense. And you're going to be *the* Queen, capital Q, of Therantia. Da wanted to spoil you. I want to spoil you, and the baby," his broad palm dropped to her stomach briefly before wrapping loosely around her waist. "Please, let us… Your Grace?"

At his use of that particular style of address, her chin whipped up, and she found herself staring into the most earnest blue eyes she knew. "I… I don't…" She tried on several attempts at a response, each time losing the thread after the verb.

Mischievous grin back in place, he dipped down to swipe his lips over hers as he blatantly stole a kiss. "I'll explain at the table, okay?"

Finally calm enough to breathe easily, she nodded with a quick dip of her chin. "All right, then."

Once seated back at the table, Mookie reached over and around his husband to squeeze her hand affectionately. He always stepped up when she needed him, and right then, she definitely appreciated the assist. Finn rose again and addressed the whole table.

"The King knew, when we approached him with the engagement, that in order for you to be Queen in full standing, you needed a title. The Minister of the Interior knew that as well and approached him with an offer."

A chair scraped back from the table quickly as Mos surged

to his feet, clearly agitated with wide gold eyes and heaving chest. "I'm sorry, what?" As much as her reflex was to argue with him, she found herself agreeing with her brother's disbelief. There was no way her father would have done this voluntarily without a larger plan in play.

"Your Lordship, if you'll be seated, I'll explain." Finn sounded perfectly calm and smooth, but Cora could hear the whip crack of command in his tone. Her brother's ass quickly found the seat again, and her husband carried on like he hadn't been interrupted. "The Marquise Marius LeStrange conferred this to my father, who then intended to give it to you." Dev pulled a sheaf of papers from the inner pocket of his frock coat. "These are the letters of patent, signed by the Marquise and my father, as his last official act prior to his death." Staring directly at Mos, his smile became a little smug. "It's a done deal. I'm the messenger here. And as such," he turned back to her with the softest and most affectionate expression she'd ever seen, "will you remove your hat, my love?"

"I'll take that, thank you."

Bless Venus, who was at her chair immediately, removing bobby pins and the hat pin she had in place to keep her pillbox hat positioned correctly in her hair. Cora knew she couldn't do it, as her hands were suddenly numb. She had no idea how Finn managed to pull this off. Her father was not a man who admitted to mistakes or apologized ever, but her husband had managed a miracle tonight. She flexed her fingers as her assistant removed the hat.

"Pretty sure you don't need this right now. You'll get it back shortly," the giggling woman whispered as she resumed her seat at the table next to her brother.

Finn tipped back the lid of the parure box, this time carefully removing the diamond and ruby tiara with both hands. "Though you'll be my queen in a few short weeks, you'll now be the Duchess of Corbeau forever."

The weight of the tiara was immense, maybe a bit heavier due to the baggage that came with it. This was the last act of the King, his concern for her. She couldn't help but tear up a bit, even as she heard her brother on the opposite side of the table quietly seething.

Her husband took her hand and kissed her fingers as he pulled her from the chair to stand beside him. "My Lords, ladies, gentlemen, may I present to you Her Grace, Lady Coretta Ashai O'Casey, the Duchess of Corbeau." He wrapped his arms around her then, cradling her back to his chest as her friends, family, and even the wait staff applauded and cheered.

There was only one more thing she needed.

FINN

Their dinner came then, right on time, and everyone sat and drank, celebrating the happy couple. To his surprise, she kept the tiara on, even when he'd offered to put it away. She wanted to show off his present, and that pleased him immensely. He also loved that he got to meet the people in her life she'd only spoken to him about. Seeing her found family in action brought joy to his soul, knowing that even though her blood family had abandoned her, she wasn't alone.

And now, she'd never be alone again, if he had anything to say about it.

They talked, he told Cora the story of the jewels, their history within her family line, how he'd come to have them. Mostly, he told her how hard it was to keep this secret under wraps and under constant guard without her finding out, even though it was only a couple days. She was uncanny in her ability to suss out a lie or tease out a secret from him. He was glad they'd be ruling together, because he knew he'd end up telling her all the state secrets later anyway.

His queen. She was his queen, and he could not stop smiling. He was sure the pictures would later show him as all teeth and dimples, because this day was beyond perfect. Vasi really came through for him.

After they cut the cake, Cora rose and addressed the table. "I am so fucking happy, let me start there." They all chuckled at her candor, because even though she was now titled once again, she was still very much herself. "I never even contemplated getting married, much less in a fairytale setting like this. You kill me, Finn. And Vasi?" She looked around her husband to his best man, who wore a self-satisfied smirk. "Good job." The smirk became a beaming grin as he nodded in acknowledgment.

"Thank you all. For being here on such short notice, for supporting us, even if we did have to practically drag some of you at gunpoint." Her eyes slid to her brother, who was all gold eyes, folded arms, and mighty scowl. Honestly, Finn couldn't give a fuck what the angry Corvid felt about the situation. It was a decision made above both their paygrades. He was here, and this was the very least he owed his sister.

"And, not to be outdone, husband...gods, I love calling you that." Finn leaned up as she leaned down, sighing into the brief but affectionate brush of his lips against hers. "Anyway," she straightened and smiled brightly, "not to be outdone, but I got you a gift as well. Mooks?"

The giant man, who frankly looked too large to be a Felid, produced a distinctive turquoise blue box tied with a white ribbon from his pocket. As he passed it to his husband, the Canid frowned and quickly untied and freshened up the mildly flattened bow before passing it over. "I love you, babe, but come on. Really?" Finn had to squelch a grin at the quiet chastisement and the flushed, but chagrined, shrug from the big guy.

Cora kissed Sam's cheek as he handed it to her with a whisper of something that sounded like "'good luck.'" On guard, he regarded the box in her hand with grave suspicion.

He wasn't reassured when she heaved a great sigh as she set it in front of him. "Go ahead and open it."

Eyes narrowed, he plucked at the white ribbon and tipped open the box, revealing a navy-blue velvet box. "What did you do?" He echoed her question as he dumped the box out of its official blue encasement.

With a tiny roll of her shoulder, she grinned so broadly her dark eyes sparkled with it. "Just open it."

Still highly skeptical, he eased back the hinged lid to find a bracelet. It was a platinum ID bracelet with a chunky, flattened-out chain, and a plate engraved with his first name and a stylized chess king. "Okay?" At her pursed-lip look of consternation, he lifted it from its cradle and examined it more closely. The back of the identification plate was engraved as well, with the word '*Chessmen.*' "I don't get it."

Cora reached up and held her tiara on as she stared at the frescoed ceiling and sighed to the heavens. "Look in the bottom of the box."

"Feelin' a little like Brad Pitt at the end of '*Se7en.*'" He snickered as he tugged on an errant piece of silk to lift the display stand of the bracelet away from the box.

"This is way better, swear."

Underneath the velvet pillow thing was a picture, in black and white, of several odd shapes like a Rorschach painting. The only defining features were the bright red circle around a bit in the middle and an 'A' in the top right corner. Underneath was the same thing, only with the circle moved slightly and labeled 'B' and 'C'.

Holding all three up like a flared hand of cards, he studied his wife's expectant expression. "Now I *really* don't understand."

She gave him the longest slow blink in history before Cora snorted so hard her shoulders jumped as she laughed. "Really?"

The way her assistant Venus was practically vibrating in her chair and Vasi's eyes were both bright orange and almost too big for his face were incredibly concerning. "I got nothing."

Gracefully slipping back into her seat, his wife—just the idea of that made him smile—took his free hand in both of hers and gazed at him with the most serious expression he'd ever seen on her outside of a dire emergency. "You referred to me earlier as the mother of your child."

"Right?"

Her dark eyes darted to the pictures in his hands before returning to his with a tentative grin painted over her lips. "Okay. Well, it appears our numbers were off. By a few."

"By...a few," he repeated slowly, tasting each word as he immediately scoured the images in his hand once more. He held up each one, absently passing them off Vasi after he'd finished thoroughly examining the picture. "I...trip—how? Are we—?" The tears burning in his eyes were both unbidden and absolutely unexpected as he collected them and looked them over again. The implications of it were enormous, so vast and far-reaching, he didn't even know how to process. "Really?"

Thankfully, she didn't comment on his breathless voice or exceptionally wet face that was probably streaking red in places. "Really." Cora plucked one picture from his hand, turning it over to reveal writing on the back. Labeled 'Knight 1-3', it all began to fall into place in his head.

"Chessmen," he breathed, and she nodded.

"A King, a Queen, and three little Knights. Congratulations, Daddy. It's a family."

He had no idea how he ended up away from the table, laughing as he twirled a giggling and squirming Cora in his arms, but their friends were hollering encouragements, and the flashbulbs were enough to bring him back to the current plane of reality. "A family. *Our* family."

Her fingertips were gentle on his cheeks as she framed his face with her hands. "I know this won't make up for everyone you've lost..." She trailed off as she touched her forehead to his. "But I'm here to tell you, going forward, we are your family. Always."

That was a thought that stopped him cold, and then reduced him to damn near sobbing with his face pressed into the crook of her neck. He hadn't expected Cora to get so flowery and effusive in her affections. Maybe it was the hormones, or the whole event, but either way, he'd take it.

Bending her over his arm in a deep dip, Finn kissed her like his life depended on it, like it was the last thing he'd ever do and wanted to get it right. Against her lips, he whispered, "Overwhelmed doesn't even begin to cover it. I hate you so much right now." His watery chuckle as he said it belied the harsh words.

His raven squeezed him tightly, pressing a gentle kiss to his temple. "I love you, too."

VASILY

Maintaining his cool and jaded facade was tough in the face of such overwhelming joy and love. This was the kind of thing that sealed families together, a kind of broadcast to the fates and the gods that this moment of joy was worth whatever trials they threw at them. This moment was theirs, and they stood united.

Watching Finn kiss Cora, and her fall into his arms like the delicate damsel she sure as hell was *not*, Vasi rubbed his chest at the slight but sharp pain in the vicinity of his heart. Oh, he didn't begrudge his best friend this moment, this latest-in-a-series of life-altering new adventures. Truly, he didn't. Couldn't be happier for him if he tried. He just, for a moment, in the tiny part of his heart still capable of wanting such things, wondered why he didn't get to have the same.

He wasn't so repressed that he couldn't admit that this had, at one time, been a dream of his. A home, a marriage like his sister had, a family, a life beyond…well, the palace was as much a home to him as his own apartment, but it definitely wasn't the same. Maybe before he joined the Corps. And now, well, he didn't have time to dwell on what might have been and would probably never be again. He needed to look after his friend and his new family and figure out the scope of Prince Brendan's plans.

But for now, he wasn't here to lament the sorry state of his love life, so with the celebratory champagne flowing like water, he threw back his drink and snagged a waitress for a refill. It was only when she asked if he heard any buzzing that he realized his phone was ringing in his pants.

It was his personal number, not his work cell, so he was concerned. Almost everyone who would have reason to call him was in the room with him.

"Brețcu." The silence that greeted him was unnerving, and he had to look at his phone to see if they were connected. "Hello?"

He was just about to hang up when he heard a shaky inhale. "Vasily?"

A feminine voice, one he almost recognized, even as it was impossible. An echo through time so sharp his breath caught. "Who is this?"

"Forget me so soon, my fine, feathery friend?" The delicate rasp of her voice, soft and rough at the same time, kind of took his legs out from under him and sent his heartrate into the stratosphere. It was definitely not a voice he thought he'd hear again.

"Excuse me, Your Highness, Your Grace." He held up the phone as proof and quickstepped out a side entrance to a service hallway. "Sweets? You there?"

"I'm here. It's been a long time."

Understatement of a lifetime. "I..." He swallowed hard, blowing out a quiet breath as he slid down the wall just outside the door. "I'm not sure what to say. I'm surprised you called."

"I am, too."

Her admission did nothing to calm his steadily escalating nerves. "You doin' all right, Cherry?"

"Been better." A whole world of memories churned up in the silence that followed that answer. "A lot going on here."

"Anything I can help you with?" A part of him wanted to snatch the words back as soon as they were uttered. Good thing he was used to living with the consequences of bad decisions, thanks to princes Brendan and Finn.

He waited, ticking off the seconds as he listened to her deliberate over explaining her answer. It was clear from the moment she'd called that she needed something from him, and as much as his instincts were very much against doing anything at all for her, he knew whatever she asked of him, he'd do. Because 'that was who she was to him.

"I need you, Vasi." Her tone sounded equal parts resigned and relieved.

"I'm yours."

He heard her sharp intake of breath at his vehemence, but then, his devotion to her had never been the problem. To be fair, though, hers to him, as well. Finally, she sighed deeply. "Can you come?"

"Where?"

"Anchorage."

"Oh? You went home." That was new. Or at least, new to him. He wondered what would have led her back to Alaska when she'd told him more than once that she hadn't wanted to return to the cold if she could help it. And truthfully, he'd gone out of his way not to know her whereabouts, solely to keep the temptation to reach out to her at bay.

Her grunt of impatience made him smile despite the circumstances. He could almost picture her scrunched up nose and pout. "It's been a few years, Feathers. Now, can you come or not?" She paused, and Vasi couldn't say for sure, but he got a bad feeling about the silence that followed. In a voice he knew could and would break his heart until the end of time, she whispered, "I need you."

"What's goin on, Sweets?"

"I...have a situation. There's something really fucking weird going on out here, and I need your help dealing with it."

The tight notes of agitation in her voice were hard to miss and given that her threshold for "'real fucking weird"' was pretty damn high—at least it had been in the past—he was more than a little unnerved but still had some questions. "That's vague. Do I get a clue? Something?"

"Something..." She sighed deeply, ending in a growl. "Something bad happened to me, Vasily. Really bad."

Questions and rage layered in his head into this weird kind of white noise. A coppery scent very much like blood snared his senses and honed his focus to a fine point. There would be time for questions later, he decided. He had people he needed to kill now.

Of course, he couldn't tell her that. That sounded crazy, possessive, obsessive. The idea that any harm had come to her in his absence incensed him. Feelings that he should have long let go of where she was concerned came flaring to the front of his mind. He would burn the world for her. "Did you go to the cops?" he asked softly, doing his best to keep his tone gentle, concerned but not overly so. He didn't want to frighten her. Seemed like she'd had enough of that already.

"Yeah. They don't seem much interested."

"I'm sorry?" Rage was a flavor on his tongue, and he had to fight to keep his talons in check.

"They said there wasn't enough evidence to make an investigation worth their time and effort. Something something, tiny department. Something something, limited resources. Something something, they're just shifter women, so why should we care?"

He almost felt bad for the involuntary growl in response to that. Once he helped her, however she needed, he was going to go make some rounds. Explain in excruciating detail that her requests, her pain, were nothing to trifle with.

"Honestly?" He could hear a frustrated sigh, and then a second that was less so, but more resigned.

Finally, in a soft voice, Cherry stated, "I'd feel better if you looked into it. Not that I don't trust them, it's just you're...well, you."

Her self-conscious chuckle at the end was what got him. As much as he knew he should stay away from her, for his heart's sake if nothing else, he truly couldn't deny her anything. "All right, Sweets, I'll see what I can do."

Her sigh of relief washed through him over the phone lines. "So, you'll come? Please?"

"Yeah, I'll come." Even if he wasn't currently listed as 'Injured, On Duty', the simple fact of her asking would have him moving Heaven and Earth before she even finished the request.

"Thank the gods. How soon can you get here?"

He looked at his watch and then at the door beside him. "I'll call you back in ten minutes with a better idea of my itinerary, okay?"

"Thank you, Vasily. Thank you so much."

He smiled, rolling his eyes toward the fluorescent lights in the ceiling. Damn, but he was soft for her. "Anything for you, *inimioara mea*."

"You ever gonna tell me what that means?"

"Nah, Sweets." He chuckled as he got to his feet and straightened his frock coat. "You'll figure it out eventually."

They said their goodbyes, and he tucked his phone into his pocket as he returned to the private dining room. His mind was already running through calculations and scenarios. He walked in just in time to hear, "Here's to many more years on this journey."

They all raised their glasses, and Cora sipped her tonic water as he did his best to slip into his seat unobtrusively.

"You good, man?" Dev asked quietly as he took the seat next to Vasi. "You were gone for a minute."

"Yeah. Um…I'm still considered on leave, right?"

"Yeah." The Day Watch Commander drew the word out and nodded slowly, suspicion plain on his face.

"Good. I gotta be gone a few days. Nothing serious, I just gotta take care of something for a friend."

"Sure, man, sure. Take all the time you need. Let Finn know, 'cause you know how he worries."

Did he ever. He stood and buttoned his coat, clapping his friend and compatriot on the shoulder. "Thanks, man. See you in a few days."

"Call me if you need me."

"You know I will."

Finn rose from his chair with a grin as he approached. "Vasi, man, I cannot thank you enough for all this. Your brother-in-law Alphonse, too. This was beyond perfect."

The vaguely tipsy prince pulled him into a tight hug, and he patted his back awkwardly. "It's okay, big guy. It was no problem. I'm happy it worked out for you and Her Grace." Cora made kissy faces at him from behind the wolf's back and mouthed her thanks as well. "Look, I gotta be gone for a few days. Dev and Xander have all of this covered, but I'm flying out in a few hours, and I wanted you to know."

"Everything okay?" she asked, her now-gold eyes honing in keenly on everything he wasn't saying.

The owl nodded. "Yeah, I have a thing I need to take care of."

"Well, I'm here if you need me, you hear?"

There was no doubt in his mind if he called her, Cora Westgate-O'Casey would show up on his doorstep armed, armored, and ready to fight, pregnant with triplets or not. "And I appreciate that, Your Grace. See you in a few days."

He was on his phone the moment his back cleared the dining room. "Yeah, Zeke, it's Breţcu. I need a favor."

WINGED GUARDIANS

Chapter 4

GWEN

After the interminable train ride out of Basque country and into Paris, the Maybach Town Car that Dmitri sent for her was a slice of heaven and nothing short of what she deserved. Under ideal circumstances, she'd be traveling with her valet and her assistant who would arrange such things for her. But these were not, in any way, ideal circumstances—at least not yet.

Traveling solo was the only way to ensure her whereabouts remained unofficial and off the record. The last thing she needed was to draw attention to herself and make it easy for the Guard, who— if they weren't looking for her now, it wouldn't be long—would be more than happy to scoop her up and remand her back to the palace where she'd remain in custody until the trial. The accommodations would likely be quite the downgrade from her usual.

The same, however, could not be said about Dmitri's house. Chateau, really, thirty or so kilometers outside of Paris, his little *pied-à-terre,* as he called it, was actually a stunning example of well-preserved French Baroque architecture by Jules Mansart himself, from the quaint gatehouse at the back entrance to the property to its sprawling but exquisitely tended gardens with oddly spike-shaped topiaries and two-story fairytale facade with open bright royal blue shutters on all the windows. All that was missing were the hoop skirts and powdered wigs.

Gwen smiled as the car slowed by the dual stone staircase outside, with a familiar face descending as they arrived. "Dima, my love."

The tall, silver-haired man in the impeccable Huntsman suit kissed her cheek as he handed her out of the car and onto the cobblestone while the driver took her bags into the house. "My pet. Your beauty is truly timeless."

"And your flattery absolutely shameless," she teased as she moved to his side and wrapped her arm around his waist.

His patrician features were like carved marble, pale and delicately veined, but a pretty face could not hide the truth, he was made of stone. Dmitri was a stone column with a Savile Row tailor, and given what he did for a living, well, he could definitely afford it. Russian by way of Lucerne, Dmitri was the guy people went to when they needed things done, for a nominal—or not so nominal, depending on your needs—fee. Launder money? No problem. Hide a body? Didn't even break a sweat. Alibi in a foreign country? No problem. New identity with paperwork so ironclad the government didn't question it? Not. A. Problem. He was a good man to know, friendly, if taciturn, but he was an invaluable business asset.

"I appreciate you taking me in on such short notice," she purred graciously as he led her to the salon, with its gorgeous original tapestries on the dark wood paneled walls and antique silk upholstered Louis XIV chairs.

"My dear, but say the word and I'll take you wherever, and however," he smirked as he took a seat across from her by the fireplace, "you would like." A member of the staff appeared out of nowhere, bringing a silver tray of tea and biscuits with porcelain china so delicate it was translucent in the light.

She couldn't suppress the giggle. "Ever the charmer, Dima." Something about the man, the lynx, made her giddy as a schoolgirl around him, though she'd refrained from indulging thus far. His flirtations were just as much a currency for him as money, and there had been more than one occasion when she'd been tempted to pay the toll.

He waited to speak until the servant closed the door behind her, choosing instead to pour out some tea and place a biscuit on her saucer. "I was terribly sorry to hear about the death of your brother." His lips twitched, but he didn't look up from his task. "You have my deepest condolences."

"Thank you." Even as she said the words, she couldn't keep the sly smile from curling her lips while she accepted the drink. "It's been a most trying time."

"I'm sure." He sipped his drink, watching her over the rim of the teacup. "And what of your nephew?"

Her lip curled involuntarily in disgust. "Which one? The rightful regent or Richard the Third?"

The silver lynx snorted. "His kingdom for a horse, no?"

"Well, you know what they say. 'Accidents will happen,' and sometimes they need a little assistance."

His deep laugh sent a teasing shiver down her spine. "I've always loved that about you, Gwendolyn. You have no desire to mask your intent where your enemies are concerned."

She dipped her chin in concession to his point. "Only to my closest friends."

"Oh, and is that what we are? Friends?"

"Among other things," she replied coyly, nipping off a corner of a cookie.

Dmitri held her gaze for a moment longer, dark eyes flashing with a silver sheen. "And to that end…" He went to the rolltop bureau across the room and unlocked it, only to return with a briefcase. "I have the items you requested, plus some I thought would be beneficial to you in your endeavors."

"I do love a man with a plan."

"Then you'll love what I have to offer you next."

VASILY

Pulling his leather bomber jacket tighter across his chest, he sighed. The damp chill of the early Seattle spring seeping in around his jeans and through his Henley and t-shirt was much more pronounced than he remembered.

The anxiety and tension he felt crackling over his skin was unexpected as he hoisted his bags into the back of a black de Havilland Beaver two-seater then climbed aboard. His ride over had been fairly uneventful. The majority of his time was spent tending to Finn and his ceaseless pre-'official'-wedding freak-out texts and updates from Xander and Dev.

The time spent not receiving updates on the Fielding diary was passed dealing with questions from his best friend like 'Would your mother mind sitting on Cora's side? It's a bit thin', and 'Should we invite members of both the Seelie and UnSeelie Courts? We're allies with one and diplomatically neutral with the other and we really don't want to alienate either. Whose side do we put which on?'

That Cora had given the wolf any wedding responsibilities at all was a blue bloody miracle, and he wanted to help as much as he could. The answers, in order, were, 'Yes, his mother will be happy just to be invited,' 'Yes, so long as they're seated on opposite sides of the venue and have monitors in place to keep them separated, and UnSeelie goes on Cora's side. Wedding today and we can broker peace talks between them later,' and finally, 'If you're looking for someone who can relate to the bride, it's definitely the Goblin fae.'

The future king of the shifters didn't really appreciate the humor in that one, but Vasi chalked that up to lack of caffeine on his end.

Maybe it was the coffee he'd grabbed when he'd landed, but he was all but buzzing by the time he and his friend Zeke, the bush pilot who was transporting him up north, were wheels up. Keeping his leg from bouncing as he shifted in the tiny plane seat was becoming a fulltime job.

In FORECON, he'd been the first one to accept an owl to his fireteam. A Pandionine, he figured Birds of Prey should flock together. Sure, Zeke had always been a little weird, one of those frighteningly smart dudes who seemed to be completely at one with the universe and its workings. The phrase used most often was "'spooky,'" but he was a damn fine tactician and close-quarter combat operator, in addition to being a pilot, so the spookiness was more welcome than disturbing. Most of the time. Exactly the kind of person you wanted when Hell decided to drop in for afternoon tea. Retired from the Corps for a few years now, he was entertaining, and loyal, and he'd been more than happy to make the four-hour trip with his old buddy up from Seattle to Anchorage.

It was all Vasi could do to keep his mind from running in circles about Cherry. All the times he'd wanted to reach out and to see her, the surge of hope burned in his chest even as it was restrained by the practicalities of distance and the time they'd spent apart. They were practically two different people now, and as tempting as dipping his toes in Lake Might-Have-Been was, his pragmatic side won every time.

"So, is she pretty in real life?" The distinct low country twang of the pilot over the headphones effectively ended his little jaunt of self-flagellation.

"Who?"

The green-eyed osprey glared at him as he pushed his grayish-blond bangs behind his ears. He'd gone shaggy in much the same way Vasily had, long hair and golden beard scruff, but even then, there was no disguising the fighter's build or the sharpness of his gaze, not even with jeans and a faded orange t-shirt with a Grateful Dead bear dancing on the front. "The new queen. I hear she's a real looker."

His lips twitched before giving way to a guffaw. "How *old* are you? A looker, Zeke...for fuck's sake..." He snorted and rubbed his head. How to describe Cora... "She's pretty enough." At his friend's amused hum, he followed up with, "What? She's my best friend's girl. I'm pretty sure I don't get to have that kind of opinion."

"Eh," he scoffed as he glanced out a side window over the

expansive ocean, "at least not share it out loud. So, what's she like?"

"Mean as shit, honestly." He cringed as the words practically leapt out of his mouth. While he and Cora had arrived at a certain level of grudging affection, that truth could not be overstated. Shifting in his seat, he faced his friend across the console. "She'd give some of our D.I.s a run for their money in the brass balls department. Her Grace does not fuck around." With a fond grin, he concluded, "You'd like her."

Zeke snickered and guided the plane into a gentle bank left up the coast. "Good." The osprey nodded absently as he flicked a gauge with his fingers. "Good. She'll be good for us, then."

"I think so." The whole reason she'd come had been to protect Finn and preserve the crown. She was here for king and kingdom; he could say that with certainty.

The silence that fell between the two men was companionable. Even though they hadn't seen each other in a long time, it was very easy to let their rhythms sync back up. "What are you doing on this side of the world? You mentioned this wasn't palace business. You need help with anything?"

Given that Vasily didn't know exactly what he was riding into, he was reticent to speculate. "I'm going to see a friend, and she asked me to come help her with something. I'm sure it's nothing." It's not that he didn't appreciate the offer, but he didn't feel like this kind of situation merited additional firepower. At least he hoped not.

The older man nodded slowly; eyes full of speculation. "All right then, but if you change your mind…"

"You'll be my first phone call."

They fell into an easy banter back and forth, catching up on their lives since they'd last seen one another. It was one of those friendships that could absolutely weather the sands of time completely unfazed. Didn't matter if they hadn't spoken in two weeks, two months, or twelve years, they could pick right back up without missing a beat.

They landed not long after that, and by the time Zeke's truck pulled up in front of the address Cherry had given him, they were all caught up on Zeke's divorces, plural, kid, singular, and a curly-haired mutt named Earl he'd found on a supply run who was currently at doggy daycare, as well as Vasi's limited supply of palace gossip. Normally, Earl was the copilot for all of his friend's adventures, but the owl appreciated him making room.

"I'll be back up this way in a week or so, unless you need me sooner." The aging osprey looked meaningfully at him as he tossed him the sea bag that had traveled with him since bootcamp.

Vasily smirked at his friend's eagerness for mischief. "Will do. Shouldn't need it, though. This should be just a low-key situation." Even as he said it, he set his bag on the damp concrete curb and dug around until he pulled out the case for his pistol.

Zeke nodded with a wry grin as he watched Vasi slip the gun in the holster at the small of his back. "All the same..."

"I'll let you know." He hoisted his bag back onto his shoulder, ignoring the dampness seeping into his jeans.

The osprey nodded and slapped the roof of his car before getting in. "Right on. Be safe. I gotta go get my dog."

Vasi watched the taillights of the truck fade as they moved on down the block, the chilly rain giving the whole street a kind of Impressionist sheen. Normally, he would have gone and dropped his stuff off before heading into a case, but this, as with all things in his life related to Cherry Belmont, was definitely an exception.

This was unlike any op he'd been on before, no groundwork beyond the online history of Cherry's digital footprint and career. She was well on her way to becoming the legend she'd sworn to him she'd be. Won a Peabody, considered for a Pulitzer, twice. She was thorough, relentless, and if her pictures were to be believed, still the most stunning woman he's ever seen. She was a fire goddess, and he had been a very willing sacrifice.

To be fair, he'd had nothing but misgivings since she'd reached out, but he could not deny her asking him for help. After all the fuckups lately with the King, Finn, and Cora, he couldn't let her down, too.

Feeling like he couldn't stall any longer, he entered the building and made his way up to Cherry's apartment. The dark-haired man with a serious glower who answered the door was not what he'd expected. His confusion must have shown on his face, because the giant in the shearling-lined blue buffalo check flannel shirt frowned even more ferociously.

"May I help you?"

From behind him, a feminine voice asked, "Daniel? Who's at the door?" A blonde head peeked around flannel-guy's shoulder, a face from the distant past. "It's you!"

Nodding slowly, his eyes never left the Aquiline between them, or the pistol holstered on his hip. "It's me. Been a long time, Pacey." He'd only met the bottle blonde once or twice when she'd worked shifts at the bar with Cherry, but he could tell she hadn't liked him then, and the intervening years clearly hadn't changed her opinions any.

"She called you?" she demanded; green eyes narrowed to suspicious slits.

When he dipped his chin, the flannel giant looked over his shoulder at her. "You know this guy?"

"Yeah," she confirmed, her eyes never leaving his. "He's the one she dated in college and then just up and ghosted on her."

Rolling his eyes, he sighed. "I got deployed, and she and I agreed to part company. Not that it's any of your business."

She crossed her arms and leaned against the doorframe. "Uh huh. Well, someone should have probably told her that. What are you doing back, anyway? Done playing soldier?"

"Have been for quite some time." As much as Vasi relished the idea of trading snarky barbs with the obviously still pissed off overprotective best friend, he had shit to do. Hoping it would speed things along, he pulled out his wallet and showed his credentials. "Is Cherry here or not?"

The boyfriend suddenly looked a lot less menacing. "Watch Commander of the Royal Palace Guard? What are you doing this far out?"

It was work, but he suppressed a growl as he took back his creds and pocketed them. Working with wolves had apparently rubbed off on him. "Cherry called me. Wanted my help with something. Is she here?" He was not usually the kind of guy who liked to repeat himself, but the duffle bag was starting to wear on his good shoulder, and he could tell that losing his temper here wasn't going to do him any favors.

"What the hell would she call you for when I'm right here?" The big guy sounded mortally offended.

"Holy gods, just let him in the door already."

A wave of gooseflesh washed over his skin at the sound of a voice he still heard in his dreams. He entered gingerly when the couple stepped back to allow him inside. His initial focus remained on the number of weapons in the room, his and the guy at the door, Daniel's. Not to mention improvised weapons. Pacey, being a non-shifter, always made him a little wary. He didn't want her to get hurt inadvertently.

Of course, she was dating an Aquiline, so he wasn't sure how that worked. Whatever. Wasn't his business anyway.

The apartment itself was eclectically furnished with none of the overstuffed couches or chairs in the living room matching but covered in granny-squared crocheted afghans. One wall was completely dominated by a massive flatscreen and the rest covered in tapestries or photographs he'd bet money Cherry had shot herself.

Cherry rose from the couch, a vision in white JAWS t-shirt and lived-in jeans. His lungs felt constricted, and he could barely look at her. Like looking at an eclipse, she was beautiful, but incredibly dangerous to his emotional well-being. He practically ached with the longing to touch her borne of years of separation.

Her mahogany curls were past her shoulders and down to blonde at the tips. Her eyes he would gratefully drown in. A little paler than he remembered, but then, they didn't get a lot in the way of light up this way. No matter, though. From her lips to the tips of her metallic turquoise toenails peeking out from the cuffed ends of her pants, she was Venus rising from the seafoam, perfection personified.

His mating bond seemed to sing within him at her proximity, years and miles between them be damned. She was his, and he could feel it, from the way his breathing calmed around her and her heartbeat synced with his. There was no denying the connection.

Clearing his throat, he attempted to shake off his inappropriate reaction. Offering his hand to the large, hovering hulk, he gave his best smile that didn't look like he was planning a homicide. "I'm sorry, where are my manners? Vasily Breţcu."

The dark-haired man examined his hand like he might be a vector for a cooties infestation before taking it and pumping it up and down once. "Daniel Williams. I'd say it's nice to meet you, but…" His shrug was surprisingly eloquent in finishing that sentence.

He let a little bit of the murder slip into his smile. If he was going to be a dick, there was no reason to pretend to the contrary. "Of course." Stuffing his hand in his pocket, he took in the room. "Moving in or moving out?" he asked conversationally, eyeing the few boxes left on the counter.

"Pace is moving in with Daniel," Cherry answered with a look requesting he ease back on his resting murder face.

He turned with a bright smile that could be charitably described as feral and he knew would annoy both of them. "Mazel tov." The blonde's response was an obscene hand gesture, so about what he'd expected.

"Am I gonna need to separate you two?" Cherry's honeyed voice was colored with amusement even as she telegraphed her anxiety loud and clear for him. The way she bit her lip and stretched and flexed her fingers even with her thumbs hooked in her pockets said a great deal about her state of mind.

"We were just leaving," Daniel announced as he inserted himself between his very human girlfriend and the owl.

"Unless we *weren't*," the blonde snarled at the eagle as she frowned down at his hand on her arm. She looked meaningfully at Cherry, who rolled one shoulder.

"I'll text you later, Pace, okay? I'm good, I promise."

Her best friend's eyes narrowed for a moment, then she shook off her boyfriend's hand. Vasi watched her cautiously as she stomped over and got right in his face. "If you hurt her again, there are a lot of ways to disappear up this way," she hissed with no small amount of murder in her eyes. "You'd do well to keep that in mind. Clear?"

He nodded once. "Crystal." Yeah, he had maybe eight inches and seventy-five pounds on her, but meanness should never be underestimated. His mother and grandmother didn't break five feet and could still quite easily break him.

"We're a phone call away," Daniel promised as he gathered the last of their belongings and tugged at his girlfriend's wrist.

She bared her teeth at Vasi as they left after she hugged Cherry. The silence left in her wake could rival a tomb. "She's still a joy."

She smiled fondly at the closed door before snaring him in her dark gaze. "Sorry about that."

Vasi shrugged. He was glad she had a best friend like that. Hell, normally, he *was* that best friend. "No worries."

"She means well."

For a rabid chihuahua. "I'm sure she does."

The lack of chaperones added a layer of intensity to the situation he wasn't prepared for. Alone in her space, he found himself—not on guard exactly, but certainly uneasy.

"So…" He rocked back on his heels with his hands stuffed into his back pockets. He could feel every bit of her scrutiny from his long hair to his steel-toed boots.

"Been a long time, Feathers," she murmured.

CHERRY

"I've missed you." His eyes widened like he hadn't expected the words on his mind to come tumbling past his lips. If memory served, he had not been a man given to excited utterances, but there was a first time for everything.

She felt her cheek tic into a smirk but ruthlessly squashed it. It wasn't that she didn't return the sentiment, gods forgive her, but the moment he walked in the door it had been like a shockwave passing through her. Vasily Brețcu was fucking beautiful and always had been.

It wasn't fair how pretty he was, with his chiseled jaw, and sensually pouty lips, and bright blue eyes. Maybe her memories had dimmed with time, but they were never as blue in her mind as they were in her living room. They weren't a regular blue either, but an overcast, cloudy gray with the blue sky just begging to bleed through. They peered at her, seeing through her, past her defenses to the softest parts of her she kept from pretty much everyone. Coupled with the long, dark hair that begged for her fingers and his broad, muscular frame, and she was basically a piece of candy left to languish in the heat of the sun.

"Nice hair," she blurted, apropos of nothing except her train of thought. When she'd met him, he'd been Marine Corps regulation perfect, and now…dark brown waves, almost black and shot through with a couple streaks of silver, cascaded to his shoulders and maybe a little beyond and gave him a bad boy quality her libido so did not need. Her whole body heated at the thought of touching him.

"Thanks." He ducked his head with his cheeks dusting pink as he ran a hand through his locks. Gods, if this could get more awkward…

"Want a beer?"

"Yes, please," he breathed; eyes wide as he seized the verbal life raft she'd offered.

She wasn't sure when her manners decided to snap back into place, but she gestured to the table as she went to the kitchen to grab a couple bottles. Once out of his sight, she leaned against the kitchen counter to collect herself with a sigh of self-disgust. *Holy gods*, she grumbled as she looked down at herself in her stupid JAWS t-shirt and, according to her reflection in the closed microwave door, no makeup. In a surprisingly effective metaphor, she was entirely without armor where he was concerned.

Rather than dwell in her frustration, she popped two tops

and returned to find him sitting in her dining room frowning at his phone. "You good?"

He blinked up at her, a quick flush on his cheeks as he stuffed the phone in his pocket. "Yeah. My best friend's getting married and is a basket case." He took her offered beer with a nod of thanks and took a sip. "Is there such a thing as a groomzilla?"

She smiled slightly, happy to know he had a relatively happy life back home in Boston. "I'm sorry to take you away from all that."

He shook his head and drained half the bottle in three gulps. "Don't be. You're doing me a favor. Besides," he set the bottle down and gazed at her with the most earnest expression she'd ever seen, "I'm happy to come out if you need me. I'm glad you called."

And just like that, the anxiety that had been coming and going in waves coalesced in her chest again, choking off her words. She could still hear the woman screaming as they beat her, smell the humid, fetid stench of all of them kept together in that room. Fucking horrible. She closed her eyes and focused on the cold glass in her hand to ground herself, only to be startled by the warmth of Vasily's gentle fingers warm against the skin of her wrist.

"Hey, there." He ducked his head to catch her eye, smile full of a kindness she was pretty sure she didn't deserve from him. "You were gone for a second there."

Cherry blinked. "Um…yeah. I'm sorry. I'm just…I thought I was ready to talk to you about it, but…" She trailed off, feeling so stupid and hating that she felt so emotionally weak.

Instead of being pissed off at her sudden hesitancy, the damn owl smiled, patted her wrist then drained his beer. "I get it. More than you know. So, here's what we're gonna do."

He got up and stretched, and she wasn't at all admiring the way his shirt rode up just a bit to tease her or the way his jeans framed his ass to perfection. Nope. Noperino, she absolutely was not.

He pulled his phone from his pocket and tapped on the screen. "I'm gonna get an Uber and head out to the cabin I rented, give you some space."

Gods, she was a selfish cow. Keeping him when he was clearly tired and then not even having the courtesy to tell him why she needed him. "Shit. I'm so sorry. You've been on a plane for twelve hours. I'm a terrible hostess."

"You're fine. Quit apologizing."

"I will, on one condition." His quirked eyebrow of intrigue touched of memories of the mischief they'd found together. "Let me drive you."

WINGED GUARDIANS

Chapter 5

VASILY

The ride to the rental place was a little less fraught. He teased her about the ska in her playlist, and she laughed at his stories about being at the palace. Around any other reporter, he'd be a functional mute, but he trusted Cherry. Even after all this time, that was one thing he never, ever questioned.

The one thing he could not stop thinking about was the haunted look in her eyes. His imagination had supplied him with an endless array of horrible images when he thought about what had happened to her. The fear for her, the concern, it simmered under his skin as surely as his feathers did. She wasn't ready to talk about it, and he wasn't going to force her, but that didn't preclude his worries. He shook off the dark thoughts as they pulled to a stop at their destination.

Dev had really hooked him up in terms of accommodations. His cousin's wife's sister's third husband or some such person had this cabin in the woods on AirBnB, and now he had his own log cabin fantasy to live out for the next couple weeks. Hell, he was just a few days' beard growth away from going full lumberjack. It fit in with the whole rustic vibe, right down to the ancient, beige Land Rover Defender in the garage with the rack on top and silver driver's side door.

"Holy crap, this place is so big it has an echo!"

He watched the wolverine prowl around the living room exploring the place with a small smile. And there was a helluva lot to explore.

One giant room that encompassed the living room, dining room, and kitchen, and then a luxuriant bedroom and a bathroom with an obscenely large tub. This place was easily twice as large as his apartment, and nicer than any hotel he'd been to before that wasn't for work. There was even a stone hearth fireplace in the middle of the main room large enough to heat the whole house and maybe half an acre around it besides.

After stowing his gear in a room with a bed large enough to accommodate a bear shifter—in animal form, he returned to find her sprawled out on the couch, lost among the comfy-looking throw pillows. "Please, make yourself at home."

"A couch this comfortable? Good luck getting me outta here." The crimson pillow on top of the pile giggled as she gestured with her free arm.

He snorted and headed into the kitchen to check out the food supply. Expecting a paltry showing, he was glad to find a stocked fridge right down to his favorite beer. "You hungry?"

"Not unless you are."

"I could eat." Literally everything in the fridge, but 'who was counting? Travel always made him hungry and being on a plane all day had him ready to start munching on the counter if she didn't want to get food.

Cherry groaned as the pillow slipped from the couch, an arm thrown dramatically across her face. "I don't think anyplace delivers out this far. We'll have to go back into town."

"I could cook," he offered. Upon receiving her skeptical eyebrow in response, he scoffed. "Don't be like that. I know my way around a stove."

"Since when?"

Ignoring her disbelieving tone, he set about throwing together some french toast and bacon. When in doubt, breakfast for dinner was always the way to go. He'd have to buy more groceries if he was going to cook all week, but for now, this would do nicely.

The scent of bacon drew Cherry to a stool at the breakfast bar with its siren call. "I'm impressed."

He felt his cheeks flush as he poked at the contents of the skillet. "It's french toast, not beef bourguignon." Her hum of amusement drew his eye over his shoulder. "What? You got something to say?"

"Nope," she answered airily, making the 'p' pop and draining her beer decisively. "I mean, just because the last time I saw you, you managed to scorch a pot of boiling water..."

Dropping a plate full of buttery, bacony goodness in front of her staved off the rest of her specious accusations. "Eat your breakfast."

CHERRY

She'd forgotten how easy everything was with Vasi. He made her laugh, he was inherently thoughtful and sweet, and he honestly treated her like a princess. She wasn't ashamed to say she still didn't know how to interpret her feelings on that but being with him for the previous few hours had brought her more joy than she'd experienced in weeks. The food wasn't bad, either.

With a belly full of carbs, she crashed out on a corner of the couch among a vast collection of throw pillows with her feet on the coffee table. Vasi started a fire in the fireplace, though the room was plenty warm without it, then joined her by flopping over on the mountain of pillows until she shoved him over to the corner.

"You're a literal child," she huffed around her giggles as he made himself comfortable at the other end of the couch.

Vasily tossed a black furry throw pillow at her head, which she deflected with a scowl. "Eh, it's one of my finer qualities."

"Whatever." His self-indulgent grin notwithstanding, she was pretty sure he'd never been an actual child, not even when he matched up chronologically.

They sat in silence, feet facing the fire, warmth, food, and actual peace drifting over her for the first time in weeks. She finally felt… safe, for lack of a better word. Regardless of how complicated their situation was, Cherry understood at a level commensurate with her soul that Vasily would keep her safe, and she could feel the strain of hypervigilance slipping off her shoulders for a moment. "I feel stupid calling you out all this way."

"Why?"

"Because." She exhaled sharply through her nose when all he did was raise an eyebrow for her to continue. "Because you have a job, an important job, and a life back east. You shouldn't have to come out all this way because I'm up in my feelings."

"I could have said no."

Eyes the color of ice watched her every breath as she formed and discarded a retort several times. Damn him for being fucking logical. "Maybe you should have."

He shook his head and scooted over to the cushion next to hers. "Why *did* you call?"

Cherry felt the anxiety spark to life under her skin even as it was muted by the safety of the location and the company. She stared at the fire for a long time, the only sound their breathing and the occasional crackle and pop of the flames and kindling as she let the warmth soothe her mind as she decided how to answer him. "I…" she took a deep breath to collect her thoughts and attempted to drop into 'reporter' mode. "I was looking into a story. Shifter women going missing around here. They leave the house and never come back. It's been happening for the last six months or so, and no one seems terribly interested in their cases. I know they're connected."

Vasily was quiet, unwavering slate blue eyes on her face. Being the object of his impressively focused gaze was fairly unnerving and quite the effective interrogation technique. "And the cops told you what, exactly?" he asked, his voice barely above a growl.

Haltingly, Cherry recounted everything from her attempts to track the missing girl to her capture and the time she'd spent locked in that room. At some point, he covered her hands with his, moving closer as the conversation dragged on, until, finally, the weight of her guilt broke her.

"Two different departments, two different versions of 'not my problem.' These women weren't priorities to them. They are to me." She swallowed hard, exhaling a broken breath as she whispered, "I left them. I saw a chance to get out, and I escaped. I left them to whatever fate had in store for them."

Her first sob found her wrapped securely in Vasily's arms, pulled into his lap as he tucked her head under his chin and rocked. Whispering words, she didn't understand, punctuated with tiny kisses he pressed into her hair, he held her as all the stress and trauma washed over and through her. At some point, he'd flailed out an arm to the end table to press a box of tissues into her hands, and even then, he didn't let go. She hadn't really let herself feel any of it, focused more on the need to right a wrong done to others as opposed to acknowledging what she'd been through.

When her tears trickled down to a few hiccups and sniffles, he leaned back against the couch cushions, arranging them more comfortably, she assumed. She felt drained, her whole body leaden and sluggish. "I'm sorry. For...all this."

She could feel him shaking his head above her before he murmured gently in her ear, "You have nothing to apologize for, gorgeous. You need me, I'm here, just how this works. We're going to get this figured out."

And there he was again; honoring promises they were too young to make and probably shouldn't still speak of. But there was something so restorative, so comforting being here with him, basking in the safety he represented to her. Her mind wandered as the space between her blinks stretched out, her body slowly giving in to the relentless pull of blissful slumber.

The last thing she heard before sleep claimed her was his

voice, barely a growl, murmuring, "*Te iubesc din toata inima. Inima mea îţi aparţine.*"

WINGED GUARDIANS

CHAPTER 6

VASILY

He was grateful the couch was comfortable.

After Cherry fell asleep on his shoulder, Vasily had a long time to sit with the revelations of the evening as he stared into the fire. He couldn't even get up and go get his laptop to distract him. White hot waves of rage and protectiveness washed through him in time with her soft breaths on his neck. Those who harmed her would die by his talons. Those who ignored her would answer to their gods. He was so far beyond incensed, her whimpers in her dreams had him holding her tight and comforting her until she relaxed once more.

Vasily carried her to the master bedroom, both to make her comfortable and to give her some space. Them sleeping together was nothing new, not in the grand scheme of things, but given that they'd only reconnected that afternoon, and he didn't feel right taking advantage of her emotional vulnerability.

And that was how, on first night of vacation, and he slept on the comfy couch, but it was the best night of sleep he'd had in years. Just being in close proximity to his mate gave him such a level of comfort, his whole body melted into the cushions in front of the dying fire. Maybe it was the travel, or the emotional upheaval of the day, but he was worn. Not so much he didn't check the perimeter before getting out his pistol to chamber a round prior to fully committing to sleep. He wasn't a heathen, and absolutely no one was getting to his mate so long as he drew breath.

That morning, she was reserved, and he was unsurprised. She'd never really been a fan of emotional displays, and the night before had been a lot, for both of them. He pushed a mug of coffee across the marble top of the breakfast bar as she poured herself into one of the bar stools around it. Dressed in her shirt and jeans from the night before, he wondered idly if he should give her something of his to wear home.

"How does sleeping so well leave you tired?" she muttered as she sipped. Her nose wrinkled at the lack of sweetener, and she set off to explore the cabinets for some sugar.

"I'm just glad you slept well." Even as she shook off her sluggishness, he could see her feeling a little more spritely, eyes were a little brighter. She was beautiful in general, but in the morning sunlight blazing through the window and casting a golden aura around her, she was luminous. Angelic. Perfection.

Cherry straightened slowly and gingerly walked back to reclaim her cup of coffee. She didn't look at him, even though he could tell her attention was firmly on him. "I'm sor—"

He slammed the laptop he'd been half-assed reading closed decisively. "Nope. If the words 'I'm sorry' leave your mouth, I won't be held responsible for my actions."

Eyes full of surprise snapped to his face, examining him closely. "But—"

He abandoned his seat to take up the spot next to her and cradle her warm, soft hand in his. "No 'but's. Here's the deal, I don't mind helping you, and I don't mind looking after you when you need it. You have literally nothing to apologize for, okay?" It was a little early in the morning for declarations of unwavering devotion, and while that skirted a little closer than he meant to, the fact was, he *did* mean every word he said.

Her dark eyes dipped to their hands, both of his giant ones enveloping her delicate paw, and he caught the dimple in her cheek as she grinned briefly before facing him again. "Thank you. For everything."

He flashed her a quick grin before moving back to his spot across the table from her. Being in her space for too long was the kind of thing that let his imagination hope, and that was not something he could afford. "Think nothing of it, *draga mea.*"

The moment her mug was empty, Cherry was on her feet and making noises like she had to leave. "I'm gonna get my research together so you can see the case notes I've been making, okay? They're on my laptop at home, and it's gonna take me a minute, but I'll have it done by tonight. I mean...if you want to come back to my place?"

Not that the idea wasn't appealing, but he was wary of intruding too much on her space. She seemed skittish enough as it was without crowding her into a reason to bolt completely. Yes, she called him, but he had no problem being respectful of her boundaries. "How about I cook for you tonight?" he called after her as she unlocked her car and had one foot inside.

"You cooked for me this morning," she challenged, leaning on the door with a teasing little smirk.

"Maybe it can be my *day* to cook?"

Cherry snorted as she shook her head. "All right, you win. See you tonight around seven?"

"Perfect."

She nodded and climbed into her car, and he stood in the driveway with his hands in his pockets until she was down the drive and well out onto the county road. Then he fished out the keys to the cabin, grabbed his laptop bag and binoculars, and locked the door before heading over to the beat-up baby Land Rover thing. It wasn't a matter of not trusting her, but given what she'd told him last night, he damn sure didn't trust anyone else.

XANDER

If it wasn't managing and coordinating the tiny details of the coronation T-minus forty-eight hours and counting, it was the upcoming wedding, and all of that was on top of his responsibilities to his daily shift. When Vasi got back, he was planning on taking the longest vacation in the history of ever. He and Dev usually split the responsibilities of keeping their troops happy and coordinated and the royal family safe. Now, Dev was managing Vasi's shift on the overnights—bless him for taking that over because, criminy, that shift left him drained and strung out—and he was the solo Day Watch Commander.

Vasily getting shot was the slimy maraschino cherry on the shit sundae of uncovering a potential plot against the crown with insiders who were ranking members of the Guard. Literally everyone was a suspect, and a large part of Xander's day was coordinating the internal investigation, polygraph tests, and interrogations. He was pretty sure his bed would be filing for divorce on the grounds of loss of consortium if he didn't get some sleep, and soon. He barely had time to keep his plant watered and groomed.

And then there was the little matter of the side investigation. Vasily had been looking into a different angle on the King's death, one that played right into the conspiracy at the highest levels of shifter government. He balefully eyed the locked safe in the corner of the room under his plant. Inside, in an appropriately marked evidence bag with a bright red label, was the personal diary of the late Bedelia Fielding. Her murder, and the subsequent implication of Prince Brendan in it, led to some highly unsavory speculations, several of which were proving true.

So far, he and Dev had been able to pin down her relationship to the prince through both her notes and some substantiated palace gossip, but there was another part to the relationship, the plot to kill the King as well as hints of something much, much darker. Something that made him worry even now about the coronation and the royal family.

He hadn't been able to save King Niall's life, but he would be god damned before he let something happen to the crown prince or duchess. His heart hurt thinking about the night he found the King's body bleeding out. Gunshots he could protect against, but sickness, that was truly fucking terrible. It was a guilt that would likely travel with him for the rest of his days.

The 'new mail' chime on his computer was a welcome distraction from the paperwork in front of him.

At least it would have been, had his desk phone not started ringing on two lines and his cell phone text alert going off.

"Is the world ending?" he asked as he picked up the handset to answer Dev's call.

"Did you read it?" His normal partner sounded harried and more than a little breathless.

Rolling his eyes, he kicked back in his chair and stared up at the ceiling like he might find his patience there. "I would have, but my phones went crazy, and I wanted to make sure nothing was wrong. So, is something wrong?""

His office door banged open as Dev hustled inside like he was trying to outrun demons. He looked a little sickly, suit hanging a little too loose on his body with bags under his eyes large enough to accommodate a body. It wasn't like him to pop out of his coffin this early, and he looked severely spooked. "You need to read it."

The email was from the state medical examiner in conjunction with the King's personal physician, Dr. Moallem, the only two people on the planet they trusted to conduct the autopsy in the dignified and respectful manner befitting a king. The first part of the report was pretty standard, died of blood loss and organ failure, the massive hemorrhaging coming from his longstanding illness.

The second page required that he read it through twice, with one more reading added just to make sure he understood clearly what he was seeing. "Heavy metal poisoning," he whispered, feeling like his lungs couldn't get enough air in. "Copper poisoning."

"Exactly like Cora said," Dev confirmed, arms crossed as he leaned against his best friend's desk. "Long term, heavy metal poisoning. Maybe lasting a couple years."

Thinking back over the years of decline King Niall had suffered, life stolen not by an illness beyond his control, but felled by the machinations of another. "That's so fucking cruel."

"It is," the falcon agreed. "You know what else it is?"

He shuddered to imagine what else there could possibly be and shook his head without answering.

Dark eyes bored into his as Dev turned the chair and leaned down to get right in his face. "Not your fault. Nothing you did or didn't do could have changed this."

As much as he wanted to meet his friend's earnest gaze, he couldn't, focusing instead on his lap and his hands as he flexed and stretched out his knuckles. It was one thing to see it on paper; it was another entirely to reconcile that with weeks of self-blame and recriminations. That was not something he could just let go of in an afternoon.

"I can't believe Brendan would do this. His own father." And maybe his heart broke a bit more because he would have given anything to have a father who actually gave a damn about him, the way the King had looked after his sons. He hadn't let his sorrow consume his life at the expense of his kids. It was unconscionably ungrateful.

"I don't think Brendan acted alone. I think there's still a part of this out there we're missing."

"We have to call Vasily. He needs to know."

"Agreed."

CHERRY

She was not a coward, despite her feelings at the moment. In her soul, she was a warrior who fought. Didn't matter if it was demons, injustice, or herself, she was the physical embodiment of "'this far and no farther.'" And yet, as she paced around her place—

and, man, did life without a roommate suck—everything felt too big, every sound was a little too loud, and just too much in general. Jumping at shadows was not a good look.

Cherry had never had a problem with being alone, but loneliness was a whole different animal.

A shower and change of clothes hadn't really fixed her disposition any. It hadn't taken but a minute or so to gather up her notes, her laptop, and the external drives she kept as backups for her work. She could have, in theory, gone straight back to Vasi's cabin and spent the day there with him, but she needed room. Well, *she* didn't need room so much as her head and her heart needed some breathing space.

Just being near him, hearing that voice, all sexy and deep, and seeing the confident and ridiculously good-looking man he'd become were enough to rattle her to her foundations. Her whole being, silenced for years by distance and time, called out for him. *Ached* for him. If she was going to get this done, find the women and keep her sanity, she needed the occasional timeout from the emotional maelstrom that was Vasily Petre Brețcu.

She didn't know how long she'd been prowling about the house, but it was long enough for her stomach to have opinions on its lack of sustenance. A cursory glance through her cabinets and fridge told her that while she had some stuff, she wasn't in the mood to actually make any of it. The anxiety that was her constant companion these days had eaten her attention span, and she really didn't have it in her to make a box of mac n' cheese.

"Takeaway, it is," she sighed to herself.

Well, it wasn't takeaway, exactly, but she could get some easy stuff at the Eastern European Store and Deli, and it wouldn't even be a twenty-minute round trip. She went straight to the counter and placed an order for pelmeni when a familiar figure caught her eye over by the coolers.

From behind him, she could take her time appreciating his form, from the dark hair streaked with the occasional shimmer of silver that brushed his strong shoulders down to that ridiculously perfect ass and those thighs. She blew out a breath. In jeans, they were a level of perfection that bordered on obscenity.

Seemingly lost in thought with a plastic basket over his arm, Vasily stood in front of the glass door contemplating something... vaguely pickled, and paid no attention to her creeping up behind him at all until she reached out to grab his arm and he turned, pulling her into him with a cheesy grin and a kiss on her forehead before turning her loose.

"What the hell, Feathers!"

Standing there in his black pea coat and jeans with his lips pursed and blue eyes wide, he looked so angelic he could tempt the devil himself. "Who, me, Sweets?"

She shoved his shoulder and scooped up her basket that she'd dropped in her flail when he startled her, after her attempt to startle him. "How'd you know?"

"Perhaps you're unclear as to how mirrors and reflections work," he snarked as he tilted his head to the cooler door, showing her silhouette very clearly in the fogged-up glass.

"Well, hell," she pouted.

"Aww, don't be like that. Just having a little fun." He threw an arm over her shoulder and hauled her into his side with a cheerful giggle. Even through the layers of warm wool of his coat and hers, her body seemed to glean its warmth from him. Seeing her brooding owl all sunshiny and happy was...it did things to her. Warm and melty things in the vicinity of her heart and points farther south.

Shaking off her distractions, she grinned up at him. "What are you doing here? Your cabin's nowhere near here."

His sudden pallor and wide eyes were concerning, but he recovered quickly, brushing wisps of bangs back out of his face. "I was in the mood for some *brânzoaică*." He held up the bakery bag in the basket at her skeptical expression. "Plus, I needed some groceries if I'm gonna make dinner tonight."

"Uh huh." She didn't believe a word of it. The more she thought about it, the more she realized he had absolutely no reason to be this close to her place that didn't involve her. The questions piled up in her mind.

"Really," he placed his hand over his heart, "groceries, I swear."

Cherry refrained from commenting further and they checked out, so dazzled by him speaking Russian to the cashier that she missed him sneaking her groceries in with his until he'd already paid and was herding them out the door with all the bags in one hand and the other at the small of her back. "You didn't have to do that. How much do I owe you?"

Vasily rolled his eyes, a slight flush coming to his cheekbones that had nothing to do with the chill in the air. "I saw a liquor store next door. I need to stop there. I'm outta beer."

"Fine, then I'm buying."

After a jaunt to his ride to drop their stuff, their mutual teasing carried over into the liquor store and down to the cooler in the back. His taste in beer was questioned, her preference for moscato judged harshly. It was when she turned to head up to the register that the floor dipped out from beneath her feet.

"Him," she whispered in horror, staring at the man up the aisle from them looking over the bottom shelf rum selection. Chucklefuck Number One, not in his brown canvas union suit like she remembered, but in jeans and a blue shearling jacket, just out here, living his life. *Just down the way from her house.*

Her own wool coat couldn't stave off the trembling that rocked through her person. Her pulse hit the roof immediately, and her claws and teeth followed. It was a miracle she didn't drop her bottle of wine. It was everything she could do not to fully shift in the mixer aisle and go rip his face off. Grabbing Vasi's arm, she pulled him back to the cooler and over an aisle, directly out of Chucklefuck's line of sight.

"What did you see?" His voice was low, deliberately calm as he slowly set down his twelve-pack to free up his hands. Blue eyes washed bright orange, and in his leather jacket and jeans he looked bigger, taller somehow, and more filled out, dangerous. Like the Bird of Prey he was. He wouldn't need the gun he had on him to take care of that asshole.

When she felt like she had a little more control over her emotions, she exhaled a deep, shuddering breath. "The man in the next aisle was one of the men who held me captive."

Vasily blinked, and his talons came out as he turned on his heel to go after the guy. Cherry was right there with him, holding him back with both her arms wrapped around one of his. It wasn't that she wanted to protect the guy, but the number of witnesses in the middle of the afternoon at her neighborhood liquor store was concerning, especially when contemplating what would likely be a very messy homicide. And it wasn't like she wouldn't be participating.

The warmth she typically associated with him left his eyes as his jaw firmed so hard, she could hear his teeth grind. He took her hand, gaze penetrating and implacable. "I'm not gonna kill him," he growled, even as he didn't fight against her hold on his arm. His eyes never left the guy's back as he sauntered up to the register to pay. "I'm going to make him sorry he's still breathing, and then if he's lucky, I'll let him die. But I won't kill him."

It shouldn't have been comforting, but his rage on her behalf was like a shield, keeping her from the terror that stalked her mind. "Feathers. Witnesses," she breathed, watching him carefully, feeling the twitch of his muscles beneath her fingers.

"Unconcerned. Let's move."

She glanced over her shoulder to see the man heading to the exit, and she knew their window for identifying the guy was closing. Vasi took the bottle of wine from her without looking, setting it on a shelf and walking out in one smooth motion. The way he moved was otherworldly, poetic violence, and people moved out of his way, like his aura exuded bloodlust. They hit the parking lot in time to see a rusted-out Ford F150 pulling out onto the street.

He didn't even pause, pivoting to the Jeep-type thing he was driving and hopping in to gun the engine. Unsure what to do, Cherry tumbled into the passenger seat beside him, fighting to fasten the seatbelt as he peeled out to follow the truck.

"You got a plan?" she asked after they pulled onto the interstate with a comfortable three cars between them and him.

"Kind of." He fished through the console and pulled out a small notebook bound in a leather folio. He blindly pressed it into her hand. "Flip through there. It's a couple pages in, but I know that truck. I think I wrote down a plate."

Confused and more than a little concerned, she quickly scanned his exacting block print, seeing times, vehicle descriptions, driver descriptions, and plates. "What is this? Where were you"— she looked down at the notebook—"at eleven this morning that you saw the truck?"

VASILY

He glanced at the passenger seat, taking in the full weight of her suspicious glare and lips flattened out to a disapproving line. "What if I were to tell you I wasn't simply in the mood for delicacies from the old country?"

Her jaw dropped, and he looked away, preparing to take the brunt of her anger at him while still maintaining their pursuit of the vehicle. "I can't believe you."

She huffed and growled quietly in the seat next to him, and when the tirade he'd expected didn't come, he hazarded a quick look in her direction. Her delicate jaw was set at such a firm angle, she would have looked carved from stone except for her eyes. Obsidian dark, sharp, full of irritation and accusation, he was surprised none of those feelings bled over into words.

"So, what now, Feathers?" Her voice was barely audible over the road noise, but still, her barely banked annoyance shone through.

"I'm gonna keep following him, and you, Sweets." He dug his phone out of his pocket and unlocked it before handing it over to her. "You're gonna send a text message to Xander with that license plate and truck information and ask for a rundown."

"And then what? We follow him until he goes home?" Her fingernails clicked on the glass screen as she texted. He rolled his shoulder in answer, as it seemed pretty obvious to him. "And what if he doesn't go home?"

"Then we'll see where he goes and who he talks to." He wasn't normally given to explaining his actions, but then, he also wasn't normally given to engaging in subterfuge with civilians in play.

"What if he goes back to the place they held me?" The slight quiver of fear in her voice as she asked the question was the only indication, she gave of her feelings on the matter of seeing the man again, and for that alone, he would die.

Fingers flexed on the steering wheel, even as he kept his foot to the floor. "Then we'll know where we need to send for backup."

"What if he sees us?"

Never in his life had he been so sure of his feelings and motivations as he was in that moment. So long as he drew breath, Cherry would never have any reason to fear anything ever again. "Then he should hope he's right with his god, because they will be meeting. Directly."

His temptation to respond to her wide-eyed sidelong glance was interrupted by his phone ringing in her hands. Seeing the name on the screen when she held it up, he nodded for her to put it on speaker.

"You're slow."

"New phone, who dis?" Xander's voice filled the cab from the speaker, colored with gleeful mischief.

Vasi snorted. "Asshole."

"Commander, it *is* you!" Dev sounded just as giddy. Bunch of heathens. "You never call, you never write..."

"It's been twenty-four hours."

"And we've missed you this whole time," Xander teased. It was actually good to hear from them, because just knowing his brothers had his back, even all the way across the country, was a comfort that helped to ground him and rein in some of the rage. And Cherry's giggles at their antics were like warm sunshine on his skin.

"Oooh, we have an audience?" the hawk asked eagerly.

"Vasily, you have a girl in the car?" Dev sounded positively scandalized.

"Fucking heathens," he muttered, frowning as he made to drop back to put one more car between them and the truck. They were nearing an exit, and he had a signal on, but that didn't provide them with a lot of cover.

"Cherry, these two idiots are my colleagues, Xander Colgrove and Devon Chilton." The two men responded with a mocking chorus of hellos. "Now, before you dumbasses get any ideas, you have info for me or not?"

"It's a fleet truck for a not-for-profit group out of Anchorage. I sent the info to your email, along with the particulars."

"Excellent. Run it down?" Vasi took the exit behind the truck and followed the sign that pointed to Black Moon Creek.

"Already on it," Dev replied automatically. "Wait, you're not really working, are you? Is this part of that *thing* you had to take care of?"

As much as he appreciated his friends' concern, he didn't have time to address it as the car between them and the target turned off, leaving the two of them exposed if anyone bothered to look. Fucking hell. "It is, I gotta go. Get me as much as you can, and I'll call you later."

"Please do. We have movement on the other situation as well."

"Clear." He disconnected without saying goodbye, abruptly pulling into a gas station at the edge of town. The way the truck was positioned at the gas pump, he still had a line of sight down the street to follow the pickup, but it looked like he was turned and looking at Cherry. Admittedly, she was kinda distracting. "Three blocks, give or take, he turned right."

"And that's it? We're done following?"

"For now. We're too obvious out here. A town this small, a random vehicle makes news. We don't want to make news."

"So, then, what? We post up here?" Her agitation was clear, but their need for a more strategic approach outweighed his desire to accommodate her desires.

Vasi shook his head and pulled back out on the street that headed back to the interstate. "We go back to the cabin and do some reconnaissance." When she opened her mouth to argue, he shook his head and laid his hand over hers in her lap. "This isn't quitting, this is regrouping before we commit too far with incomplete intel."

Cherry didn't respond beyond a growl, but he'd take that over actively arguing in a moving vehicle.

CHAPTER 7

CHERRY

Maybe it was petulant, but she didn't speak the whole way back to the cabin, including the brief stop at the closest liquor store to make up for the beer they didn't buy earlier. Continuing her perfectly reasonable grumbling, she kicked off her boots at the door and threw herself onto the comfy couch to stare at the vaulted ceiling. They were so close and he just...pulled back. It was enraging, and to add insult to injury, he seemed perfectly content as he stowed the groceries away and cracked open a beer. Before her stewing could really get started, though, a wine glass appeared in front of her. She growled, making no attempts to hide her fangs, even as she accepted the delicate glassware from him.

"Consider it a peace offering." He folded his long frame into the corner of the couch opposite her as she sat up. He'd ditched his coat in favor of a black t-shirt and a blue plaid flannel shirt with the sleeves rolled up to show off his forearms. Which were not sexy in their definition at all, she reminded herself.

"Which wouldn't be necessary if we were out there actually pursuing our one good lead." She pushed the baggy sleeves on her oversized sweater up to her elbows as she increased her comfiness and nestling.

His insouciant shoulder roll only served to raise her hackles further. "Perhaps." Sharp silvery blue eyes pinned her down as he sipped his beer. "What happens when you get them?"

"What?"

"The girls. You set them free, and then what?"

Cherry gave herself a couple swallows of wine to parse out what his real question was, though he wasn't making much sense. "What do you mean, 'and then what'? Expose these assholes, force this malignancy into the light of day. Take the festering rot and debride it."

"Online. In the papers." She nodded, unclear where he was headed with this line of questioning. "I see." He drained his beer in a few swallows before setting the empty carcass on the table on a coaster she hadn't noticed before, steel gray eyes pinning her down as he smoothed his bangs behind his ears. "Then why am I here?"

It was a question posed without rancor or malice. Hell, he was even smiling as he asked, like he had some grand secret to impart.

"You said no one believed you, but you know you don't need their validation."

The people who were supposed to protect them, save them from predators like these men, weren't inclined, and so she would. With or without help at this point. "What I need, what those women *need*, is for them to do their jobs. That's not too much to ask." The full weight of the offense and rage she felt burbled beneath the words, still so fresh in her mind and heart.

The smile never left his lips, though in some imperceptible way, it was sharper now, harder than she ever remembered seeing it. "You don't just want to expose the people in charge, though. You want retribution. You want someone to pay for what they've done."

Hearing her innermost desire spoken so plainly rendered her mute but for blinking.

"I mean, it makes sense," he continued with a conciliatory hand up, though she hadn't moved or made a sound to argue the point. "I'm not mad. Believe me when I tell you that those who wronged you, who hurt you, they will suffer for it. I'll make sure of it. But let's be real here. High and mighty ideals of justice and whatever don't really have a place here. This is vengeance, and vengeance requires planning. Haste leads to fuck-ups. Fuck-ups lead to jail."

He rose from the couch then, snagging his bottle as he made his way back to the kitchen. "Now, did you want me to make your pelmeni or did you want to do it yourself?"

The soft flickers of memory layered against the hard-edged man in front of her were a jarring juxtaposition but not unwelcome. Head full of ghosts, Cherry watched Vasily flit around the kitchen, handily sorting dinner, letting her mind wind its way around a long-ago memory of a tiny apartment with terrible wallpaper and Concrete Blonde playing on a small tape player on the windowsill above the sink. It was surprisingly easy to let her mind pick through these images; ones ruthlessly curated to keep from the light of day. Fragile, ephemeral, only now allowed out in the fresh air and only in the company of the one who shared them.

In her mind, he was still twenty-six, with short hair and a quick grin. A man of infinite gentleness and affection as well as honor and duty. Walking a tightrope of contradictions. There were shadows of that boy in the man in front of her, the one who moved with confidence and promise. It was becoming increasingly difficult to remember why she was pissed at him to begin with.

"I forgot you spoke Russian." It was kind of a conversational ceasefire, if she squinted and maybe cocked her head to the side. She sidled up to the breakfast bar to watch him work, shamelessly ogling his broad shoulders and strong back beautifully displayed in the soft-looking flannel of a clearly well-loved shirt.

A quirked eyebrow, a smirk over his shoulder as he manipulated the frying pan at the stove with a dish towel thrown over his shoulder. "That's what does it for you, huh?"

"Maybe."

To be fair, everything about Vasily did it for her. From the soft, teasing lilt in his tone down to the lips she wanted to test drive again and bright blue eyes that missed nothing ever, from long hair to steel-toed boots and every perfectly sculpted t-shirt and denim-clad inch in between, he was her definition of Mr. Right. No one else could hope to compare.

"Eto khorosho znat', moya vishnya vlyublena."

"Which means…?" She crossed her arms as she eyed him skeptically.

"I'll keep that in mind." He winked and whipped the towel off his shoulder, plating up the food and setting it in front of her at the breakfast bar. "Sour cream?"

The mood between them lightened considerably as they ate, the hangry vibes receding between them. Last thing anyone needed was two predators at each other's throats. She was sure the wine helped a bit, too.

"Any word from your colleagues?" Cherry hoped the question sounded as innocuous as it was intended. She was too tired to pick any more fights, especially with him.

Face lit by the phone screen, Vasi scrolled with his thumb. "Just the bare minimum. Do you know anything about Matryoshki Limited?" She shook her head. It wasn't anything she was familiar with at all, but Russian words and names in Alaska wasn't exactly cause for any concern. Rolling a shoulder, he pocketed his phone again. "They'll figure it out."

"Are they the ones on your phone?" An eyebrow rose in a silent request for clarification. "On your lock screen. The barbecue?"

All at once, color flooded his face, and he ducked his head with a toothy grin quickly obscured by a veil of dark hair. The picture in question, of him and two other fairly jacked shirtless guys in shorts gathered around a grill, looked like a magazine spread right down to the apron he was wearing with a goofy saying. It was actually pretty cute in its own way. "Ah. Yeah. Xander's the tall blond, and Dev's got the dark skin and the tats."

"'Don't make me poison your food,' huh?" She may have been teasing about the phrase but seeing his beautifully honed and chiseled chest and abs wrapped in a silly apron was an ovary-decimating event that had her clenching her thighs.

His little smirk as he drove his fingers through his hair was not helping her situation. "I'm descended from Borgias. Occupational hazard."

"That's fair." She swirled the wine in her glass as she watched him stoke the fire in the hearth. She was curled up among the couch cushions, positioned in a spot she was beginning to think of as hers. "I'm sorry about before."

He shrugged, a motion he made look elegant as he tossed himself down onto the opposite corner of the couch from her. "No need to apologize."

His quick dismissal of her asshole behavior was nice, but she still felt like a jackass. "I've been a bit jumpy since all this happened." It was an excuse, a flimsy one, but she didn't want him to think that was who she was now.

"Understandable."

"I didn't call you only for retribution." Just so he was clear. She had a laundry list of reasons she called, but that certainly hadn't even made the list at all.

A languid smile stretched across his lips. "I know that. It's a perk."

Her eyes closed as he huffed out a quiet chuckle at his attempt at humor. Just having him here with her, and she felt like she could finally exhale for the first time in forever.

"Wanna go for a night out?" His silver eyes glittered as his full bottom lip slipped from between his teeth all pretty and shiny before curling into a wicked grin.

"What'd you have in mind?"

VASILY

Maybe he didn't think this all the way through.

His thought process had been for the two of them to blow off some steam. Maybe he wanted to take some time and relax after the intensity of the afternoon, a deep breath before they dove into the recon work necessary to tease out more leads.

And he was, well, on vacation such as it was, he mused as he took off his shirt and stepped out the front door. The gathering shadows of evening collected in the screened porch area were a sharp and definitive punctuation mark on the chill in the air. The cold was a statement here, and even though he planned to shift momentarily, the faint breeze that caressed his bare skin was like icy razors.

"You coming?"

He smiled over his shoulder at the woman hovering just inside the doorway, still ensconced in the warmth of the house and her clothes. Liminal space, Cherry looked warm and soft in her baggy sweater with her hands in the pocket of her skinny jeans. Comfortable. *She looks like home*, a voice deep inside him whispered. She was the embodiment of his efforts to straddle his two worlds, his duty and his desires. The threshold of his life, and the harbinger of so much change.

The reddish and blonde highlights in her curls caught the light as she tossed her head back on a deep sigh that seemed to roll through her from the ground up. "A night run."

"Yeah, get a little fresh air. Relax for a bit. Then we'll come back and tackle everything we need to. But just let off some of the leftover..." He gestured vaguely.

"What happened to your shoulder?"

The laser focus of her gaze was almost a tactile sensation. He followed it down to his newest adornment, a stellate scar just below his collarbone. "Occupational hazard."

Her irritated growl drifted out the doorway to him as she bared her teeth. "You good to fly?"

It was all he could do not to beam at her grudging show of concern. "Come on," he held out a hand to her, "show me a good time."

He felt her dark eyes drift over every inch of his exposed skin, the gooseflesh erupting on his flesh having absolutely nothing to do with the chill in the air. He wouldn't push if she dug in her heels, but he really did want to do this with her. Having their animals out and free was a very different dynamic than just their human bodies.

She was dangerous in so many ways, to his person, his heart, his soul. It was easy to forget himself around her, forget the distance and time and their respective boundaries. Still, he'd await her reply, up or down, didn't matter, and go from there.

Blowing out a deep breath, she nodded, and he had a blink before her sweater was over her head and draped over a chair on the porch. It was a race then, the abandoning of clothes on the porch then off to play in the great outdoors. The forest called to both of them, and they each dropped into their varying animals quickly to take advantage of the night.

Wings outstretched, Vasily took to the trees in a silent rush of wind. This was his favorite part, the sky, the freedom, all of it. As an owl, he could see so sharply, hear so well it was like having another life. In his daily existence, his attention to detail and his ability to see and hear more than most of his colleagues came in very handy, but this...was light years beyond anything he could accomplish in his human form.

His shoulder protested, but only a little. He healed a lot faster in this form, his body naturally acclimating to the feathers of his eagle-owl and behaving accordingly. This was kind of the last step for him to consider himself "well," at least well enough that he could comfortably return to work. He was also glad he'd decided to test his mettle out here instead of where his friends could see him in case he failed. The last thing he wanted was to fail, even temporarily, in front of those who counted on him the most.

Below him, he could see and hear Cherry tearing it up through the underbrush. She was a demon that stalked the night, her wolverine a thing of beauty and a goddess to be feared as she scampered beneath his flight path. Though they were apart, doing this together gave him a closeness to her that made his mating bond with her sing.

The smell of cold, the sweet odors of pines, and maybe, eventually, coming spring, plus the varying animals bedding down for the night, all of it filtered through his senses as the winds glided silently over and around his wings. Deceptively light footfalls below him, quick and nimble, were the hallmark of his wolverine, keeping pace with him.

From under the canopy of trees below him, a sound wafted up that set all his predator urges on high alert. A cry, a bellow, outrage, injury, whatever it was, it was going down for the count, and his instincts honed in with a desire to take a look. Heart in his throat, he looked for Cherry's shadow but didn't see any sign of her. Coming to alight on a tree limb some seventy feet in the air, he was well hidden from any prying eyes below as he watched three men, two in red caps and mossy oak camo, and one man in a canvas coverall corner and take pot shots at a wounded caribou.

There were several things wrong with this picture, not the least of which was that caribou hunting season was a ways off— he'd looked when he was researching the area for Cherry—and these guys weren't trying to actually kill the animal, but tormenting it by firing at it to make it scream.

Fuck that, he thought as he leapt from the branch. He was an avenging angel, death on silent, celeritous wings. A five-foot-tall owl with an eight-foot wingspan, he'd brought many a man closer to his faith with rapier claws and a speed that rendered him almost invisible to the human eye. Especially at night.

Unprotected flesh gave way quickly with a slash of his talons as he passed. The cartilage of an ear clung to one toe until he scraped it on a tree before another strafing run. From the corner of his eye, he watched as a brown, furry buzzsaw came snarling out of the darkness, and there were even more screams. The complimenting scents of terror, piss, and blood were gratifying.

They took several more passes, ripping clothes and rending flesh, chunks of tissue bitten out and tossed aside, rifle reports echoing through the forests with shells flying blindly and easy to dodge. The terror of their attack quickly drove the men away from the downed animal and back to their ATV to flee, and Vasi took a few more runs at them just to make sure they stayed gone.

When he returned to the caribou, she was struggling to her feet, watching Cherry warily. She smelled...odd, off. Of sickness and death and something strangely chemical. This was no ordinary caribou, but a woman, a *shifter* woman, who had been pursued, hunted through the forest by these assholes for sport. The very idea of it enraged him.

Though she was much larger than he was, she cowered away when he landed in a swirl of dust and dead pine needles. His desire to reassure her outshone his modesty, and he dropped his feathers in front of her. He knew Cherry would keep her form in case the men regrouped and returned.

"Are you all right?" he asked, keeping his voice soft, delicate because he didn't want to spook the woman further. "I'm not here to hurt you."

She watched him closely as she got her legs under her, becoming more confident the longer their staring contest went on. He didn't know why she hadn't shifted back yet to talk to him, so he tried again.

"I work for the King. I'm with the Guard. I can help you."

But all his words seemed to do was to rile her up, eyes widening as she backed away from him. Her breath fogged the air and that was the first time since he'd stepped out, he'd really noticed the cold. He reached for her again, but she bolted, taking off into the night, leaving behind the smell of sheer terror tinged in blood.

Vasily had no idea what was going on, or why she had been out there being chased by those men in her animal form, but coincidences did not exist in his world. Now, he was terrified as to what could have happened if Cherry hadn't escaped.

WINGED GUARDIANS

Chapter 8

CHERRY

Reassuming her human form after that was a nonstarter. She couldn't stop pacing in front of the door to the porch, the adrenaline still a sharp flavor on her tongue. It was the shit out of nightmares, the things her grandmother would tell her about in a language Cherry could no longer speak fluently. The idea of humans hunting shifters violated human rights laws, shifter rights laws, and several negotiated treaties and conventions between the two groups. It was indecent, obscene. This was the kind of shit that could bring down a government or set the night on fire across the country.

She scented him on the breeze before she saw him. It was easy to admire the graceful way Vasily dropped his shift midair, coming to rest in his human form, his absolutely luscious human form, on two feet in front of her. He was beautiful, made of the night, moonlight and shadows delineating his sharp jaw, statuesque cheekbones, and gorgeously sculpted muscles as he moved into the house and made a beeline for the fireplace.

"I couldn't find her anywhere. I went all the way down to the clearing by the river, and no sign of her or them. I have no idea where they went. Are you okay?" he rasped, still a little breathless as he forced some additional warmth into the room. She snarled in response after she followed him inside on all fours.

Her eyes followed Vasi as he threw on his jeans but didn't bother with the zipper, and it was only after she watched him check the perimeter of the house that she felt the adrenaline ease back enough allow her to resume her human form. He wrapped her in a blanket the moment she dropped her fur, holding her close with his arms around her and her head tucked under his chin.

Vasi smelled like blood and sweat and cold, and his slow, steady heartbeat was the most welcome sound she'd ever heard. He was warm, safe, solid, everything her frayed nerves needed to allow herself to ease back from the edge. It wasn't hard to imagine what could have happened to her had she not gotten free. It was horrifying, and she felt a shiver chase down her spine, only to be answered by a comforting squeeze of his arms around her.

"I need a shower," she whispered into his chest.

"We both do," he rumbled with another quick squeeze and a kiss to her forehead. "You first, though."

"You sure?"

He nodded, and twenty minutes later, she was curled up on the couch in a pair of beat-up black USMC sweatpants rolled up at the ankles and cinched in as far as the waist would go and a t-shirt that would have better served as a dress. Hair tied up in a pineapple with curls flowing off the top of her head, she was as comfortable and ready for bed as she could be.

"Here." He pressed a steaming mug into her hands before he took over the couch cushion next to her. His shirt still hadn't reappeared, but he'd ditched his jeans for a pair of flannel pants that looked incredibly comfy even as they rode low on his hips, the wet trail of his braid sending a rivulet of water down his shoulder. "Did you recognize them?"

"The guys? I don't know. Maybe. They weren't the guy from the liquor store, but they could have been with him." That much she could speak to, but she knew there were more than a couple other people there at the building with her. It hadn't been the kind of operation that would have worked solo.

"And the woman? Did you recognize her?"

She frowned as she sipped her drink. "Maybe? We were kept in a dark room and chained. I can tell you I smelled a caribou there, but I don't know if it was her." Fuck, but she *hated* not knowing things. Especially something like this. She rubbed her eyes hard before pulling a hand down her face in an effort to release some of her tension.

"Why didn't she change back?" Steel gray eyes watched her over the rim of his own mug.

That one she could speak to, kind of. "I don't know, but I had the same problem. I wasn't able to get myself together for several hours after I escaped. When they took me, they injected me with something, and when I woke up, I couldn't shift back. I don't know what it was, but it was terrible." Setting her mug down on the table, she curled up in the corner with her arms wrapped around her knees. "There's so much about this I just don't fucking know."

Vasi scooted over, leaning into her space with his arm around her shoulder. "Hey, it's okay." Pressing a kiss to her temple, he growled softly in her ear, "Here's how this is gonna go. You're gonna go get in bed and get some sleep, then we're gonna hit it hard tomorrow when we get up."

Sounded like heaven. "Where are you gonna sleep?" He nodded to the other end of the couch, which didn't work for her at all. She needed a little more comfort than simply knowing he was in the same house with her. "Dude. Fuck that. Come on." She rose and held out a hand to him, staunchly ignoring the butterflies in her stomach as she took in his sweetly open expression in addition to the pinup-worthy chest and abs all the way to his v-line. She may have needed reminders that they weren't together anymore, but damn if he wasn't still the kind of hot that melted her panties.

When he didn't move immediately, she barked, "Chop-chop, Feathers. Let's move, Marine."

VASILY

He scrambled to his feet, allowing her to drag him into the bedroom with her hand around his wrist. He only dug in his heels at the doorway, at once at war with himself. On the one hand, he wanted nothing more than to be near her, to feel her skin warm and soft against his, and on the other hand...well, Cherry's boundaries were inviolable in his mind, and he did not want to manipulate his way around them or have her think that was his intention. "You don't have to..."

She cut him off with a raised hand as she threw back the sheets and slipped underneath them, turning over to look at him expectantly. The curls dangling in her face and the dimple in her cheek as she smiled softly at him just about killed him. "Get the light on your way in, yeah?"

He had no idea how she was being so chill about this. It was like the mating bond was a throbbing brand in his chest with her every breath and plunging the room into moonlit darkness was doing him and his emotions no favors. The sheets were cool and itchy, like new feathers, and every minute adjustment from her side of the bed registered on his emotional Richter scale. There was no way in hell he would be able to sleep tonight.

"We've both had a hard night. Let's just get some rest and pick it up in the morning." Her murmured rasp held a tinge of fond amusement.

If he was startled that she'd read his mind, Vasi wasn't going to show it. He snorted. "Shouldn't I be the one reassuring you?"

Her quiet snicker ended in a sigh. "You are. Just by being here." Her hand slipped over, displacing the blankets for just long enough to brush her fingers against his.

He turned his head to find her dark eyes glittering in the muted light. "I don't remember you being this mushy."

Her quick grin and eye roll warmed him more than the blankets did. "Fuck off. You love it. You know you do."

Well, she had him there.

The pounding that woke him the next morning was not, as he'd hoped, in his head. Peeling open both eyes, it took a second to orient himself to the situation. It was early, or at least it felt like it was, though the light streaming in the window told a slightly different story. There was a weight on his chest, something tickling his chin, and as he moved, coming back to consciousness, he was suddenly exceptionally aware of the woman with her head pillowed on his chest. The tickling on his chin was her riot of curls, and Cherry was, for all intents and purposes, crashed the hell out never to return from the land of Nod.

It was a startling development, but pleasantly so. His body immediately cataloged the feeling of her soft skin against his, warm and smelling like his soap from the shower, and everything about it aroused possessive urges within him. Unfortunately, right then the pounding resumed, and from what he could tell, it was someone at the front door who appeared to have some law enforcement background. It was a very distinctive knock.

Cherry groaned as he slipped out from beneath her, deciding to forego changing into jeans and just keeping his sleep pants on as a matter of saving time. He didn't want to give whoever was at the door the opportunity to make decisions that would negatively affect his security deposit.

The bright sunlight was like a slap in the face as he opened the door to three men, one of which he'd already been acquainted with. "Detective Williams, how can I help you?" Pacey's boyfriend was as imposing and thoroughly unpleasant as he remembered, only now in a suit that likely required extensive tailoring, the other two men were in uniforms, one blue and one greenish brown.

"Fancy meeting you here." Daniel nodded, letting his eyes travel from Vasi's half undone braid down to his bare feet. "May we come in?"

"No." His mate was asleep and vulnerable, and he damn sure was not letting more people into the house. "Why are you here?" He could blame his lack of tact and manners on his lack of coffee, and that was the story he would stick to.

"There was an incident that happened not far from here, and we were canvassing the area for witnesses," the man in the blue uniform informed him. He was as tall as Vasi but maybe thirty pounds lighter, though some of that was likely made up by the overladen gun belt he wore around his waist. What was interesting about him was his face and hands, both visible around his jacket and both liberally covered in scratches, gouges, and a very obvious bite mark that was partially bandaged and shiny with antibiotic ointment.

"I see. And you're with whom?" It wasn't hard to keep an impassive expression when he was wholly unimpressed.

"Jerome Benedict, Black Moon Creek Town Marshal, sir." He fished out his wallet and showed off his badge and identification. "The report came in to our station."

"I see. And you? Park Ranger, I'm assuming?" The kid—and really, he looked younger than Xander by a bit—but was all big puppy eyes and cornfed size.

"Were you out last night?" The eagle's sharp eyes never left his face as he brought Vasily's attention back to him.

"Yes, why?" His eyes flickered to the other two men who hadn't really moved and seemed to be watching him intently. The one in blue smelled vaguely like a deer of some kind but the base scent was clearly human with hints of Neosporin and peroxide thrown in, and the other was distinctly human.

Ignoring the question, the detective made a note in his book. "Did you run into anyone last night?"

He could see exactly where this was going, and he was in no mood. The fact he had to leave Cherry in his bed to come entertain this foolishness was *prostii*. "Why don't you just ask what you came here to ask?"

"Where were you last night from, say, nine to maybe eleven, eleven thirty?"

And there it was. He should have expected it after having everything go to shit the day before, and yet he figured the woman would be grateful for the assist instead of sending the cops to look for them. "Do I need a lawyer?"

"I don't know, do you?"

"He does not." She wrenched the door out of his hand and muscled her way into the doorframe with him and slightly in front. Even barefoot with her hair done up, her murder face was a thing of absolute beauty. All three men at the front door took a step back, with the one in blue's bandaged hand casually resting on the pistol on his hip. "He was here, with me. Any more questions, Daniel?"

To his credit, the Aquiline didn't even flinch at the obvious threat she posed, even in her shorter human form. Her animal form was one that even non-shifters knew to steer clear of her if she was in a mood. That mood being "wishing a motherfucker would," or the default wolverine state. "None at all, thank you, Cher. Do me a favor?" he asked as he folded his notebook up and slipped it into his pocket. An eyebrow raise was the only reply. "Text Pace and let her know you're okay, please. You know how she worries."

She dipped her chin sharply once. "Will do." Looking beyond him to the two cowering in the background, she demanded imperiously, "Gentlemen, anything further from you?" Her tone did not encourage any further interactions, and wisely, they shook their heads. "Fantastic. Have a great day."

Vasily watched her ramrod straight back as she all but slammed the front door, marched into the kitchen, and proceeded to lay siege to the coffeemaker.

"Um, Sweets?"

"Caffeine, clothing, conversation. In that order."

"Yes, ma'am." And if her growly demeanor made him grin a little bit, well, who could blame him? She was adorable, like a fuzzy, lethal kitten.

XANDER

He'd been eyeball deep in research since he'd gotten to the office. Vasily's favor had become an ever-blossoming flower of fuckery. The company he wanted the intel on was a subsidiary of a ton of shell corporations. He was on number six so far, this most recent one located in the Caymans. Getting more information was becoming difficult, and every name he chased seemed to vanish into the ether the more he looked.

His door opening drew his eye to the clock at the corner of his screen. "Unless you come bearing food, I'm busy." He wasn't normally given to being rude, but he was frustrated, hangry, and half-tempted to order in some delivery so he could keep working through lunch. There had to be a lead here; he just had to find it.

"I was told you're the Watch Commander? Am I in the correct place?"

"You are." Xander scrambled to his feet to greet the dark-skinned man in front of him. He was easily as tall as he was, impeccably dressed, and looked…familiar. "Lord LeStrange?"

His lips twitched in what could have been a smile if he put effort into it. "Yes. I was looking for Vasily, but I was directed to you."

The future queen's brother and the Deputy Minister of the Interior was a highly unusual visitor. After brushing imaginary wrinkles from his pants, he hurried to close his door. Whatever brought the raven to his office probably was not for bullpen consumption. "Commander Brețcu's out of the office on leave, Your Lordship. I'm happy to be of whatever service you need." He gestured to the chair across from his desk. "May I get you anything?"

Nicodemos shook his head and took a seat like he was perching on a throne. "No, but thank you."

"Of course." He resumed his seat, hyperaware of the mess of his desk, the scent of stale coffee in the air, and his overall sense of dishevelment. Shoving all that aside, he put on his best Supervising Watch Commander front. "What can I do for you, My Lord?"

"I have received word that someone in your office has been looking into Matryoshki Limited." The way the man spoke gave the appearance of both dislike and disdain, with a healthy dose of disinclination. Toward him, the company, or the circumstances that brought them together, he couldn't tell, but he was immediately on guard.

All the blood in his head drained south below Xander's collar. For a minute, he pondered the merits of lying but decided against it. He shuddered to think about what Vasily had gotten into that would bring the attention of the Interior Ministry but going to jail was not on his agenda for the day. "I see. I take it that's a problem?"

"Not yet, but there are several operations in play outside of the Watch Command's purview, and the situation is quite fluid at the moment." His lack of follow-up indicated the weight of the previous statement, and Xander could almost hear the alphabet of agencies indicated by his few well-chosen words.

"Uh huh." It was only because he kept the room slightly chilled to accommodate his violet, Brunhilde, that he wasn't sweating bullets. He suspected the reason for Mos's appearance in his office was merely a formality. The last thing he wanted was to run afoul of the Interior Ministry, but at the same time, he wasn't terribly concerned he'd uncovered state secrets. Yet. "That was me."

The only acknowledgement he received was a slow blink. "I see. And what put them on your radar?"

"It came up as part of an investigation." He wasn't in a hurry to give up the whos and whys if the Baron didn't know enough to ask. He'd done enough interrogations and cross-examinations to know how to answer only the question asked and to volunteer nothing. "What's your interest in it?"

"Classified." If he didn't blink, the Corvid minister could have been mistaken for a statue. "How far have you gotten?"

"Not very," he admitted. Bouncing around shell corporations didn't really count as progress until he could tie actual people to them. "Should I stop looking?"

The silence that crept into the room after he'd asked the question was cloying, heavy and fraught with potential bad outcomes. He knew he shouldn't have tempted fate and brought that option to Mos's considerable attention, but if he was going to break rules, he needed to know which ones they were.

The raven's bright gold eyes looked him over, examined him in a way that could only be described as clinical. Xander had no idea what Mos was seeing, but he could outwait the best of them when the notion suited him. "No. Not at the moment."

He rose to his feet, a study in style and grace, and Xander's training managed to get him to the door to hold it for the minister in short order. "Thank you, Your Lordship."

"Don't mention it." He was two steps out the door when he turned smartly on his heel and faced Xander again, a strange little grin playing at the corners of his mouth. "Do you know what matryoshki are, Commander?" The smile only grew when the hawk shook his head. "Russian nesting dolls. Just something to keep in mind."

The Day Watch Commander's eyes followed the tall raven down the hall until he'd left the Guard Post. He was the kind of man it behooved a person to keep in front of them. His whole body unclenched as he watched the minister glide out the front door of the post.

Heaving a deep sigh, Xander went back to his desk and slumped into his chair. He was decaffeinated, hungry, and he knew his brain wouldn't fully come back online until those two states were addressed. First order of business, though, was to text Vasi. The owl should know the kind of attention he was receiving before he drew a target on his back. The Right Honorable Nicodemos LeStrange showing up in his office was no coincidence—if anything, a shot across the bow.

Whatever was going on, he reasoned as he fired off an email and threw in a delivery order online, he'd lay odds that LeStrange was—for the moment, anyway—on their side, and the nesting dolls were a clue.

CHAPTER 9

VASILY

Dressed and substantially less surly, they both fell into research mode, checking the layout of the town of Black Moon Creek, hypothesizing about where Chucklefuck had been headed. Where the police station was in relation to the route the guy drove. How the cops were possibly involved.

"I guess that explains why they weren't interested in taking my report." There was no mistaking her bitter tone as she checked street addresses for names and possible links to Matryoshki.

It was tedious, but then, he was making notes on the five sworn, two reserve, and two civilian members of the Black Moon Creek Marshal's Office. Chasing down someone's digital footprint was something he enjoyed, seeing it as part of the hunt, and as an owl, the hunt was life.

"I know, *iubi*." It was exceptionally high on his list of things to *handle*, right after finding the girls. Those who took them, hurt them, enabled this travesty...he blew out a deep breath as he reeled in his rage. That was of absolutely no help here.

"He had my bite mark on his hand."

His lips twitched as he caught her dark gaze. He couldn't help the pride that swelled inside him at that knowledge. "I saw. He's lucky you didn't take his hand off at the wrist."

She dipped her chin with a shy smile that made him want to pick her up and cuddle her senseless. "Probably should have, in hindsight."

"Eh." He shrugged. "Live and learn." He went back to his searching and startled when his pocket buzzed with a text. Xander's name put him on alert. Reading the quick warning, Vasi felt a chill run down his spine. This was clearly a lot larger than either of them knew about.

"Good news?"

"Maybe." He dialed the comm center and gave his code, immediately put through to Lord LeStrange. "You rang?" he asked as he put the phone on speaker and took up his pen.

"How's Alaska?"

Vasi snorted. *This asshole.* "You psychic or having me tracked?"

"Neither. I'm just that good." The raven's quiet chuckle did nothing to ease his anxiety. "I thought you were on vacation."

He shrugged and then remembered Mos couldn't see him. "It's more complicated than that. And actually, I have some questions for you."

"Oh, I'm sure this is going to end badly." The background noise on the phone died down to utter silence except for the sound of the man kicking back in his chair.

"It's not about your sister this time."

"Small mercies."

His cheek ticked in a smirk, and he turned over a fresh sheet in his notebook. "So, what can you tell me about nesting dolls?"

"Not as much as you want. The board reads like a who's who of shifter aristocracy, and yet we can't figure out what exactly it is they do. They're supposed to be a not-for-profit helping, I don't know, homeless puppies and kitties or some shit, but…" He trailed off with a sigh and some typing in the background.

"But?" he prompted after the stretch of silence got awkward.

"Let's just say their donations and disbursements are a little… suspect. Or a lot suspect."

Okay, so it's a front for money-laundering, sure, but that doesn't explain the missing girls. "Any chance I could get your notes on all this?"

"None whatsoever. What's your interest in this?"

"It's…complicated." A movement caught his eye as Cherry held up a sign that said 'Tell Him' with a gratuitous number of exclamation points and additional underlines. He would never willingly reveal her secret unless she allowed it, but in this case, the minister needed the whole story.

"More complicated than international money laundering and possibly funding non-sanctioned clandestine operations?" Only Nicodemos could sound almost entertained by the notion.

"Are you sure?" he mouthed to her, only to receive back an emphatic nod. Vasi cleared his throat. "Is the trafficking in shifter women on *your* radar?"

"…Huh." The silence that followed made Vasi wish he could see Mos's face. The old bird was a hard-ass and a political monster when he needed to be, but he was not heartless. "And how did this come to you?"

She was nodding for him to speak before he even turned to look at her. "Cherry Belmont."

"The writer?" The look of mute shock on her face as she stared at the phone would have been hysterically funny under other circumstances. "How are you acquainted with her?"

"She's my mate." It was out of his mouth so fast, so naturally, her startled squeak and the appalled silence that followed took a second to register. He'd never been ashamed of it; it was simply not something he discussed. He would never impose his desires on her. It was enough for him that he could be there for her when she needed him.

"I...had no idea you were mated." Mos's tone was both marveling and colored with a light dose of censure. They'd been friends long enough that was the kind of thing that might have come up in conversation. He'd make it up to him later.

"Neither did I." Cherry speared him with a glance that demanded further conversation after they hung up the phone. So, he *may* have neglected to mention to Cherry that she was his mate. In hindsight, not his best look.

CHERRY

Of all the things she'd expected today... She blew out a deep breath from puffed up cheeks. Mates? Them? It was like she'd taken a bat to the head, because all her thoughts suddenly disintegrated in front of her. Her teeth clicked as she resumed control of her jaw.

"Is someone else there? Miss?"

Being addressed directly, she sat up straight and did her best to shake off her stupor. "Cherry Belmont, sir. I apologize for the lack of introduction earlier."

"Not at all. Your mate has absolutely no manners, if you didn't know already."

"Oh, I'm abundantly clear on that." Her owl's cheekbones flushed red, and he ducked his head to hide behind his hair. It was damn difficult not to pick that fight right then and there.

The man on the phone snorted in what was maybe a laugh. Hard to tell. "All right, then. What can you tell me about the missing women?"

She ran down her tale, glossing over some of the more harrowing details until he asked about them specifically. Then she ran it right up to finding the wounded caribou woman the night previous as well as their suspicions about what was going on.

"My gods, how horrifying. I'm very glad you're safe now." He sounded like he meant it.

It felt weird coming from a stranger, but she appreciated the sentiment all the same. "Thank you. Can you help us, please? There are women still out there."

"Let me…" There was movement in the background and the soft beep as a computer came on. "I'm going to look into this myself. I'll do what I can."

"I'm grateful."

"Of course. Vasily, we'll speak soon."

"Thanks, Mos."

The call disconnected, and her owl suddenly found great interest in his hands. Try as she might to get his attention, he would not raise those baby blues. "I imagine you have a lot of questions."

"You could say that, yes." Cherry dragged her chair over next to him and tilted his chin up. His eyes were denim blue and his expression guarded as he looked at her. "I'm gonna start with, who was on the phone?"

He wrinkled his nose and looked away from her again. "Nicodemos LeStrange. He's a colleague."

The name sounded familiar, but she couldn't focus on that right then. "Could you be any more vague?"

"Probably," he conceded with a wince. "It's complicated." He went straight to the fridge and pulled out a beer. "Want one?"

"No. Thank you." This man was, apparently, the god of avoidance, because he simply nodded and took up a seat on the couch like they hadn't been talking at all. "For the record, math is complicated. This is some bullshit." Cherry sat herself down on the cushion next to him, setting his beer on the table and taking both of his hands in hers. Vasily made a halfhearted attempt at pulling away, but he wasn't getting out of this so easily. "When did you know?"

His normally full bottom lip was trapped between his teeth as he bit it, let it slide out, only to bite it again. "When we got together. The first time."

She passed a hand over her mouth to keep from snarling outright as she dropped her head back. Her next few deep breaths were an exercise in forbearance. When she'd sufficiently reeled in her temper, she asked, "I'm sorry, what?" in a tone much more civilized than she felt.

"I knew when I kissed you the first time in my Jeep. It's always been you for me." The admission was a sucker punch to the gut. She couldn't help thinking back to the last time she'd seen him when they'd broken up. How he'd basically shoved her away from him without even the barest backward glance. Not that she regretted taking the job in Georgia, but they could have had everything together instead of being miserable separately.

"Were you gonna tell me?"

"No." At least he was honest about that part, even if he still wouldn't look at her.

"Why the hell not?" Cherry barked, unable to stop the razor sharpness from leaving her mouth.

His slate blue eyes snapped to hers then, bright and challenging. "You have a great life. A life independent from me, and you deserve that. You don't need to be bound to me by some archaic vestige of biology."

"Archaic vestige of biology?" He nodded, like it was a foregone fact, and she felt a stabbing pain in her chest where her heart should have been. "Then you never wanted me?"

It was his turn to be flummoxed, she figured, judging from his eyebrows shooting up and the way he reared back from her. "What?"

The sharp ache in her chest was growing, eating its way through her like a gnawing sinkhole, but she still fought to sound both calm and nonchalant. "I mean, if it's only biology, then you don't really want me for me, and you never did."

"I never said that."

"Didn't you just?"

This time he was the one who growled and rolled his eyes, throwing up his hands in frustration before driving through his hair.

"No." Irritated, he yanked a hair tie off his wrist and bound his locks back out of his face. He then took her hand in both of his, scowling at their joined hands. "It's just...you deserve more, Sweets, you know? You deserve the best of things and—"

It took a moment to remind herself that killing him outright defeated the purpose. "I swear to the gods that if you keep talking about what I need and what I deserve, I'm gonna smack the hell out of you." Dutifully, he pursed his lips and gestured for her to carry on. "Why'd you really push me away? Why do you keep pushing me away?"

"Your life is complete without me," he said like he was pleading for her to understand. Like them being apart was the most natural thing in the world when it was clearly something that neither of them wanted.

She understood, all right. She understood she wanted to shake the stuffing out of him and then pounce on him. "And what about your life?"

He smoothed the stray tendrils that had escaped his bun behind his ear and swallowed hard, asking softly, "What about it?"

She came up to her knees on the cushion, cupping his cheeks in her hands. "I was in love with you, you know. I might still be." She stopped to think about it. "Probably. But you...you still love me, after all this time?" Vasi nodded haltingly and tried to duck her gaze, like he was ashamed of having emotions or wanting something for his own. "I—you know—you're allowed to want things, Feathers. You're allowed to have things."

He shook his head, carefully removing her hands from his face. He would have gotten up if she hadn't climbed into his lap and straddled his hips with the speed of an apex ground predator. There was no way she was letting him out of this conversation, not when he dropped a bombshell that large in the middle of the room that was several years in the making. "I can't have you, though." The way he whispered that broke her heart.

"Who says?"

She was close enough that his warm scent, cedar and spice

and something warm, sent a frisson of lazy heat through her body. Giving in to temptation, she swept his bangs back out of his face, reveling in the softness as they curled around her fingers. He closed his eyes, growling in pleasure at the feel of her nails around his ear. Foreheads pressed together, she shared her breath with his, and she found she couldn't hold back anymore.

The feel of his scalding hot lips against hers was like coming home, feather soft as she brushed her lips against his sampling their plush fullness and delicate texture. Just tiny kisses, nothing intense as she reacquainted herself with the feelings of being this close to him. His hands hovered for a moment, seemingly unsure what to do when she threaded her fingers through his long, dark mane and tugged. Tilting his head just so for a better angle, she rose to meet his lips with hers more forcefully.

She moaned softly against his mouth as his hands settled on her hips, pulling her closer to him, his tongue teasing the edge of her lips before slipping inside to tangle with hers. Her hands now braced on his shoulders, she wriggled in his lap until she was pressed against him chest to chest, his growing arousal snug between her thighs. His lips tasted like sweet coffee and lust, and she wanted nothing more than to drown in his ardent kisses.

Vasily smelled so good, like woods and coffee and that unidentifiable thing that made her feel like he was hers and hers alone. When they separated for breathing purposes, she nestled her face into the crook of his neck with a quiet chuckle.

"Should I apologize?" She mumbled the words into his skin even as she made no effort to move.

He tightened his grip on her hips, digging his fingers into the tender flesh as he shifted her closer. His nose grazed her cheek, and he pressed a tiny kiss to the spot just in front of her ear. "For? Doing what I've wanted to do since I got off the plane? Um, no."

Cherry growled and pushed herself up on his shoulders. "You can't say shit like that, man."

Vasily looked debauched, swollen lips, blue eyes blasted dark with lust, slashes of flush across his cheekbones. In short, he was glorious, and she found herself melting a little more the longer she stared. "Shit like what?"

"Like you want me. Like you've *always* wanted me. Like we haven't spent the last few years apart because *you* broke up with *me*." Shoving her own hair out of her face, she moved back a little from him, still on his lap but no longer pressed together. "How am I supposed to know how to act around you when you have this whole other narrative going on in your head? What is that about, anyway?"

Blinking slowly, Vasi licked his lips, which was alarmingly distracting, before exhaling a sigh that moved them both. "I've...seen what happens with mating bonds." His blue eyes looked troubled as he searched her face before letting them slide to the couch cushion next to them. "How the needs of one person can be totally subsumed by the needs of the other in the name of the bond, and I...can't. It's not fair to ask someone to give up the life they know for me, just because I've bonded to you. So, I didn't say anything."

She could scent his apprehension in the air as much as his intense desire for her. He was nothing if not confounding. "Lemme get this straight, you're not afraid I'll say no, you're afraid I'll say yes," she clarified, kneading her claws in his shoulders slightly as an act of self-soothing. It was that or shake some sense into him. When he shrugged under her hands but didn't say anything else, she didn't need more of a hint. "All right, then."

Extracting herself from his lap, she went back to her seat at the breakfast bar. "When you figure out what or how you want, you let me know. In the meantime, I'mma go back to work."

VASILY

It was hard to imagine that particular situation going so exceptionally well only to slide right back down to exceptionally poorly. *Words have consequences,* a voice that sounded not unlike his mother reminded him. Of course, silence had consequences as well. And now the consequences he attempted to shield her from would likely claim them both.

The Mob of wolverines had a different view on mating, she'd

told him once, with one male taking many wives, which was, essentially, the opposite of eagle owls. Mated for life was a helluva thing to someone who was raised or wired that way. And then there was the matter of the bond itself.

He'd seen the bond in action with his parents, the sacrifices his mother made that were seen as expected and normal because of the bond. Vasi wanted a union of equals, not someone to subjugate. And maybe that was why he was so gone over Cherry, because he knew his Sweets would never allow for such a thing.

Her phone chirped in her hand, followed by a whispered, "What in the fuck?"

"You all right over there?"

The phone chirped again in response, and again. "Um, Feathers? You might wanna come see this. It's weird."

She pushed her phone across the table to show him the screen. The first message was '667 4' then an owl and cherry emojis. The next was a crocodile with a name behind it, and the one after a tiger and a name. There was no number attached to the messages, and the name was merely 'You Know Who This Is.'

Vasi shook his head at his friend's theatrics. "God damn, he is extra."

Cherry held up the still beeping phone. "What *is* this?"

"They're from Mos. The 667 spells out his name and also shows he's the neighbor of the beast." At her confused look at his tiny joke, he just shrugged. "It's the list of names he couldn't give us directly. He probably spoofed a phone line to send that out."

Reading through the thread again, she snorted. "He takes that spy shit very seriously, doesn't he?"

Vasi rolled his eyes. "You have no idea." He watched as more and more names popped up on the screen, fourteen total. "He's a lot more cloak than dagger, but yes, definitely."

She flashed him a grin and wrote down all the names so he could have a copy, and though he probably imagined it, her fingers seemed to linger with his on the handoff. Then she went back to her research. "Sounds like an interesting guy."

Looking through the list, he could recognize a couple straight away. "He's a dick, but he gets shit done. Getting results makes him tolerable."

"Can't imagine why you'd get along," she mused airily while scrolling through her phone.

Some of the tension he'd been keeping in his body since their kiss melted away with her teasing. If she was snarking, she was smiling. He'd take it. "Shut the hell up, Sweets. I'll take the bottom seven if you take the top, yeah?"

She nodded. "Already on it."

They worked in silence through the afternoon until he turned on his eighties playlist, and then he got to listen to Cherry pretend she didn't know all the words to *Come On Eileen* and *Bringing On the Heartbreak,* even as she whisper-mumbled the lyrics. She got up for a beer after a bit, and the only reason he knew was because she left a cold one by his hand on her way by.

"Thanks, *iubi.*" He sipped his drink as he watched her from the table. She was wearing another one of his t-shirts, black this time, but back in the jeans that did incredible things for her ass, hair twisted up on top of her head and secured with a pen. Every once in a while, her blonde tipped, dark curls would dangle in her face as she wrote things down, and she'd blow them back without even interrupting her thought. She was so fucking perfect for him, his heart hurt just looking at her.

"Any luck on your end?"

He'd been so lost in his musings about her, it was like his brain was running a fifteen-second delay. "Um...not so much. I mean, I know several of these names from working at the palace, vetting them before they meet with the King and whatever, but as far as how they're connected to this? Yeah, not so much. You?"

Cherry shook her head and grimaced. "No." She spat the word like it offended her. Standing from her spot, she pocketed her phone and stretched her back. "All right, I'm gonna go see about some food, and I'll trade you my list of names to see if you have better luck.

Deal?"

Vasi nodded, diving back into his research to the sounds of pans clanking together and the varying noises that accompanied kitchen work. Before too long, his stomach growled loudly. He looked up as she slipped a steaming bowl of tuna noodle casserole onto the table next to him with a shaker of celery salt.

"How the hell—?" he demanded in disbelief as he picked up the spoon in the bowl and tasted her cheesy goodness.

She grinned wickedly, blowing him a kiss as she returned to her side of the marble bar. "Because I'm fucking magical."

A truer statement had never been uttered. "Fair, but where did you find all this?" He shook out some seasoning and slid it in her direction.

She caught the bottle before it slid off the table next to her and shook out her own salt then turned her attention back to her phone. "It's a home staple, Feathers. Every house has the components. Question..."

He watched her check her phone and her notes against the list of names. "Yes?" he prompted when she didn't follow up after a moment.

"The town marshal who stopped by earlier. The one I bit. His last name was Benedict, right?" The way she spoke, he could tell her hackles were up, and he was instantly on guard.

"Yeah. Why? You got something?"

"Maybe." She brought her bowl around to his side of the table and shoved him over to make room for her as she set out both the list and her phone. "This name, Jerome Benedict, shows up on the board. It's not a common last name, so I looked into it. He's a veterinarian, living outside of Black Moon Creek, in one of those massive mansions near Chugach. It's his home and his practice both. According to his website, he works with the parks service, too." She pulled the pen from her hair, shaking down the sexy mass of curls as she tapped the pen against her delectable bottom lip and looked around the room. "I like him for this."

"Go on." He spooned some of the noodles into his mouth to hide his smirk.

"A vet knows how to deal with animals, right? And since he's got that big house out in the country, he's got room to stash people if he wants. Plus, since his practice is there, he's got the meds necessary to sedate animals and whatnot."

Cherry started rocking a little on the chair as she eyed the ceiling, clearly still in working through the threads in her mind.

A couple bites of food later, she picked up her train of thought. "His son being on the police department and also an accomplice makes this easy, really. No one is gonna come looking for these missing girls, or if they are, the investigation will only be cursory at best." Her dark eyes glittered, her fangs showing as she finally looked at him with a frighteningly hostile grin. "We got him."

He would have been impressed, but her work made her as research-oriented as he was, so he was merely proud. Her intuitive leaps and ability to construct a sound theory of the case was goddamn breathtaking. She was getting shit *done*. "I love it so far. What do you have to back it up?"

The mischievous curl of her lips and the wrinkle on her nose was so damn cute, he was momentarily distracted. Long enough that she was able to commandeer his laptop and pull up Instagram. As a matter of course for work, he wasn't one for posting pictures of himself in too many places. Just a hazard of the work he'd done for most of his life, being too social on social media had the potential for fatal consequences. So, she logged in as a "No Thatsnotmyname,"— which, *cute*—and pulled up the public page for one Jerome Benedict of Anchorage Alaska.

"And behold. Chucklefuck Number Two, also known as Junior." She clicked the first row that popped up, revealing a picture of two men, one of them clearly the mustachioed cop from this morning, shirtless and holding up a string of fish in front of a mountainous backdrop, the other looking exactly the same but a bit more weathered and gray.

"I'll be damned. You want a job?" Xander would be overjoyed at handing over deep diving to someone else, and it was clear she had a knack for it. Goddess as his witness, he'd put her on the payroll today if she wanted.

Cherry snorted, a dimple appearing on her cheek in a brief flash as she dove deep into her bowl. "Appreciate the offer, but no."

Eh, it was worth a shot. "Our loss." He gathered up his things and packed away his laptop. "Okay, we need a plan."

WINGED GUARDIANS

Chapter 10

CHERRY

She left him to planning the details of their reconnaissance mission in favor of taking care of a small fire. Well, a small fire that would in no time at all turn into a conflagration if she left it unattended.

After popping back home for a quick shower and cleanup, Cherry threw on a cute burgundy turtleneck and a black maxi skirt that clung to every single curve with some tall boots to meet up with Pacey at Le Grec Bar & Grille for drinks and stuffed grape leaves.

Her best friend was sitting at the far end of the bar in the corner, a usual table for them, and she waved as Cherry ran the gauntlet of boozed-up frat boys, harried waitstaff, and tall shoes.

"Hey, stranger." The blonde kissed her cheek as she grabbed a seat.

"It's only been a few days, Pace," she chided, but feeling guilty all the same. Normally, she'd be over at the new place she shared with Daniel helping them get unpacked and settled. Pasting on a smile, she gave her drink order to the waitress who stopped by their table with Pace's cosmo.

"Sue me if I'm used to talking to you every day. How you been?"

"It's been…" She trailed off, trying to settle on a description that wouldn't elicit massive amounts of yelling from her friend. "It's been."

She looked serious for all of a moment before laughing into her pink martini. "For a writer, you sure do have a shitty command of the language."

"Fuck off, would you?" Of course, she snarled right as the waitress returned with her pomtini, and the poor girl startled so badly she splashed most of it onto Cherry's shoulder and arm.

"Oh shit! I'm so sorry, ma'am!" She started blotting her shirt immediately, eyes giant and fearful like she was going to sprout her fangs and rip off a chunk.

"Hey." She gently took the napkins from the flustered waitress and attempted her gentlest smile. "It's fine. No harm, no foul. It's not even gonna stain. Just grab another. It's fine. Relax." The woman nodded and swept the drink away. Watching her recede into the crowd, she sighed. "I'm not normally terrifying, am I?"

"Normally? No. Today? You're a little intense." Shimmering blue eyes watched her over the rim of her drink. "You wanna talk about it?"

The innocent tone of the question would have totally obscured the intent behind it if it had come from anyone else. "Why ask if I want to talk about it when you're just going to interrogate me either way?"

The blonde tossed her hair over her shoulder like the very question was beneath her dignity. "Feigning politeness. Now, tell me about it. What's going on with you? I spoke to Daniel—"

"Oh, here we go."

"You were at his cabin this morning, Cher." Of course, that was the moment the skittish waitress returned, all fear pheromones and Juicy Couture, with undertones of spilled vodka. She set down the fresh drink and the plate of dolmas before backing away like she was terrified to turn her back on them.

Her best friend watched the young woman with barely concealed annoyance at making her wait to continue her barrage. "What was he supposed to think?" she hissed as soon as she was out of earshot.

"That it's none of his business." She bit into her grape leaf dumpling and chewed defiantly.

"We care about you, sweetie." She laid her hand over Cherry's, effectively blocking her ability to snag another snack with an onslaught of sincerity. "We know how badly this went last time. You can't fault me, or him, for worrying."

As much as she wanted to lash out, she knew her friend had made a decent point. "Fine. I'm sorry."

"He said he went to the cabin to ask the owner some questions, and you were there. How the hell did that even happen? Is Vasily helping you, at least?"

"He is," she confirmed, throwing back her ice-cold drink in three sharply bracing swallows. "So, here's how this went down."

Dinner with Pacey left Cherry feeling a lot more grounded. Her best friend had a way of clearing all the clouds in her head and making her thoughts a great deal clearer. By the time she got back to Vasily's cabin, she was centered and ready to go with whatever plan he'd put together for them.

Finding the vet practice info had been a cake walk, and according to Google maps, it was much larger than they imagined. It was a sprawling collection of buildings including the practice, connected to the main house and a few barns where he could house some of the larger animals that came in as rescues or for rehab.

This was going to be a much larger operation, so they grabbed supplies from her place and worked out a rotation. The next few days were spent with one of them sitting in the wood line during the day as their respective animals as they observed the comings and goings at the compound, the other tracking the officer from his work to his home. At night, Vasi flew overhead, cataloging everything with a pulse on the ground, and Cherry patrolled around the fenced-in perimeter, looking for a way in.

The fence was the first clue that something was a little off there. The front of the house that faced the street, where clients would come to bring their animals, was quaint. Old school with hints of Tudor charm, it was cute with its curves, leaded glass windows, and a weathered split rail fence that surrounded the front of the property and ran right up to the much larger chain link one.

Both Vasily and Cherry agreed that even if they were merely treating larger animals in the back for varying local rehabs, there was no call at all for double layers of concertina wire at the top and along the bottom interior. It all looked fairly new, too, which was a little suspect. Literally everything weathered quickly here with all the cold and wind and snow, and the chain link was pristine, shiny and new.

There had been nothing really out of the ordinary until the weekend, when a newer Porsche SUV, the super nice one with a paint job that let the vehicle almost blend in with the twilight of fading midnight sun, pulled onto the property and drove immediately behind the vet practice. Cherry and Vasily watched as three men got out, carrying long guns and wearing camouflage.

"This looks bad," she whispered, shifting back and crouching behind his massive owl. His animal form was majestic as hell and twice as large. It never failed to impress her. "I think we might need to call for some backup."

The owl did the creepy thing, swiveling his head around almost a hundred eighty degrees, blinking at her and whistling softly. She nodded in understanding and reclaimed her fur, taking off back through the forest to the trail where they'd left Vasi's Land Rover. She didn't have to speak Owl to know what he wanted. Changing back into her clothes, she grabbed her cell phone and fired off a text to Zeke.

Vasily had explained his relationship to the osprey and the man's offer to assist if they got into a tight spot. Truthfully, when he was describing the guy, all she could think of was the father from *Taken*, with the same scarily lethal skill set. He answered promptly with an ETA, and she sat back in the passenger seat, trying to get a handle on her emotions.

The idea that she could have been hunted like the caribou woman—like all those other women—caused a hot wave of nausea to wash over her, and she worked to breathe through it. She knew she could share her fears with Vasi, but it was another thing entirely to do so. Since the kiss, they hadn't really had a chance to be *together* like that, and that was really just as well. It was very possible that neither of them was prepared to commit to that level of vulnerability with one another. Some hurts just cut too deep.

That didn't mean she didn't want to, though. When she thought about the idea of being his lifelong mate, she wasn't possessed with an urge to flee the country and change her name, which was a remarkable change from her usual M.O. where people with dicks were concerned.

Lost in her thoughts, she sprouted claws and fangs when a knock sounded on the window next to her head. "Fucking hell," she muttered, unlocking and opening the door.

She wasn't sure what she was expecting when Vasi told her about his friend, but it hadn't been a thinner version of The Dude. In his quilted flannel, with his thick ash-blond ponytail at the base of his skull and sharp features, he was at once very mundane yet distinctive-looking.

"Miss Belmont, I presume."

"You can call me Cherry, Zeke."

His eyes widened, though even with the dome light lit behind her she couldn't tell the color. "You don't say." His smile was speculative, so disconcertingly *knowing*, and just this side of entertained. "Where's our boy?"

She nodded toward the darkened forest straight ahead. "He's posted up by the fence in the treeline."

He shrugged out of his coat and folded it across his arm. "Then, what are we waiting for?"

Cherry had no idea how she'd managed to end up running around with enormous frickin' Birds of Prey, but holy shit were they impressive. Zeke's bird was huge, as big as Vasily's both in height and wingspan. Black body with a white chest, he was uniquely suited to prowl the darkness and blend into the canopy overhead. He trailed behind her as she ran, following the scent path she'd left from their last position.

Once the three met up, they crouched down to confer in human form.

"It's cold as fuck, so I'm gonna be brief," Vasi began. "Two side-by-sides rolled out of the compound out of a back gate, one pulling a trailer. Everyone had rifles, so far as I can see. Zeke and I are going to track them and see where they go and what they get up to." When she opened her mouth to object, he held up a hand. "I know you're a fucking amazing tracker, *dragostea mea,* but I'm not going to put you in a position to be caught, retraumatized, or both, by whatever we find. Just not gonna happen, and I'm not sorry. I need you to watch the perimeter. If anyone else shows up, comes out after us, if anyone seems unduly interested in you, you bug out and come find us. I know you're fast and strong, but you're not equipped to repel bullets." His silvery eyes caught the moonlight, jaw set at a truculent angle that practically begged her to argue.

She snarled in response but didn't put up a fight. She appreciated he was trying to keep her safe, and she'd allow it. For now. She wasn't some shrinking violet or a hothouse flower incapable of taking care of herself. "Fine. You get hurt or don't come back, I swear on all that's holy, I'm killing everyone and burning this place to the goddamn ground."

It was hard not to love a woman like that. "*Şi eu te iubesc.*" Vasily grinned and threw an arm around her shoulders and pulled her in to kiss her forehead. "Zeke, you good?"

The man, who was watching their interaction with an expression that bordered on fondness, nodded. "Recon unless engaged. Got it."

"Let's move out."

Vasily and Zeke took up their feathers once more and spread their wings, leaving her in the wood line with her fur and her rage. It was all she could do to summon her patience. Someone would pay for this, but not at the moment.

VASILY

He didn't need to be psychic to know Zeke was bubbling over with questions. About Cherry, both in the past and now. The problem was he didn't know exactly how to answer them. Everything between the kiss and the present moment felt like both an incredible dream and an unattainable fantasy.

Every time he closed his eyes, he could feel her lips on his, smell her scent, cinnamon, sugar, and a musk that was all her. She always smelled warm and so perfect, and he was suddenly glad for his bird form because he was pretty sure his human face would have done that thing where it slipped from vaguely homicidal to absolutely besotted without prompting. And the memory of the softness of her body cradled in his arms and on his lap, his heart could barely stand it.

Dropping out of his silent flight, he alit onto a pine bough that offered him cover as he watched the goings-on below. His ears told him that Zeke had landed a couple trees away, and the osprey ducked his head when they made visual contact.

From high above the scene, the night was quiet except for the men's voices below. They were discussing a hunt and preparing their guns by the back of a white covered horse trailer. Vasi's heart tripped into double time as they gathered around the doors of the trailer and they swung open.

Into the night, a stark white, horned sheep of some sort stepped out of the trailer on uncharacteristically wobbly legs. If there was one thing he knew, it was that goats were steady on their feet. In mute horror, he watched as Benedict, in canvas coveralls and visible from the way his bright white bandage on his hand lit up in the moonlight, smacked the animal on the ass, startling it and sending it skittering off into the night.

The men down below laughed at her shocked bleat and cheered as she darted off through the trees. Once they'd given her enough time to consider it sporting, they took off on foot after her, tracking her path with guns ready and evil intent.

Silently, he descended to the ground below, within sight of the trailer but far enough away to not draw any attention. Zeke followed immediately, dropping his feathers with a look of horror that Vasi hadn't seen since they'd been overseas.

"The fuck did you bring me into?" his friend demanded urgently, lips barely moving and eyes eternally scanning for threats.

"These are the assholes who took Cherry. She escaped, but we're pretty sure they were going to do this to her. They're taking shifter women and hunting them down for sport." Just saying the words enraged him almost to the point of bloodlust.

They both stiffened at the sound of a rifle report in the not too far distance.

"We need to kill a lot of people," Zeke observed, looking surprisingly comfortable with the idea. Vasily was glad he called him.

"Then we're gonna need a plan."

Cherry had been all questions when they returned, both somber and angry, having watched the monsters haul the sheep carcass back to the trailer, blood showing night black on its white fur. Vasi and Zeke herded her into the truck without a lot of commentary, and the consensus was they were headed back to the cabin to work out how to proceed.

Once inside, he skipped over the beer and headed straight to the liquor cabinet for a full bottle of whiskey and three short, squat crystal tumblers. After pouring for each of them, he roughly gathered Cherry to him and sat there in silence for a moment with his arms around her as she sat still in his lap with her head automatically going to rest on his shoulder. It was several deep lungsful of her scent before he felt his body relax enough to contemplate calming down.

"Do I wanna know?" she inquired softly.

"No," Zeke and Vasi proclaimed at the same time.

Zeke threw back his glass without so much as a flinch and immediately poured another. "Okay, so, this is an infiltration and extraction, right?" When Vasi nodded, he pulled out his phone, scrolling through until he showed them what he had on his screen—the vet's hours of operation. "I have a way in, but only one of us can be obviously armed."

Cherry sat up and grabbed her and Vasily's glasses, pressing it into his hand as she got comfortable in his arms once more. "We're listening."

CHERRY

They'd offered to let Zeke stay at the house on the couch, but he declined, citing his dog Earl's bathroom needs, but he appreciated the offer all the same. And maybe she wanted the buffer of him between her and the smoldering ember that was Vasily. The way he looked at her was like he could burst into flames at any moment, and honestly, she wouldn't mind terribly being consumed.

He leaned his head against the door after he showed Zeke out with a plan to meet the following day. All at once, the darkness outside seemed to bleed in through the windows, even with the fire blazing in the fireplace and the overhead lights glowing like they normally did.

"I can't do this," he whispered, his quiet words ricocheting off the wood frame easily picked up by her sensitive ears.

Cherry watched him from her spot folded up into the corner of the sofa with her arms wrapped around her legs and coffee mug resting on her knees. His eyes were closed, body in a position of defeat, shoulders rounded, and head still bowed against the door. "You can't do what?"

"I tried to stay away, you know," he replied, avoiding her question. "I wanted nothing more than for you to be happy, and I couldn't see how that would be possible with the mating bond hanging over our heads like a damn sword." He pushed off the door and trudged over to sit next to her on the edge of the couch, not crowding into her space, but definitely close enough to touch if she wanted. "I wanted..." He huffed a mournful laugh, the smile on his face anything but happy.

"Whatever you want, I'll give it to you," she promised, reaching out to touch his arm with one hand as she moved her mug to the floor. Everything about him was broadcasting his anxiety and agitation, from the way his normally silver blue eyes flashed orange and back, to the notes of pepper in his normal scent. His skin was hot to the touch, like his bird form was waiting just beneath his skin to burst forth. He'd changed out of his flannel shirt into a blue Red Sox t-shirt with a rip in the neck and left his feet bare.

He flicked his silvery gaze to her with a quick smirk that he squelched equally as fast. "You don't know what you're saying."

"Then tell me what you want, and we'll negotiate." Taking a chance, she slipped a little closer to him, unfolding a leg behind him on the couch, arms looped loosely around his waist, face pressed to the solid strength of his shoulder. She could imagine that soft pink scar under her lips beneath the cotton. "Please," she murmured, "tell me."

His turn to her was sudden, but she wasn't startled. He braced his right hand on the cushion by her hip and leaned into her, his left-hand weaving into her curls, lips claiming hers and tongue demanding immediate entry. Her breath caught at his vehemence even as she acquiesced, slipping her tongue past his lips to slide against his.

His growl was a visceral sensation, vibrating through her as he pressed her back into the cushion at the arm of the couch. Her left hand teased the hem of his shirt in back, nails scraping against the soft skin just above his jeans even as her right hand cradled his jaw gently.

Vasi broke the kiss to press his lips briefly to her palm before he rested his forehead against hers. "Need you," he breathed as his hand at her waist stole under her shirt and raced up her ribcage. "Please."

Cherry answered with a shaky nod. "Have me."

His shirt tangled around his shoulders, her lips drawn to his collarbones and up to bare her teeth against the flesh of his neck. He tasted like fire on her tongue, the burn of memories so hot and addictive she could barely resist biting down. His scar, so delicate and pink, drew reverent kisses as her fingertips explored the vast expanse of muscles from his chest down each rib to trace over his abs. He had been gorgeous from the moment she'd laid eyes on him all those years ago, but in this moment, she couldn't contain the wave of sheer want that coursed through here as her center clenched in response.

Legs wrapped around his hips, she ground up against him, her body instinctively seeking the friction that would relieve the ache between her thighs. Her own shirt had evaporated somehow—she wasn't quite clear—and the cups of her bra were peeled down, revealing breasts that were now the sole focus of his attention.

His happy sigh made her giggle as he buried his face in her soft flesh, the teasing scrape of his stubbled jaw making her squirm even closer to him. Clever lips glided over her skin, sealing around her nipple to draw it deep into his mouth, but moving away the moment her back arched to bring him closer. It was as arousing as it was maddening. Her fingers found purchase in his long hair, and he whimpered the moment she tugged the handful wrapped around her fist.

It wasn't pain, though, no, his hips grinding down to meet hers, his cock hard and more than evident even in his jeans. "So good," he praised even as he unwound her fingers from his tresses. His lips trailed down her belly, tongue an unexpected tease as it circled and dipped into her bellybutton.

Hips rising to chase the feeling of him moving back from her, he pushed up on his hands and knees, sitting back to examine his lascivious handiwork. She knew she presented quite the picture with her hard nipples glistening with his spit and her lips parted on quick pants that were just short of moans. Legs spread lewdly, open and casually draped around his hips, he dragged his fingertips from her knees up to her inner thighs to her waist, avoiding where she wanted him most.

His lips twitched at her outraged groan and accompanying

pout. Fingers resting on the button of her jeans, he cocked an eyebrow, silvery eyes now bright orange, considering her. "I..." He swallowed hard; his voice not nearly as steady as it normally was. "Is this—I mean, do you want—"

"Feathers, if you do not get these jeans off me right goddamn now," she warned him, but couldn't get any more words out as he leaned over her all of a sudden and laid absolute siege to her mouth. Senses awash in his smokey, spicy smell and the unique flavor of him on her tongue, she was only peripherally aware of her jeans sliding down her legs, but the feel of his denim-encased length settling down against her was enough to wrest a moan from deep in her chest. Thin, neon pink cotton and flimsy, lived-in jeans were the only things that separated them from being completely bared to each other, skin to skin.

She was the one begging now, nonsense words and half-formed pleas on her lips as he rolled his hips against her slowly and to devastating effect. His fingers preceded his lips on a return trip down her chest, pausing at her nipples for just a moment before heading south to the waistband of her panties.

There was no such thing as keeping still, her need for touch overriding her sense of modesty as the heat and wetness between her legs began to eat away at her sanity. He shushed her when she keened, his fingers dipping below the elastic to caress her mound before sliding down to tease her lips through the cotton.

Her moan when he swept the soaked cloth aside and slipped his tongue between her folds was one of both lust and relief. His skilled tongue consoled and aroused in equal measure, his touch both soothing and a brand that made her body clench. His fingers teasing her entrance before sliding into her, broke her, leaving her gasping and practically sobbing with need as her body clenched around his marauding digits.

Vasily purred in pleasure, vibration igniting the nerves in her most sensitive flesh, sending waves and spasms of completion through her as he touched off another orgasm before seeking another after that. His ruthless attention to detail left her throat raw and her fingers cramped as they clenched the sofa cushions and in his hair.

His nose, cheeks, and chin glistened as he sat back on his heels with a triumphant grin. Cherry could do little but lie there, splayed out before him like a wilted flower, petals plucked and strewn about. She reached for him, her fingers grazing the button on his jeans before he moved back out of her reach.

Her disappointed whine only made him smile more. "Another time." He kissed her fingers and placed her hand on the back of the couch. "I can't even tell you how long I've wanted this."

"And you're making me wait because...?"

VASILY

He wheezed out a soft snicker before exhaling a tremulous breath. In a million years, he would have never dreamed of being in this position. A year ago, a week ago...her gorgeous expanse of dark skin called his fingertips, the taste of her muddling his senses, burning through his veins. The tiny scrap of Day-Glo cotton drawn down her long, long legs and thrown somewhere across the room.

Not content to lie back and let him spoil her, she reached up again, her fingers dancing from the button of his jeans then down to skim his diamond-hard length before hooking her fingers in his beltloops and yanking him down over her. Her mouth was wild, soft lips and sharp little teeth chasing the sparks and spikes of pleasure over his skin, from the spot on his neck under his ear to his shoulder and clavicle and back across his jaw before claiming his mouth again.

"I need you, Vasi." Her warm breath against his ear sent a shimmer of goosebumps down his body as his hips ground down against hers.

The shuddering pleasure that went straight to his cock when she bit and sucked his neck also reminded him of a fairly pressing related matter. "I'll be right back."

Cherry pulled back, her brows arched and dark eyes wide with lust and irritation. "You good?"

Pressing a quick kiss to the tip of her nose, he pushed to his feet and dashed out of the room. "Hold that thought," he called over his shoulder as he darted into the bathroom.

"Are you fucking serious?" Her howl was tinged with laughter, and when he turned, he found her propped up on an elbow looking like she might take a bite out of him solely on general principle. "You don't carry one on you?"

"I haven't seen you in several years! I didn't want to presume." He banged around the cabinet for a moment until he found his prize. "Problem solved," he informed her, leaning against the doorjamb and holding up a three-pack strip of condoms, thankfully included in his welcome packet from his host.

"Not yet." Eyes sparkling, his sexy ground predator rose from the couch and stalked him across the floor, her walk so mesmerizing he felt himself start to sweat the closer she drew to him. Chin up, her sexy fucking strut damn near brought him to his knees in gratitude. She grazed him with her claws as she passed him into the bedroom, his stomach muscles trembling with the sensation.

Following her with his eyes, he locked his lips as she draped herself artfully on top of the bedspread. "You coming or nah?" she teased, looking up at him through her lashes.

Vasily ditched his jeans on his way to the bed, tearing open one packet with his teeth. One knee on the bed, he reached out to pull her up into a deep kiss. He smiled at her whimper when he retreated. "Not yet."

He couldn't really tell who pounced on whom at that point, because once he got in the bed, it was an all-out battle for supremacy. He kinda loved it. It was so comforting—restorative—for him to know she wanted this as much as he did.

Cherry sank her teeth into the juncture of his neck and shoulder when he slid inside her, the melding of pain and pleasure clouding his thoughts until all that was left was the two of them. Her heat, her softness, her fingers digging into the muscles of his back and shoulders, all of it was more than he'd ever let himself imagine and so, so perfect.

They moved together like they'd never been parted, her hips

rising to meet his thrusts, her back arching off the bed and offering herself to him. Being allowed to touch her and feel her against him was blowing his mind. He needed it more than oxygen, and the emotion of it was drowning him.

"*Cireașa mea, ești atât de frumoasă*," he growled as he nosed the corner of her jaw and the spot just below her ear that made her gasp. "Fucking beautiful."

"Bite me." Cherry turned her head, baring even more of her neck to him. "Please, my neck," she panted, her voice hoarse and soft. "I'm close, please."

Sinking his teeth into her neck, he was shocked at the spasm that ran through her, like an electrical shock that sent her over the edge with a sound that was part wail, part growl, and everything he ever wanted. The feel of her body clenching around him, pulling him deeper into her, wrecked him, bringing him to his release almost immediately after her as his arms gave out, collapsing him down onto her fully.

They were left drained, sweating, on top of the blankets in a room that was surprisingly cool, and all he could think was how much he loved this woman. His lips forging a path of tiny lazy kisses, he could feel the hammering beat of her heart as she slowly returned to normal beneath his lips.

"*Mă faci fericită*," he purred along her collarbone as she absently carded her fingers through his hair. "You make me so happy. I..." He trailed off with a giggle, feeling heat coalesce in his cheeks and ears. "I'm sorry for hurting you."

Despite the mellow languor that was quickly spreading through him, her deep sigh concerned him. Maybe he'd waited too long, maybe this was simply a much-delayed goodbye, maybe—

"You're thinking too much again, Feathers." She tugged his hair until he looked up at her dark eyes that absolutely held all the secrets in the universe. "Forgiveness'll be a minute, but it's definitely on the table. I still love you. Never stopped, for what it's worth."

Just hearing the words choked him up enough to need a minute. With a fair amount of strain, he pulled himself from her embrace and headed into the ensuite bathroom to both dispose of the evidence and collect his wayward emotions. Returning to the bed, he wasted no time collecting her into his arms like he had no intention of ever letting her go. "*Inima mea îți aparține,*" he whispered into her hair.

"What does that mean?"

"My heart is yours, Cherry. Always has been." Sealing his vow with a quick kiss, he snuggled back into the pillows, reveling in this turn of fortune he never expected.

"When you leave a review for the host, make sure to give them high marks for planning. This could have been a crisis of biblical proportions. 14/10 would recommend."

Vasily snorted, his chest shaking with snickers as he tried not to laugh. "Biblical."

"Noah's flood had nothing on me."

His whole body jerked at the visual. "Okay, that's fair."

He awoke to an empty bed and the smell of bacon and coffee in the air. Bless Cherry for her kindness. Taking advantage of his moment alone, he dialed Mos again. It was closer to noon than he intended, but he figured the raven would be close to winding up his day.

"*Bună ziua!* You never call, you never write."

"You and Xander both need new material." Hearing his scoff brought a smile to Vasi's face. It felt good to have a moment of normal because the rest of the day was going to be anything but. "You ready for the coronation tomorrow?" He felt terrible that he was going to miss Finn's ascent to the throne the next day, but he knew his best friend would understand. He'd send him a text once he was off the phone.

"I have to wear the fucking coronet and robes. Are you kidding me? How do you think I am?"

Vasi could almost see the face he was making and grinned in spite of himself. "Life's tough when you have a title. Take a selfie."

"Fuck you, and it's tough all over." There was some shuffling in the background and a female voice wishing him good evening and hoping he would have a good weekend. "As much as I appreciate you calling, I have things I need to do to get ready for tomorrow, so since this isn't exactly a social call, what's going on?"

"Can you speak freely?"

The ambient background noise died immediately after a click. "I can now." With a sigh, the owl looped Mos in on their findings and the things they'd seen the night before.

In response, the raven blew out a deep sigh. "What do you need from me?"

"Sanction me. I'm going to take care of this whether you do or not, but it's a fucklot less messy if you do. Off the books until the job is done, and then you can claim you were coordinating a clandestine op, code word compartmentalized. Attach it to the case you already have, whatever. I don't care."

The wheezing laugh that answered him was not encouraging. "That's a tall damn order. What do I get in return for such largess?"

He rubbed the back of his neck in irritation as he thought about it. He wasn't in the habit of explaining himself to anyone but the crown and hadn't been for a while now. "The knowledge those shifter women have been set free isn't enough for you?"

A derisive snort echoed over the phone. "Not by a long shot."

"What do you want?" He didn't mean to come across as a dick, but he hadn't anticipated having to negotiate this part.

"Intel. Paperwork, cloud networks, hard drives, phones. Everything you might find comes directly to me." The fact he didn't mention witnesses or persons of interest did not go unnoticed.

"Naturally. I was planning to do that anyway to thank you for your help with the other thing." Even if they were on encrypted lines, there was no reason to get careless. If anything, they found helped further whatever the minister had brewing, all the better. "Do you have any contacts at the embassy who can be trusted for this kind of thing? Someone to come in afterward and sweep up the place?"

Mos hummed, his tone sliding from annoyed to resigned. "I'll have some people read in and on the ground in four hours. Good enough?"

He felt the thrum of anticipation shoot through him as the logistical side of his brain was appeased. "That works for me."

"You have enough people?"

Vasily knew better than to tease him about the notes of concern in his voice. "Yeah."

"If it's just you and the wolverine, I can send some people to back you up."

Mos's ability to suss people out never ceased to amaze him. "I appreciate your concern, Nicodemos, but you're not the only one with people on the ground." At this point, the fewer people directly involved, the better. He could speak to Zeke and Cherry's loyalty; anyone else wouldn't make it through the vetting process in time.

"Feathers, you up? Zeke'll be here soon," Cherry called from the kitchen.

"Sounds like your keeper is calling."

If being kept by her was the worst thing that could happen, he'd be doing all right. "Be out in a minute, *iubi*," he replied out the door. On the phone, he muttered. "I gotta go. Details forthcoming. We'll be in touch."

"Understood. Be careful and know this. If you fuck this up, this call never happened."

"Clear. direct." Slipping his phone into his pocket, he moseyed out to the kitchen to kiss his mate on the cheek and steal bacon from her plate. "Nicodemos says hello."

"Uh huh. Were you planning to tell me we were talking to the Deputy Minister of the Interior last night?" She held a spatula up in accusation.

"What?" he asked, all big, innocent eyes and pout as he slathered his toast in blackberry jam. "I thought you knew."

WINGED GUARDIANS

CHAPTER 11

XANDER

"Have you spoken to Vasily lately?" Finn asked as Xander escorted him back to his quarters from the throne room where he'd spent the better part of the day working on the dress rehearsal for his coronation. This should have been Vasi's job, and Finn's nerves were fraying without his best friend to lean on.

"Not in a couple days or so, no." Which was entirely true. Other than the search request, they hadn't really spoken at all. The Commander's approach on assignments was always 'no news is good news,' so until he was told otherwise, Xander chose to assume all was well.

The crown prince frowned and pulled on his cufflink. "I see. I just sent him a text, and he hasn't answered. I mean, he knows what tomorrow is, right?"

"I might have a reason for that, Highness," a deep voice piped up from behind them, making both men jump. How the Deputy Minister managed to appear out of thin air was anyone's guess. It just added to his creeptacular aura.

"Fuck me, Your Lordship. With all due respect, I think someone needs to put a bell on you," the prince exclaimed, clutching his chest then smoothing down his tie like he didn't just leap a foot into the air in shock. Normally, sneaking up on a wolf was hard, but downwind and preoccupation had obviously worked in Mos's favor.

Try as he might, Xander couldn't contain the snort of laughter in response. "I don't think that would work out the way you intended, Highness."

Mos's lips twitched, but otherwise he didn't react. "Be that as it may, I think I might have a reason for Commander Breţcu's," he paused like he was groping for the word, "distraction." He held the door for them as they entered the antechamber to the prince's quarters.

"Other than him taking some off to help out a friend?"

It was the prince's last night in them before moving across the palace to the section reserved for the Regent. Though most of his personal effects had been moved out, the furniture would remain. They entered the room to find his wife stretched out on the couch with her feet up and a Kindle in hand. The moment she saw her brother, she rolled her eyes and got to her feet.

The look on the minister's face was far too self-satisfied to lead to anything good. "A friend, hmm? I think he may have left out some pertinent details that might be of interest to you."

CHERRY

Zeke carried a truly alarming number of weapons on his person at any one time. Three knives, one pistol, and one retractable baton, and those were just the ones he told her about. There were no illusions in her mind that he was likely packing many, many more, and interestingly enough, she couldn't see any of them. It was kind of impressive. Her job was to hand over her bag and carry in any weapons he and Vasi would need for the mission.

And she wasn't naïve; that's what this was. This was covert ops all the way, from the in-person meeting to the amount of coordinated recon between the three of them. She was really only a fuzzy critter along for the ride, with the bite force to break a femur, but really, the clandestine services part of this was all them.

They'd been discussing the plan for later in the day, finetuning any questionable details when Vasi's phone beeped with a text message. And again, and again, in rapid succession. It was going off like a Monday morning alarm, and all he did was look at the screen and silence it, shoving it into his pocket with a huge sigh.

"You good?" she asked, concerned because his pocket was still vibrating quite vociferously.

"I'm fine," he replied in a tone that clearly indicated he wasn't.

She thought about challenging him on it but given the way his glower darkened with every buzz of his cell phone, she figured they were all better off if she left it alone.

Her phone ringing was a complete surprise. Pretty much anyone who knew her knew to text her rather than call, but when she saw the name, she knew it was likely important. She held it up for Vasi to see the name.

Eyes wide, he reached for her hand. "Don't answer—"

She connected the call before he even had a chance to finish the sentence. "Yes?"

The voice of Baron LeStrange was very distinctive in both its depth and clipped diction. "Miss Belmont, would you please put me on speaker?"

With all the yelling and carrying on in his background, it sounded like he was at a bar. "You sure that's a good idea?" Vasily looked surprisingly pale with a hand over his mouth, shaking his head vehemently.

"Oh, yes," the Deputy Minister assured her, drawing out the 's' like a snake.

Rolling her eyes at the owl's histrionics, she set the phone on the table and hit the speaker. The background noise died down immediately. "You're on speaker."

"Oh, good. Commander, do you know what tomorrow is?" a silky female voice inquired immediately. Under other circumstances, she'd feel jealous, but the look of abject horror on Vasi's face eliminated that as an option.

"The Coronation, Your Grace."

Cherry looked from Vasily to Zeke, who was making the same face she was, big eyes and vaguely terrified. "Your Grace?" she mouthed to him, and he nodded grimly, acknowledging she wasn't crazy.

"And I'm told you have a good reason as to why you're not here for it? Supporting your best friend? The one who is freaking the fuck out and driving me insane?" Cherry flinched when the duchess casually dropped an f-bomb, wholly unprepared for the level of familiarity there.

"You've been mated this whole time?" a male voice cut in, and surprisingly, Vasi looked even worse. "How did I not know this? Were you gonna tell us? What the fuck, man?"

"Finnegan, you just took away all my fun. I never get to bust his balls."

"You were taking too long to get to the good part, Angel."

The female voice continued, undaunted. "And that's another thing. My asshole brother had to come with this news? Really?" A lightbulb went off as Cherry remembered her first conversation with Mos.

"I didn't *have* to tell you," Mos interjected.

"Should have gone with that urge, Nicodemos," Vasily muttered darkly, for reasons that made Cherry deeply curious. "Can we do this at another point in time?"

"Uh, *no*." Vasi braced himself at the sound of hurt in Finn's voice. "Really. I've known you since you first came to the palace. How many years is that, now?"

"A lot." He sighed dejectedly; head bowed like he was getting reamed out in person.

"And that whole time, you were mated and said nothing? The

fuck, man!" Finn, she liked this guy. He sounded like good people.

"Maybe he has a good reason, love."

"To not tell his best friend? Something like this? After all we've been through?" Yep, she definitely liked this guy. He was asking all the right questions and surprisingly getting no answers.

Listening to them argue with each other on the other end of the call was trippy, however, there was one point they all seemed to be missing. "Um, hi. I'm sorry. I'm not trying to be rude, but who are you and why are you busting Vasily's balls on *my* phone?"

"Wait," the new male voice answered. "He didn't tell you about us, either?"

With a greatly aggrieved sigh, Vasi rose from his chair and grabbed the phone. "I will call you back in fifteen seconds," he snarled and hung up, pressing her phone back into her hand and pulling his own from his pocket. "Fucking hell."

Cherry could hear the weird ringing that indicated a video call and then there was more yelling.

"Look," he grumbled as he stared into the screen. "I'm alive. Is that enough?"

"Are you fucking kidding me right now?" the female voice demanded. "You got something you need to say?"

Looking very put-upon, he marched over to stand next to Cherry and wrapped an arm around her shoulders. It could have been perfunctory, but the way he pulled her into his side and brushed a kiss over her temple said otherwise. On the tiny screen in his hand were several people all jockeying for position around the camera. One she recognized from his lock screen, but the man with the beard and the dark-skinned woman in his lap needed no introduction at all. Aside from the eager grins and furtive little waves, she didn't need to be told she was suddenly having an audience with the future king of the shifters while wearing a black *Star Wars* shirt she'd borrowed from Vasily and frayed jeans with holes in the knees.

"Your Highness, Your Grace, may I present Cherry Belmont, my mate." He sounded annoyed, but one look at him and he was smirking like he couldn't contain his happiness. It was an unsettling juxtaposition, but she opted to for the optimistic view.

Impossible as it seemed, the smiles only increased in wattage and affection. "Cherry, these intrusive assholes are Finn and Cora, the blond is Xander, and the permanently grouchy-looking bastard is Mos."

"You're one to talk," the man in black snapped back but looked almost like he could be smiling? Maybe in an alternate universe?

She held up a finger. "Quick question. Am I supposed to curtsey?"

NICODEMOS

"I cannot believe that asshole," Dev muttered as he dropped down into the armchair next to Xander. Both of them had already talked to Vasi, making small talk with him and Cherry because this was definitely not the time to discuss case notes.

"Leave it to Vasily to mate with a damn wolverine—holy gods!" Xander agreed vehemently. He was, by far, the most stunned by the revelation that the Strigine had taken a mate. His reaction to the news seemed almost jealous, Mos noted, information that may prove useful at another point in time.

He, at least, had had a moment to process it before springing it on everyone, so keeping his reactions schooled was a lot easier, and he could enjoy the show. Finn was a bundle of emotions on a good day, and him being hurt by this omission from his best friend made sense. Cora simply liked to be the one with all the secrets and insider knowledge. It was a trait she shared with Mos, though he'd be plucked bald before he admitted that openly. The rest of the hurt and shock were totally understandable. They were a little cadre, a node of power, a family as such, and Brețcu just doused the lot of them in hot water.

And then there was the matter of Cherry herself. She was an unusual choice for a man like Vasily. Of course, she was pretty, maybe a little more laidback than he would have pictured for the notoriously hard-nosed Commander, but she had a decent sense of humor and seemed to be moving well for having an owl wrapped completely around her little finger. She lived her life exposing secrets and forcing dark actions into the spotlight, and he was... well, the nature of his job meant he kept a good deal of darkness around him at all times.

"Right?" Cora chimed in as she draped herself across her husband's lap and the couch simultaneously. "He had a lot of damn nerve coming after *me* for keeping secrets when he was sitting on something like that."

Mos snorted derisively, leaning against the door to the antechamber. He didn't want to come any farther inside than was necessary. Closeness with others was never a high desire on his list. "To be fair, yours *did* have some fairly grave implications for the affairs of state."

The glare she leveled at him was hot enough to remove feathers, but he would never give her the pleasure of a reaction. "We're not talking about me—"

"There's a shock," he bit out, the sniping between them more out of reflex than actual antipathy.

The future queen of the shifters had an impressively eloquent glower, packing it full of curses, invectives, and pejoratives with but a twitch of an eyelash. "...Anyway," she grumbled, turning her head away from her brother like he no longer existed, "Vasily had a mate. One none of you all knew about. Can we talk about that for a minute? What the hell?"

"You're missing the bigger picture, Commander," Dev piped up.

"Which is?" Finn's voice was equal parts exhaustion and dread. This kind of thing was exactly what they didn't need the night before the coronation.

"He left to go take care of something for a 'friend.' That's what he told me, told all of us. And now he's out in Alaska with his mate? What's he got going on that he needs to be out there for her right now? What is she into?" He shifted back to relax in the chair again, crossing his legs with an ankle on his knee. "You know damn well he's married to this job. We couldn't even keep him out of the office with a gunshot wound, so you know he would not be missing the coronation for anything short of the apocalypse."

The room sat silent with his proclamation, and Mos had to admire Dev's mind. Five moves ahead at all times, and it was fucking impressive to see. He made a mental note to offer him a job at the ministry if this one got too mundane. Thinkers like that were priceless. He was also alarmingly accurate in his hypothesis, though if Mos said as much, there'd be many, many more questions than he was comfortable answering.

"So, I guess we need to know what kind of horseman he's facing, right?" Xander asked.

"Doesn't matter." Cora swung her long legs off the couch and turned to face the man who would be king. "I'll go get him. I can have him back here in ten hours, less if you don't ask questions as to how."

"Angel…"

She held up a hand even as Mos watched her slip a foot under the table to corral one of her high heels to put it back on. "I mean it. I will go and deal with his problem and bring him and his mate back here if that's what you need. Say the word, and I'm gone."

And that was the other problem that came with coming clean with what he knew. The difference between Cora and a Valkyrie boiled down to merely ethnicity. If Mos so much as breathed a hint of what the owl had going, there would be no stopping her from riding out to descend like a plague upon the state of Alaska and everyone in it.

"Your Grace." The whole room turned in stunned shock as Mos reinserted himself into the conversation in such a spectacularly provocative fashion, reveling in the quick looks between each other and the estranged siblings.

It wasn't often he got to thoroughly rock someone's world in person. Especially Cora, whose mouth opened in mute astonishment at him acknowledging her as anything but a disappointment or a hindrance, much less by her new title. He may not have approved of how she'd gotten it, but he wasn't so stupid as to spit directly into the face of the man who would be King or on the memory of his father. The issues between him and his sister were not for public discussion, and so he could be polite because that was his job.

The silence in the room dragged on, a clear line in the sand between the two of them that no one else dared approach. After a minute or so of waiting for the waspish reply he'd expected, he cleared his throat and began slowly rubbing a spot over his eyebrow in response to the mother of all migraines brewing as he ticked off his list.

"Overlooking your rank, your pregnancy, your duties and engagements as the fiancée to the future head of state—and, oh, yes, your position as *the future Queen*—I'm going to forbid that level of intervention. There will be no unsanctioned and illegal uses of magic and witchcraft here."

"Oh, you forbid it?" Her deft fingers were fastening the buckles on her fashionably over-tall stilts.

He nodded slowly, eyes never leaving her, in case she decided to take one off and lob it at him. "I do. It's a kind offer, if a bit misguided and wholly unnecessary."

"'Misguided?' I don't give a fuc—" She would have been up and off the couch and in his face if Finn's reflexes had been a half-second slower. "Motherfucker, I will end you."

The older raven shook his head, drawing up to his full height and doing his best to sound dispassionately compassionate. "What I meant was, I will take care of this. I won't be able to get him back before the coronation, but I will have people out there to assist him in whatever he's got going, which I assume will get him back here sooner." Turning his attention solely to Finn, he dipped his head. "Is that acceptable, Highness?"

Tucking his grumbling fiancée into his side, he leaned back against the couch again. "I guess it'll have to be."

Mos nodded and turned on his heel. He had shit to do, and god help him if anything happened to Breţcu in the meantime.

"We gonna talk about how creepy he is?" he heard Dev ask the moment the door was closed at his back.

"Unfortunately, that's a family trait," Cora muttered, and Mos smirked as he stepped into the shadows of the hallway. They would never be close again but hearing that they still had a scant inch of common ground between them made him happy, or some approximation thereof.

VASILY

He could *not* get them off the phone fast enough, holy gods, but it had gone surprisingly well. Dev even showed up toward the end, so all the major people in his life got to "meet" Cherry. The owl could not deny the warm feeling that knowledge gave him.

His friends meant well, he knew, but fuck, they were overbearing as hell. Everybody had questions for Cherry, which was expected, and there was a fair amount of yelling at him as well. He expected there would be a great deal more when he got back home, but then, that was how family worked. He wanted to be angry at Mos for selling him out, but Vasi suspected this was a little bit of payback for the debacle involving Cora, so he decided to let it go.

Cherry had been surprisingly chill about "meeting" royalty for the first time. She'd said just treating them like his friends made it easier, and he believed her. The fuck-load of questions he knew she had for him were tabled, however, when they settled down to finish running through the plan from top to bottom. The seriousness of the situation was underscored when he got the text from Mos that the cleaner was on the ground with a crew and awaiting deployment.

She'd been drawing in on herself all afternoon, even without the phone call. He didn't know if it was pheromones or a matter of knowing her intimately, but he could feel the tension and potential violence coiling just under her skin as the minutes ticked by. Truthfully, he wanted to run this as a two-man operation of only him and Zeke—not because he doubted her abilities but to minimize the potential for trauma, but the potential for failure skyrocketed without her with them. Not to mention she deserved the opportunity to exact her own measure of vengeance. It was only fair.

The ride to the veterinarian was silent except for the classic rock station playing on the radio. This was the calm before the storm, the moment of tranquility before the first waves of violence. He was well familiar with the feelings, and rather than allow himself to get hyped, he focused on his breathing and keeping his pulse rate low.

Everything from their observations of the property and the fence showed the easiest way was through the front. According to their website, they had a very liberal walk-in policy, with no restrictions on the animals brought in. That kind of thing should have been a red flag, but if one was not in the habit of looking for demons, it wasn't likely they'd find them.

They pulled over at a deserted overlook for Zeke to shift forms. In addition to needing to be naked, if for no other reason than to preserve the clothes, going from arms to wings and feathers was something that required sufficient room to accommodate all the changes involved.

Deciding who would be the animal infiltrator was really a matter of pragmatism. Neither of them wanted Cherry to be the one, but Zeke took the plunge because it was more believable that someone might hit an osprey with a car in Chugach Park than a Eurasian eagle owl, at least in this part of the world. They carefully wrapped his shifted form in a blanket they'd snagged from the linen closet and proceeded to the hospital like the concerned citizens they were.

The vet's office was brightly lit, populated by numerous comfy chairs and occasional displays of prescription dog food. Walls were covered in pictures of pets and animals available for adoption and requests for donation from the local animal shelters.

There were a couple free range cats who perched in the windows catching the last rays of the western sun, but there was a distinct lack of humans. They were taking their chances with only two cars out in the lot, but the moment they had entered the building, Cherry only scented two humans in the place, and no shifters.

Vasi carried Zeke in, wrapped in a pile of blankets, as Cherry went to the counter to ring the bell.

"May I help you? Holy crap!" The vet tech who came up from the back was a thin man who couldn't have been older than twenty-one, not too much taller than she was, and who was distinctly unclear on facial hair maintenance. He and his sideburns rushed out of the back of the building to Vasi's side, brown eyes huge as he watched the massive bird shiver a wing and kick out a rapier-taloned foot. "What the hell is that?"

CHERRY

"I hit him with the car," she replied, cringing and doing her best to appear cute and unimposing as she hiked her backpack up on her shoulder. "I don't know what happened. I was driving through Chugach with my boyfriend, and he just fell out of the sky and hit my windshield. I don't know what's wrong with him, but I couldn't just leave him there."

The kid nodded seriously. "Of course. Right, you're not a monster." He gingerly lifted the edge of the blanket and saw the massive, theoretically passed out, osprey. "That might be, though." Shaking off his apprehension, he seemed to remember there were people there, as well. "Let's get you a room, okay?"

They allowed him to lead them to an examination room at the back of the building. It was unremarkable, doors on either side, one leading back to the lobby and the other to the testing area. Vasi sat on the bench seat along a wall, still bearing Zeke in his arms.

The vet tech—Brian, according to his nametag—looked a strange combination of eager and nervous. "May I take him from you?" Honestly, he didn't look strong enough to carry a lunchbox, much less a larger than average raptor, but Vasi agreed and handed him over. "I'll be back in a moment."

When the door closed, Vasi fired off a text to the cleaners, letting them know to post up nearby and wait for the signal. Bright, silvery eyes watched her as she took a deep breath and went to the door leading to the lobby.

"You got this?"

She knew if she said no, he wouldn't think any less of her. It was a comfort. She also knew that no matter what happened with this, he'd fight for her, so she gave the only answer she could. "I'm good."

He was across the room in a flash, wrapping her in a tight embrace and lifting her into him for a deep, but brief kiss. "Keep yourself safe, Sweets," he whispered against her lips, his forehead pressed to hers. "However, you have to. Promise me."

"Pinkie swear, Feathers." She nodded and ducked out of the room to head down the hall 'in search of a bathroom.' In truth, she was headed to find the doctor's private office in hopes of digging up the trail of the missing women. She'd bet money they were on the property somewhere. It was like she could feel it, the irritating itch of familiarity under her skin. Maybe it was the building itself, or the scents that swirled around her, but she was more convinced than ever that she would find them. How and in what state remained to be seen.

The bathroom was empty, and she crept down the hall, looking into the door windows for each exam room she passed. She wasn't much for sneaking around in human form, which didn't use her hunting skills to their greatest advantage. She came to a door with no windows and the doctor's name on it in gold. It was most of the way closed and would have passed as such if she hadn't been right there next to it.

"Well, shit." It really was that easy. She tried the knob, not terribly surprised to find it locked even as the door pushed into the room slightly. Casting her eyes up and down the hallway for either her compatriots or the other human she scented earlier, a weirdly heavy creak in the room caught her attention.

Slipping inside, she was immediately confronted by a sight equally familiar and weird. An oddly familiar man emerged from a trapdoor in the floor. The creaking she heard was it opening. The handsome face she recognized from his Instagram, tall, looking very professional in his burgundy scrubs and long white coat as he climbed out and closed the door behind him, scents of fear and unease, sickness wafting past her. "Um, hi."

"May I help you?" It was not a friendly offer of aid, despite the words, eyes narrowed, and lips curled up in a snarl. He had a few inches on her, and probably outweighed her by twenty pounds, but that never once crossed her mind as a concern.

Of course, a lot of her hunting skill came from being brazen as fuck. "What's down there?"

She watched his hands carefully as he advanced toward her, keeping himself between her and the trapdoor. "Miss, you shouldn't be back here." That was all the warning she got before he charged into her, shoulder first, hitting her dead in the solar plexus and knocking her back into the older metal file cabinet behind her. The bite of metal digging into her shoulder was distracting, but not enough for her to miss the fist he launched toward her jaw.

They tussled a bit, him swinging at her and making attempts to grab her, and her ducking out of his grasp like an afternoon game of tag. The one good hit he landed on her shoved her into the door to the hallway, locking and latching it as they pressed against it. The doctor grabbed a handful of her shirt and tried to twist her arm behind her to subdue her, and she knew her playtime was over.

Cherry grinned in his face, making to bare her teeth to him as she let them lengthen into her mouth, her vision sharpening as she slipped between forms. She could smell the moment the adrenaline dumped as his lizard brain kicked in, and he suddenly realized he was fighting for his life. His grip on her wrist tightened as he committed to his terribly lazy armbar, and when that failed, he threw himself into her again, managing to knock her off her feet and onto her back.

It didn't take much to flip them over, though, her muscles loose and conditioned to flex in ways abnormal to the human body. She twisted and rolled them over, kneeling with a knee on either side of his chest as he flailed from the floor. He reached up to grab her throat, and her instinct took over. His wrist in her mouth, she shook her head until his arm came loose at the elbow and tore free.

She figured the shrieking would alert her raptors and was

proven correct moments later when Vasi and Zeke came barreling through the door, blasting it off its hinges with their combined force. They both skidded to a halt at the sight in front of them, the man crumbled to an undignified heap on the floor in the midst of a rapidly expanding pool of blood, and her snarling with a face and teeth steeped in gore and one disarticulated forearm in her hand.

"I had it under control." She was panting and wiped the wetness from her mouth with the bottom of her shirt, annoyed when all that did was smear it around.

Zeke shrugged with a rakish grin. "Clearly." He was remarkably comfortable in his nakedness as he knelt over the doctor's body. "If he's not dead now, he will be shortly."

"Eh." She wasn't terribly interested, tossing the arm to the side and rubbing her face. The doc wasn't the only one feeling the effects of adrenaline, and now that the danger had passed, she felt the fine tremors that usually came over her after a battle.

Vasi helped her to her feet, taking in her disheveled hair, ripped shirt, and the blood she could feel running down her chin. "Are you all right?" he demanded urgently, cradling her face in his hands.

The osprey snorted and pushed to his feet. "Look at her, she's glorious." Glancing back at the body, he grimaced. "You think he'd mind? Nah, probably not."

Cherry looked on in utter amazement at Zeke's comfort stripping the good doctor of his scrub pants and donning them himself. They stopped at his shins, and even as muscular as he was—which, holy V-line and eight pack, Batman! —with his shaggy hair and scruff, he looked like an island castaway or a kid who'd been violently mugged by puberty overnight.

All right, then.

"What happened?" Vasi asked. He seemed physically incapable of being more than a foot from her at any given point in time.

She shrugged into the leather office chair that was rolled under the desk. "I found the office. The door was locked but not latched. I went inside and caught him coming out of some weird-ass hole in the floor by the plant, and he charged me." She leaned over her knees, resting her head in her hands as she collected her thoughts. Shoving her curls out of her face, she blew out a sigh. "I think if he was trying to keep his hobby a secret, it's all out in the open now."

"We just have to get to it." Zeke walked over and found the spot she pointed to immediately. Jumping up and down on it, the door didn't budge, and the floor barely gave any indication that anything was amiss, like the hinges were invisible. "It's gotta open somehow."

Looking around the room, there was nothing that stood out to her as something they could use to unlock, or pry open the door. "Can either one of you pick a lock?"

The osprey sauntered over to the doctor's body, the cocky strut looking surprisingly sexy for a dude in highwaters and bare feet. He dipped into the pocket of the white coat and came up a moment later grinning. "No, but I can pick a pocket." He twirled a ring of keys around his finger playfully.

Vasi snatched them mid-spin and went to check for some kind of external lock, sending him an air kiss over his shoulder. "Doesn't count as pickpocketing if you loot a corpse."

"He's still not dead yet, just knocked out. It totally counts," Zeke argued.

"Hypovolemic shock is not a technicality."

Their snarking was trying her patience. "Boys, can we focus? Please?"

VASILY

When no lock revealed itself, they set about exploring the room in hopes of finding a way inside the trap door. The doctor kept a surprisingly densely packed office, walls lined with file cabinets and an ornate wooden desk in the middle of the room facing the door with an open laptop on it. There was even a remarkably sized but drooping philodendron on the floor in the corner. As evil lairs went, it was all surprisingly ordinary.

"This is disappointing," Cherry grumped, putting a voice to his thoughts. "You'd think he'd want a quick escape route in place if he needed it."

He hummed in agreement and closed the door behind them to keep out the prying eyes of anyone who happened to show up, eyes catching on her as she began a thorough and systematic search of the desk exterior. Her thoroughness was impressive.

Between him and Zeke, they deposited the doctor's body by the desk and unlocked and rifled through the file cabinets. There was nothing to be done about the blood trail, but at least there wasn't a corpse sitting in the middle of the room. The cleaners would be on the property, and soon, and would likely go over this for anything they might have missed or wasn't in their purview, but at that moment, the goal was clear.

"Does this strike anyone as weird?" Zeke asked, snagging a rubber band out of the pen cup on the desk and tying his hair back out of his face.

"What?" she asked, feeling inside the middle drawer of the desk.

"Just seems too...*normal.*" He scratched his head and went back to looking.

"Well," Cherry mused while going through the file cabinet on the desk, "if this place really is a front, it helps to look like an actual front." She fell silent as she rummaged, and they all went back to looking.

"Does this drawer look weird to you?" she asked as she cocked her head like she wasn't sure of what she was seeing.

"Hey, Dad?"

The voice in the hall outside the door brought them all to a halt. His eyes met Zeke's; whose vicious grin still sent a chill down his spine after all these years. The poorly-dressed Pandionine shifted over to plaster himself to the wall next to the door, still as a statue as the sound of keys jingled ominously in the lock.

Vasi stepped to Cherry's side behind the desk as the door swung wide, doing his best to puff up and look as menacing as possible, next to his fanged and growling girlfriend.

"What the fuck are you doing here?" Deputy Marshal Benedict demanded as he stomped through the door. He was in street clothes now, flannel and jeans, but the gun on his hip was the fashion statement he couldn't live without. His focus locked on the two of them behind the desk, and he thumbed the lock off the holster as he settled his hand on his pistol.

"Hi, there!" In clear surprise, Benedict whipped around just in time for his momentum to carry his face into Zeke's swinging elbow and send him to the floor in an undignified heap. The osprey's bottom lip pooched out as he gazed down at his quarry. "That was anticlimactic."

"Tell me about it. I didn't even get to bite him again."

Vasily shook his head. *Great, now they're both sulking.* "All right, Sweets, toss him your backpack. Zeke, just…" he gestured absently to the far side of the room, "toss him in the corner." He hadn't planned on taking prisoners today, but the more he thought about it, the more he appreciated their investigative value. The vet tech was likely an innocent bystander, but it didn't hurt to double check. The marshal on the other hand… he couldn't help the cruel streak that blossomed within him as he thought about ways, he planned to extract information from him. He'd promised Cherry he wouldn't kill him, but he would damn sure make the man wish he had.

"All right, Gunny." Slipping his arms under the unconscious man's shoulders, he dragged him over to the corner to prop him up next to the planter. He, too, was divested of pants and disarmed before being left to the philodendron.

"Holy crap!" Cherry pulled files from the drawer and revealed the reason it was so randomly shallow for its size. The back of the drawer held a biometric lock of some kind. The mechanism took up half the drawer and opened with a handprint. "I need him to give me a hand." She nodded at the corpse behind her.

He winced at her terrible joke, eyes immediately falling to the dead veterinarian and his conveniently dismembered arm. Zeke guffawed at her terrible pun, almost doubling over in his amusement. "Oh, I *like* her, Gunny. If she wasn't already your girl, I'd be making a play for her myself."

He was pretty sure the blush in his cheeks undid any sternness he may have attempted to give her in his disapproving glare as he presented her with her chew toy. Other than a wink and a knowing grin, she accepted it mercifully without comment.

Carefully, she wiped the palm off before laying it carefully on the box. There was no reaction until she pressed it down firmly with her own hand, at which point each fingertip lit up in sequence, followed by the palm and a godawful wailing groan as the trap door in the floor levered open.

The sound startled Zeke and Vasily into drawing their pistols. "There goes our element of surprise," he murmured as he cautiously approached the hole in the floor. It wasn't much to look at, a darkened stairwell with metal steps leading down to a well-lit area with a poured concrete floor.

Cherry tilted her head to one side and then the other, stretching her neck and rolling her shoulders while blowing out a breath. When her eyes met his, he knew anyone they came across from this point was in for a lethally painful time. "Eh, fuck 'em. I want them to know I'm coming."

"'Look upon me and despair,' huh?" The osprey elbowed her with a wry grin before preceding her down the stairs. "Yep, Brețcu. If she wasn't your mate, man, she damn sure would be mine."

"Shelley? Really?" he asked as he followed Zeke down the steps. He noted the biometric keypad at the base of the stairs. This was all surprisingly high tech.

Zeke pursed his lips with a smug little smirk. "She seems like the literary type."

"He's not wrong," Cherry teased as she followed them into the underground area.

It wasn't until the door clicked shut behind her that the realization hit. "Fucking hell."

"What's wrong?" she asked, looking between him and the now-sealed door.

Zeke picked up on it right away and nodded grimly. "If we have to get back out this way, we're gonna need another hand." Somehow, the joke wasn't any more amusing this time than it was the last.

"Then I guess we'll have to pick one up on the way."

WINGED GUARDIANS

Chapter 12

CHERRY

Before they got to the bottom of the stairs, Zeke stopped short, fist in the air, and Vasi followed up with a hand splayed on her chest. The look he gave her over his shoulder pinned her in place as the two men advanced in tandem. For all her earlier bravado, seeing the men with guns concerned about a situation brought her up short.

The burst of gunfire down the hallway at the mouth of the staircase stole her breath as her body fought the simultaneous urges to cower out of the way and to shift on the spot all fur, fangs, and claws. Bullets buried deep in the concrete walls, sending up tiny puffs of dust and chunks of debris as Vasily and Zeke took up spots in the stairwell, returning fire around the corner. All at once, there was silence, the kind of quiet that made her afraid to breathe as the walls pressed in around her. And then came the alarms.

Gunpowder, cordite, and blood filtered into her senses, sending her already racing heartbeat higher, her ears full of the sound of rushing blood and the constant throb of an overhead klaxon as panic clawed at the edges of her mind. She couldn't breathe, couldn't think. The only feeling was her skin tingling as her body flooded with adrenaline.

It struck her then that the scent quickly dissipated. The air underground was weirdly artificial, like they had some kind of scrubbing system in place. It went from firefight to oddly antiseptic with an undercurrent of oranges, and the sense of deja vu made her stop walking to get control of the bile rising in her throat. Her skin prickled with a faint sheen of sweat as she felt the squadron of butterflies in her stomach start their bombing runs.

Part of her discomfort came from not being able to smell anyone. Normally, she could scent a building walking through the door and know the number of occupants and little tidbits about them. Were they pregnant, sick, upset, joyful? Here, though, here the growing scent of orange cleaner and raptors chilled her to her soul.

"Sweets, you with me?" The tone of his voice and the look on his face told her he'd been trying to get her attention for a minute. He had to lean closer to her to be heard, and had a hand out like he wanted to reach for her but stopped just short of touching her. Probably for the best.

Nodding shakily, she pushed away from a concrete wall she didn't remember leaning against. Making it to the bottom of the stairs, the larger, brighter room actually made it a little easier for her to breathe. "I'm good." She wasn't, but they didn't have time for her to get it all the way together.

Slate blue eyes narrowed in skepticism, but he didn't challenge her outright. "All right. I asked if this looks familiar to you."

Looking around, she made a conscious effort to catalogue her surroundings as opposed to letting her traumatized subconscious do all the work. The walls here were on the yellowish end of the green spectrum, and this floor was poured concrete without the polish, but she knew damn well this was the place. "Not yet, but it's the same place...and I don't know how many people are here."

Zeke nodded grimly. "All right, then. Gunny n' I'll take point, and you follow up. We assume everyone we come across is hostile unless otherwise indicated." She and Vasi nodded, following the osprey as he led them down the hallway, stopping at the bodies of the men they'd shot to check for a pulse and take their weapons and any spare magazines they had. Tucking a weapon and magazine in the waistband of his scrubs, he stowed the rest in her backpack as they continued on their way.

If it reminded her of the opening sequence to a video game, she wasn't going to mention it.

Vasi had his phone out, attempting to text even as they stealthily advanced down the long corridor. "Fuck!"

"Problem?" Zeke's soft tone was conversational enough, but his body language was razor sharp.

"I can't get through to the cleaners down here."

The osprey shook his head and muttered a curse. "What's that mean?" she asked. This whole 'Jason Bourne with Wings' thing was still pretty new to her.

Vasi's lip curled as he shoved his phone back in his pocket. "Well, other than the fact we have a prisoner and a couple bodies upstairs in need of transport, it means we have no backup in case shit gets hairy." Yeah, that sounded pretty bad in her mind.

"Easily solved." Zeke pulled the pistol from his waistband and offered it to her, handle first. When she grabbed it, he nodded. "No more prisoners."

The heavy weight of the gun in her hand was startling. "Wait. What—?" she asked, but they were already moving on down the way toward a set of double doors. The alarm was so loud it was starting to fuck with her equilibrium, every throb of the noise sending her stomach on a churning roll. They couldn't get that off soon enough. "What do I know about carrying a gun? I write about war zones, I don't participate," she grumbled.

"Business end goes toward what you wanna hit. It's a new day for everyone, Sweets."

The hallway was wide enough for them to walk three abreast, but she kept behind her raptor protection squad, admiring the way they moved in perfect tandem like they'd done this a thousand times. That made sense, considering. All at once, the hallway spilled into a large round room, though entry was made difficult by the absolute wall of noise.

Given the resistance they encountered when they came down the stairs, the lack of drama leading into the room was…concerning. One of the chairs was still spinning like it had been recently abandoned.

"Spooky," she whispered, taking in the whole room.

There were more file cabinets down here, monitors on the wall that showed views down each hallway, including the one they'd just come from with the bodies laid out and bleeding on the floor, and a few grayed out night vision shots of rooms with several people in them. Gaunt animal faces with shining white eyes in the infrared lights, it stoked her rage to the point she felt her claws extending from her fingers.

Shaking off her desire to kill the next person she saw; she went straight to the control panel to see if she could make heads or tails of where the people were being held. Labels on the screens had names like Cactus Bear Rose and Jenga Kickball Atom. She paused in her search for the source of the alarm to ask, "What in the actual fuck is this nomenclature?"

Zeke looked up from whatever he and Vasi were reading at one of the file cabinets. He wandered over and cocked his head with a thoughtful expression. "Huh."

Watching him pull out his phone, Cherry grew even more confused. "Do those words mean something to you?"

He held a finger and resumed his agile swiping across his screen. "Possibly." He light eyes gazed at the screen and then he swiped some more. "Huh."

"I'm gonna need a little more than that, boss," she snapped. She knew impatience wasn't helpful, but damn if she could help it. Just being in this place made it hard to keep her human form.

"Sweets come see me," Vasi called from his place at the cabinet. He had several folders open and was comparing pages in what looked like Cyrillic.

"What's going on over here, Feathers?"

"Client lists, money transfers, looks like someone's been keeping the books down here for a fairly palatial, blackmail-based retirement fund. This shit reads like Ted Bundy's resume." The rage in his voice was carefully banked, but she could smell the rising levels of adrenaline in the air as this went on.

"Got it!" Zeke exclaimed, holding his phone triumphantly aloft over his head.

"Where are they?" She wanted nothing more than to get down to the women and get them somewhere safe.

"These names are the surface coordinates of two locations in a grid format. It's like GPS but more accurate. There's this thing," he started to explain whatever his awesome discovery was—something about a three-word location—but she could barely process the words for the noise.

"One sec." Holding up a finger, she raised the pistol in her other hand and aimed at the speaker closest to them. Before she could get a round off, the room went totally dark and silent, the sudden change almost enough to make her swoon. No lights, no monitors, no alarms, nothing, it was like all the air got sucked out of the room at once.

"Everybody relax, we're fine." Vasily's voice was close behind her, and she'd never been more grateful that he was an owl than in that moment. He sounded so calm and assured, combined with the quiet, she felt her shoulders begin to recede from her ears, and her stomach calmed down.

"Was that us?" she demanded, even as she felt a hand on her wrist lowering her weapon.

One by one, emergency lights over the doors came on, over the door they'd come in through, as well as the three doors on the other side of the room.

"That wasn't us," Vasi confirmed, taking up a defensive position behind her.

As her eyes adjusted to the change, she found herself enveloped in raptors. All three of them jumped at the sound of gunshots coming from beyond the door to their collective right.

"Also, not us."

Zeke's move to the door was barely visible. "Clear."

Vasi joined him after checking the other two doors. Taking her hand, he pulled her aside. "We're gonna go see about the gunshots. Wait right here."

Her jaw dropped open. "Are you serious?"

"Best I can do. I don't wanna leave you alone, but I can't send Zeke by himself either."

"But what if someone comes out while you're back there?" She gestured with the gun toward the doors.

Zeke's pleasantly conversational tone cut through their budding argument. "Shoot them."

The owl had the sense to look vexed even as the osprey turned his attention back down the hall. "Stop them if you can. You don't have to shoot them. We'll be back as soon as we can."

He kissed her then, arm around her waist pulling her into him, molding her against him with his lips on hers like he was going off to war. It was a kiss she could have just as well done without. He pulled back only to press his lips to her forehead before vanishing down the hall with his raptor buddy.

VASILY

"I shouldn't'a left her." It was the feeling he had the moment the door closed between him and Cherry. It was more than he expected to feel, even as he and Zeke systematically made their way to the room at the end of the hall.

His friend was unsurprisingly low-key about his concerns as he moved stealthily down the hall. "Do what you need to do, Gunny. I'll be fine."

"Can't leave you either."

Zeke smirked as they carefully rounded a corner to a doorway of another node-type room. "We'll clear this and be back before she even has a chance to miss that face. Though why she would is anyone's guess."

The scent of blood and death reached them long before they got to the door. It was an atrocity, animal bodies piled on the floor, like they'd been executed, cowering in the corner.

"Fucking hell, Vasily. It's a bloodbath."

They were malnourished, filthy, fur worn in places and all wearing these kind of shock collars that incited the predator in him. When he caught this guy... He exhaled a growl.

All he could think about was their families, the people they left behind. That he could have been one if Cherry hadn't escaped. He swallowed hard against the howl of rage he was feeling and the burning sting of tears behind his eyes.

There were no survivors and only one way out, leading to a cross hall that terminated maybe thirty feet away with another darkened doorway. The first nexus they came to was a cross hall, with one end leading back to Cherry in the control room and the other leading to a staircase with an emergency exit at the top.

"Call it, Gunny."

A quick look up the hall toward Cherry's location and the eternal night up the stairs and outside, and he made up his mind. "We need the cleaners. Now. They're supposed to be positioned around the fence. Go get 'em and bring 'em in."

Zeke nodded and mounted the steps, stopping after two to turn around. "What are you gonna do?"

"I'm gonna find the rest of those women. And kill anyone else I come across."

His friend of way too damn long smirked and shook his yeah. "That wolverine is gonna eat you alive when this is done. I hope you know what you're doing."

"That makes two of us."

CHERRY

She didn't really like quiet. Her thoughts could get going too loud and fast if the quiet was strong enough, and right then, the quiet was industrial strength. The air had just started to recover its normal scents, the faint trail of raptors out the door, the humans who'd been in the room but were no longer, and farther, more indistinct, fear, blood, animals. Lots of animals.

The stark cones of off-white emergency lighting painted the large round room in oddly misshapen stripes of darkness and light. It had this kind of bizarre, funhouse feel to it, but there was nothing entertaining about her situation. The urge to go after Vasi and Zeke was a real, tangible sensation, and she actively fought it with every breath, but hell. She wasn't a gunfighter. She didn't even like squashing bugs if she could avoid it. And sure, she'd jumped in the fight to defend the caribou, but that wasn't her normal reaction. That was her animal making decisions for her.

Cherry backed herself into the darkest shadow she could find, with her back to the wall and a good sightline for all the entry points. She wasn't going to be surprised here, and it was a good place to wait for the guys' return. Her claws extended and retracted as she flexed her fingers, doing her best not to otherwise move and possibly draw attention to herself.

The exchange of gunfire made her jump and stiffen, eyes snapping to the door on the far side of the room. She could see a figure coming her way moving fast, just the one, and her heart sank even as her adrenaline spiked. Setting her backpack and gun on the floor beside her, she waited to see who would emerge from the doorway. It had damn well better be Vasily and Zeke, or she would escort whoever it was to the gates of Hell herself, the long way.

She didn't jump when the metal door banged against the wall as it slammed open. The scent that rolled out afterward made her mouth water as it washed her vision red. There was no holding back her claws and fur now. She breathed deeply as she watched him brace his hands on his knees and pant before looking behind him. The gods had seen fit to deliver vengeance directly into her lap.

Canvas union suit hanging open to his waist, he was dressed in a flannel shirt with sweat stains under the arms and on the chest. Dark hair sticking up like he'd been electrocuted and in disarray for whatever reason, he looked a hot mess, smelled even worse, a mix of flop sweat, adrenaline, gunpowder, and blood.

Cherry grinned as she dropped to all fours and stalked him through the shadows of the room. He never even saw her coming.

VASILY

It was like everything slowed down when he entered the room with the girls. The gunshot and the man standing over an arctic fox's body was the only thing he could process beyond the screaming and howling of the other animals chained up in the room. He fired his gun, but the asshole in the flannel shirt jerked before the bullet could penetrate anything other than the wall.

He was moving without even thinking about it, muscle memory dodging return fire while trying his best to draw fire away from the hostages. Of course, him coming out of the doorway left it wide open for that coward to beat feet into the hall. He turned to follow him, only to see a long line of black suits filing down the stairs heavily armed and coming in Vasi's direction.

Leading the pack was five feet of no-nonsense badass Alectorine in low heels and a slim cut suit. "Commander Breţcu, *konbanwa*." She even dipped her head slightly with a bow.

He dipped his chin in return. "Agent Nakamura, you have no idea how glad I am to see you."

"Funny story about that, actually." The crane's slight smile was as close to amused as he'd ever seen her. "We'd've been here sooner, but there were some snags."

"Just glad you're here now." And holy shit, was that an understatement. Just having her here meant more guns to deal with any remaining threats as well additional protection for the women.

Her dark eyes took in the scene behind him, widening slightly.

"This is significantly fucked up."

Between the number of animals, chains, and collars, he knew he would have nightmares for weeks. "Ma'am, you have no idea."

Everyone's heads turned at the sound of a blood-curdling scream that was cut off sharply.

Vasi was off and running without even saying goodbye. "My mate's down that way."

She nodded at the tall blonde woman behind her with a severe bun and sky-high cheekbones. "Then mine will come with. Agent Skagen?"

They fell in the door as a group—him, Skagen, a quick-footed mink from up north, and Zeke—all fanning out to take in the scene in front of them. As it wasn't the first time that day, even, he felt like he shouldn't be surprised, but coming back to find his mate with blood from her muzzle most of the way down her chest, her claws dug into the man's sides, and a gaping hole where his throat should have been was definitely something to get used to.

"*Iubi.* Really?"

She looked up the moment he entered the room, and the mink behind him stopped just inside the doorway if her heel clicks could be believed. There may have also been some fearful squeaking, but he wasn't going to mention it. Cherry in her full animal form was scary as hell, and he loved that about her.

"You good, Sweets?" he asked again, watching her carefully in case she was too deep in the bloodlust to really appreciate words.

He didn't even see her shift as she leapt from the body to his arms, covering his face with kisses and having a minor meltdown about how worried she was. It wasn't the worst of all receptions.

WINGED GUARDIANS

CHAPTER 13

GWEN

The longer she spent in Dmitri's presence, the easier it was to imagine a life with him. One of ease and intrigue, the power couple of the underworld akin to Caesar and Cleopatra ruling with both an iron fist and a velvet glove. It was a playful fantasy, one she indulged in while she relaxed in the warm strength of his embrace. He seemed to relish caring for her, and it had been a long time since she desired or allowed such a thing.

He lived to spoil her, and Gwen, honestly, enjoyed the attention. They'd spent the afternoon in Tuileries Garden, appreciating the sunshine and beautiful rebirth of the land from the cold shroud of winter, and then he'd spirited her away to Cartier to pick up a demi-parure he'd commissioned in her honor. Earrings, a necklace, and bracelet all in gold and studded with tasteful diamonds and rubies. It was the kind of day that threatened her focus, and though it took much effort on her part, she kept her eyes on the prize. Maybe once she was on the throne, she could afford to dream about more of this life, but in that moment, she did well to remember it was simply a façade.

Dinner was a late meal at Le Cinq, with beef from the chef's own Reserve Privee menu and a magnum of Petrus '45 Merlot that was possibly the best experience her tongue had ever had. In short, the whole day was long on romance and short on anything but leisure and relaxation. At least until Dima's phone buzzed in his pocket during dessert.

His ferocious frown when he glanced at the screen was there and gone before he schooled his features. Holding up the phone with a placid smile, he asked her, "May I take this?"

She nodded and smiled as a server brought around coffee service for the two of them. "Of course."

He kissed her cheek as he rose from the table and stepped into the lobby, far enough away to be unobtrusive but not so far as she couldn't hear him.

"I do hope you have a good reason for interrupting my dinner." he snapped in Russian, and the quiet menace of his tone made her smile. "I see. The accounts...?" He sucked his teeth, and she could easily visualize his sour expression. "And the women?" His deep sigh was one of both regret and resolve. "Fire sale...Of course I mean right now; do we have time for anything else? ...Yes, all of them. Move the ones you can, dispose of the ones you can't. However, you see fit. Must I explain everything to you? ...Advise me when it's done."

Dima's smile when he returned to the table was pleasant enough, only the tightness and slight wrinkles at the edge of his eyes giving him away.

"Is everything all right, my love?" she asked in Russian.

A quick flash of teeth and an equally brief brush of his lips over her cheek were his immediate answer as he settled back into place at the table. "It would appear the Ministry of the Interior and the FBI have some uncomfortable questions for some of our business partners."

"Should I be concerned?"

He shook his head, stirring a single cube of sugar into this coffee and taking a sip. "No, though it would behoove us to transition to Plan D to orchestrate your return."

Her lips twitched as she pressed out imaginary wrinkles in the napkin in her lap. "And is there a Plan D?"

The warmth of Dmitri's quiet chuckle washed over her, the feelings of affection and safety they represented blooming in her chest. "Of course, my dear. Who *do* you think I am?"

CHERRY

Sorting the whole situation out took hours, and night bled into day and then into the afternoon. Thankfully, there was coffee, but damn little else in the way of sustenance that wasn't protein bars. There had been a literal fuckton of paperwork, but more than that, there was Vasily, but not the one she knew.

Commander Brețcu was a completely different entity than Vasi. He was confident, decisive, all sharp lines and edges as he moved through that world. Not that he wasn't confident or decisive with her, but he was a damn sight softer, and she loved that.

There were so many people to inform and appease. So many. From the Deputy Minister to his coworkers, and finally, even a private audience via FaceTime with the new king and his duchess. Missing the coronation had been a huge deal, but since it was for breaking up a shifter trafficking ring, their friendship would survive unscathed.

It was crazy to imagine this was all over. That what had happened to her, to so many others in so many worse ways, was now avenged. Even if the women didn't come home, or as was the case with Bernadette, returned home shattered, there was no one else who would suffer by these monsters' hands.

The scene got even crazier when the number of agencies involved quadrupled, with Anchorage PD, state troopers, and the local branch of the FBI, even the Bureau of Land Management, the Parks Service, and the Bureau of Indian Affairs. Everybody had a piece of this giant-ass mess, and Cherry didn't envy the person coordinating the investigation.

Her editor had even called, wanting her to cover the story knowing she was local. Jury was still out on that one.

When the three of them were finally released, night had fallen again, and she knew if she didn't get something to eat, and soon, she may pose a danger to people around her. Fortunately, Zeke's cabin had more than enough meat on hand to satisfy three predators, and he was more than happy to fire up the interior grill while they cleaned up.

Vasi's running buddy was a bit of an enigma to her. Flirty, but only playfully and respectfully, obviously skilled and lethal, but his whole affect and demeanor reminded her of a laid-back beach bum. He was a contradiction, but truly, kind enough to open his home to them, so she wasn't going to look a gift sea hawk in the mouth.

Zeke's house wasn't too far from the scene of the crime, surprisingly, and it was only fifteen minutes of riding in the back seat wrapped up in blankets so she didn't stain everything before they were off the main road and driving down a path through the trees that looked barely wide enough for the Jeep.

A blast of moonlight through the trees heralded the clearing in front of them, and she watched the darkness out the windshield dissipate with a scattered handful of diamond sparks on the surface of an unnamed pond. There were lights on the far edge of the water, a barely visible distant shore they drove steadily toward.

Zeke's house was a cabin in the sense that it was in the woods and constructed out of hewn logs, but there wasn't a damn thing quaint about it. It was two stories with a steeply pitched roof and a large collection of soaring picture windows that faced the placid surface of the pond and the forest and mountains beyond. It was more chic chalet than rustic cabin, but she wasn't complaining.

Exuberant barks and howls greeted them as soon as Vasily cut the engine. They only got louder as they approached the glass-walled porch that was furnished like its own sitting room with several comfortably upholstered couches, chairs, and low tables, all of which were platforms for the sentient dust mop the osprey called a dog to use to see over the window ledges and bay so loud it made the glass shake.

The fluffy dog made a beeline for them the moment he unlocked the door, and thankfully, Zeke was able to intercept the wiggly missile before he impacted Cherry's shins and got covered in gore.

"There's a shower through there." He nodded toward a door off to the side of the porch while dodging the wildly joyful kisses off his pup. "I'm gonna take him outside, get cleaned up, and we'll get dinner together."

She headed off to the room he'd indicated, pleasantly surprised to find an unexpectedly large shower and bathtub for a man she assumed was accustomed to living alone. It took a few washes to return to a state she'd deem clean, but when she emerged from the lightly woodsy-scented cloud of steam she found a bizarrely out of place Packers sweatshirt sized for a yeti and a pair of cutoff jeans shorts sized for someone who clearly had no ass. Her own clothes were missing, though she suspected it might be simpler to incinerate them than attempt to get all the blood out.

The doorway from the porch opened to a massive room with antlers mounted on the walls and a large spiral staircase to the loft area of the second floor carved out of a single tree in the middle. The furniture was low and blocky, and she could smell the real leather through the door, from the chairs and couches to the hides that decorated the floor. It was oddly rugged, yet luxurious at the same time.

Earl's basso-profundo "woof" greeted Cherry when she opened the door, and he came to a skidding halt at her feet as she made her way inside. The floor was even heated, holy hell, and felt like heaven against her bare soles as she danced around the dog and dodged furniture on her way to the kitchen.

Vasi looked up from his vegetable preparations as soon as she opened the door, giving her a once-over and lingering appreciatively on her bare legs. "Those legs should be illegal."

In her absence, Zeke had ditched the scrubs he'd filched for a neon blue t-shirt from some annual music fest and a pair of jeans that had been washed so many times they qualified as the immaculate conception. He turned away from the fridge with a huge aluminum foil-covered platter and a lecherous smirk. "Mind the asparagus, Gunny, or you're gonna lose a finger."

"Yeah, Gunny," she teased, bending over to make kissy faces with the dog before climbing onto a stool at the breakfast bar. If the hem of the sweatshirt crept dangerously high up on her thighs, well, that wasn't her fault. "Wouldn't want you to cut off something vital. Might have a use for it later." Cherry winked and licked her lips at him, grinning broadly at the helpless whimper he'd been unable to stifle.

An ice-flecked beer bottle settled hard against the counter next to her arm, where she turned to see the osprey's cheerfully admonishing glare. "We've had enough bloodletting today. Knock it off."

Vasily set his knife down and came around the counter to kiss her cheek. "Don't cover up on my account, Sweets. Those legs are a national treasure as far as I'm concerned." The heat of his breath so close to her ear sent shivers racing through her, even as she wrinkled her nose at him. He pressed a quick kiss to her temple and whispered he was going to get himself cleaned up too. "Don't get into too much trouble while I'm gone."

She stuck her tongue out at him but giggled softly as she gently ogled his ass as he walked away. At some point, she figured she might feel bad about objectifying him, but with thighs like that, that day was a long way off. Her happy sigh was interrupted by the scratch of wood on marble as Zeke slid the abandoned cutting board in front of her.

"Less mooning, more chopping." He rapped the wood with his knuckles before tying on an apron and pulling his faded blond hair back into a half-assed bun like she'd seen Vasi do. He clicked his tongue at the dog, who retired to his bed with a highly displeased harrumph.

"Mooning? How old are you?" The question was met with crossed arms and an implacable expression. Sighing, she picked up the blade to carry on where the owl had left off. "Aye aye."

Her sloppy salute was ignored with a flick of his wrist as he attended to the meat, and she continued chopping and eventually rolling the stalks in strips of prosciutto. The quiet between them was mellow as it was companionable, and no would know they were only a few hours out from bedlam at their door and the associated cleanup work.

"So, you live here alone?"

"No." He gestured with his meat fork to the dog crashed out in his bed with his paws in the air by the back door. "Earl lives here, too."

Not what she meant, but okay. "Fair. No wife or girlfriend?" she clarified.

His bright eyes glittered as he smirked over his shoulder. "Why? You looking to expand your holdings?"

The knife she'd been so careful with came down dangerously close to her thumb. "I'm sorry, what? Holdings? No." It took a second for her mind to shake off the shock of his response to articulate her reason for the question. "Just seems like an awful lot of house for a man and a dog."

Zeke didn't look at her again, but his shrug at the stove was dismissive. "I built it myself, as is customary for my kind. I figure the mate will be along when she or he gets here."

Having run out of things to keep her hands busy, she set the knife and board aside and took up her beer bottle. "Kind of an 'if you build it, they will come' scenario, huh?"

He turned from the stove with a grin and moved across the kitchen to a large, restaurant style grill. "Something like that." Once he set the meat down on the prep table next to it, he returned for her veggies. "You good here?"

She nodded and followed him over to the grill with her stool in tow to watch the master at work. He was thorough, meticulous, timing so precise, she would have expected a stopwatch from him, but he was just that good, cooking like it was an innate skill. Clearly comfortable in his own space, and yet he clearly said he was ready to share when the time came.

"Do you normally keep this much meat on hand for impromptu

get-togethers?" The sizzle of the grill and the smell of cooking meat was making her mouth water.

He grunted a negative as he carefully tended the steaks and their perfectly symmetrical char marks. "I was planning on inviting Vasily over anyway, and whoever it was that managed to pry him out of Boston and bring him to this side of the world, as a thank you. I've missed his ugly mug."

That hit her a little sideways. "He didn't tell you why he was coming?"

The blond shook his head, unbothered as strands of bangs came loose to frame his face and scruffy jaw. "Nah, and to be fair, I only asked surface questions. We've been dealing in secrets and behind the scenes stuff for a long damn time, and I figured if he wanted me to know, he'd'a told me."

That sounded like the owl she knew and loved. Though she found it exceptionally curious that he'd left a key bit of information out of his explanation. "Did you know Vasily was mated?"

The question, one that had been percolating in the back of her mind since the Strigine had spoken them aloud, came tumbling past her lips despite her efforts to stifle them with the lip of her beer bottle. There was just something about the universal shock and confusion of his closest friends and family that didn't sit well with her at all.

He shook his head and took up a heavy-looking iron skillet to melt some butter and seasoning in before setting the veggies in for a bit of a sizzle. "No, and I have to say I was surprised, but I'm happy for him. For you, too. For both of you. It's a good match."

Somehow his felicitations weren't exactly a source of comfort. "It's not weird that this man you've known for years neglected to mention that to you?"

"Secrets and subterfuge, dear. In some circles, they're a currency. It's not personal." He nodded toward a cabinet across the room. "Could you grab the plates, please?"

It felt personal to her, and it was just as well that she had a reason to turn her back to him as she did as he asked. Setting the table gave her a minute to ruminate over the conversation without the distraction of pretending to be social. How the fuck was she not supposed to take it personally that it seemed she only existed to him when they were in vague proximity to one another?

There was a lot of old resentment that accompanied that, though, feelings she'd kinda put aside to deal with the whole kidnapping situation that picked the damnedest time to reassert themselves. The light tapping of Earl's claws on the hardwood floor alerted her to another presence right before his scent hit her. As internally pissed as she was, there was something about his scent, and the feel of his arms as he wrapped them around her waist and buried his face in her neck that made her feel loved, cared for. Wanted, even. At least for now.

As politely as she could, she shrugged out of his embrace and moved to the breakfast bar to grab the asparagus Zeke had just taken off the grill. "C'mon. Let's eat."

If Vasi noticed anything, he didn't mention it, keeping the conversation fun and light with Zeke well into the early morning hours of the next day. There was a lot of steak, enough to keep three carnivores exceptionally happy, and enough for her to rein in some of her more aggressive feelings.

In fact, they managed to stay civil and pleasant right into the living room of Vasi's cabin. "So, you gonna tell me what's going on?"

"With?" Cherry winced internally at her snappish tone but figured it was too late to do anything about it.

Vasi locked the doors and made a quick check of their perimeter before heading to the kitchen. "You. Are you okay? You had a pretty fucked-up night, and it's understandable that you wouldn't be—"

She held up a hand to stave off his verbal torrent. "I'm fine." She was too tense and too annoyed to maintain her civility for much longer, and she could practically hear a steady countdown in the back of her head. Trying to buy herself some time and some patience, she walked over to the window and stared out into the night, the forest underbrush a fathomless blackness that let the room behind her reflect in the glass. She watched the owl's approach but didn't turn to face him.

Brows drawn in skepticism, Vasi frowned. "Okay. You're fine. Great. Then why are you acting so strange?"

"Strange how?" she asked his reflection. "How would you know what's strange for me, considering we haven't even seen each other in years up until a few days ago?"

Vasily reared back, steely blue eyes blinking like she'd slapped him. "Oh, wow."

She faced him defiantly. "'Oh, wow?' That's it? That's all I get?"

His jaw came up as he straightened, his body unconsciously squaring up against her. She'd point it out, but there were bigger things to work on right then. "I'm not sure what you want from me."

"There's an honest statement." It was work to keep her voice above a growl, her hackles untufted along her back, all of it. She shifted from foot to foot, trying to dissipate some of the more bellicose energy.

"I've always been honest with you?"

Cherry squeezed her eyes shut at his questioning tone, like he had no idea why she'd be pissed at him. And maybe he truly didn't, and that made it worse. "Don't even. You were honest when you pushed me away all those years ago?"

He drove both hands through his hair and dropped his head back. "I wanted you to have a better life!"

"And you just conveniently neglected the whole 'mated for life' thing, huh? How is that better life working out for either of us, exactly?" She paced around the room, trying her best not to break anything since nothing in the place belonged to either of them. "How is it you tell your colleague, the Deputy Minister, that I'm your mate and you never came out and told me? Don't you think that's something you and I should have probably discussed first?"

"Cherry—"

It was like once that question came out, the rest came pouring behind it. "How is it none of your friends even knew I existed? Much less that I was your mate? Why claim me now, when you know you're just gonna leave again? Are you ashamed of me?"

VASILY

He didn't even have to contemplate his answer. "I have never in my life been ashamed of you. I'm proud of you." Truthfully, after the day they'd had, he had no idea how they'd even gotten to this point, much less started fighting, but he was not going to let her think he somehow didn't value her.

"So proud no one in your life knew about me. How can I be your mate when I haven't even seen you in years?"

The open scorn in her voice was hard to take, but it was a fair shot. "I'm extremely proud of you, yes, but my feelings aren't like you think." She pressed her lips together and blinked at him, and he figured he should continue before she exploded and ripped his throat out. Seemed to be a theme with her today. "You are fucking amazing. You're so smart and gorgeous and funny and…you're everything. Everything about you is precious and rare and worthy of being cherished."

"From afar, right? On a pedestal and out of the way, right?"

"Yes. No. It's…complicated."

"Trust me when I say we have the time," she snapped, folding herself into the corner of the couch with her arms along the back and side. She looked relaxed but regal, and only a fool would approach her right then.

"You've been in my mind and in my heart literally every single day since we met. You know that?" He paced back and forth in front of the coffee table, clearly trying to speak and organize his thoughts at the same time, both with moderate success. "I can't see a sunset that you're not the first person I think of sharing it with. You're my first thought in the morning, my last thought at night, and you're stolen moments in between."

"And yet we're no sooner parted and you dropped off the face of the planet. Why is that?"

He stopped with his back turned to her, his shoulders rising and falling with a deep sigh. "I had...I have a hard life, a dangerous life, and I didn't want you have any part of it."

"Because you thought I couldn't take it?"

He spun around quickly with a look of shock. "What? Noooo... Because you shouldn't have to be subjected to that. You don't need to worry about me. The bad parts of my life should never, ever come near you, much less touch you."

"But here we are, anyway."

Vasily's eyes closed as he kind of wilted with dejection. "Fair enough. The men who hurt you, the ones still alive, will answer for their crimes. This world, the next, doesn't matter. They'll be dealt with."

"So, you'll protect and avenge your mate, but you won't have me around, huh?"

"Wait—"

"For what, Feathers? For you to figure your shit out? You've had *years*, and more than enough ways to come find me if you truly wanted me."

He was not above begging. "I do, though. Want you."

"You have a whole other life, Vasily, that knew nothing about me, supposedly the great love of your life, until today. And suddenly you wanna act like we're a done deal. Assuming a permanence nowhere in evidence." He flinched at her bald assessment of the situation, and in a softer voice, she continued, "You're not an impulsive guy, Feathers, and this level of personal news is quite the shift. So, I'm sure there are more than a couple people in your life feeling a little shocked and betrayed."

He blinked in horror. "Betrayed?" That was something that hadn't even occurred to him.

"Yeah. All this time, I was, more or less by myself. Oh, I had Pace, but it wasn't that kind of relationship. I was alone, lonely, or bouncing from one meaningless cock to the next, doesn't matter." His heart hurt imagining her circumstance and lamenting how closely it mirrored his own. She exhaled deeply. "What matters is I could have had you. I could have been happy with *you*, truly happy and joyful and loved *with you*. And you didn't give me a choice in the situation. You just left without even giving me all the information. How am I supposed to feel?"

Just hearing her talk about it was ecstasy and torture at the same time. It was all he wanted and was terrified to have. "I'm sorry."

"You're sorry?" she spat. "You couldn't even tell your best friend about me like I'm some kind of illicit tryst or torrid assignation!"

"Did I miss the Jane Austen segue?"

She growled as his weak attempt at humor fell completely flat. "Don't even."

Regrouping, he pulled his hair back into a bun and secured it with a hairband from his wrist. "I need you to understand," he began haltingly, choosing each word with exquisite care. "I'm not ashamed of you." If she internalized nothing else, that much he needed her to know.

He came around to the opposite side of the couch, and he meant to perch gracefully on the edge, but the hide on the floor thwarted him and he slipped, collapsing into the cushions like an untethered puppet.

"Sorry," he blew his errant bangs out of his face and started again, "I like to keep the important things in my life, the things that mean the most to me, as close as possible. In fact, the more treasured and precious something or someone is to me, the more likely I am to keep it to myself. I don't share well."

Eyes wide, Cherry blinked a few times like he'd doused her with cold water. "Except that you all but shoved me out of your life and in effect shared me with the world."

"You didn't know my feelings."

"And who's fault is that, again?"

He got to his feet as she stalked away to stare out the window before stomping back over to get right in his face. "So, what now? Now that I know?"

He slowly got to his feet, in love and in agony all at once. "I won't ask you to choose." She had a life here, friends, family, and he would never ask her to abandon that to follow him. He just couldn't do it. As much as he wanted her, needed her in his life, the very idea of asking her to give that up stymied him.

Obsidian eyes widened in outrage. "There's no choice for me to make. Fucking hell. For once in your goddamn life—" Her words were cut off by his phone ringing in his pants pocket. No one called at four a.m. with good news, generally.

He held up a finger and answered without looking at the screen. "Brețcu."

"Commander, I know it's early there. I'm sorry, but this couldn't wait." Xander was not the kind of guy to reach out without exhausting every other option first. Whatever had him sounding so breathlessly urgent on the phone likely merited that reaction.

With a look of apology to Cherry, he asked, "What do you got, Xan?"

"Dev and I were looking over the prelim reports you filed with the Interior that somehow ended up in our email…"

Fucking Mos. "…And?"

"And some names from the documents you recovered match up with another case we have open." The meaningful pause filed in all the blanks he could have had.

All at once, it was a billion degrees in the room and his heart felt like it was going to pound out of his chest. "I'll be there in twelve hours. Faster if I can lean on Mos."

"See you this afternoon, Vasi." The relief in his voice was evident. "Safe travels."

When he slipped the phone back into his pocket, he felt the withdrawal of her feelings like a cold, black wind settling around him. "All right, then."

"Sweets—" He reached for her, but she agilely dodged his attempt.

"Nah, Feathers. We're done." She sniffed, backing away from him one step at a time. "I guess I get closure this time, so there's that. But your priorities now are what they've always been. I knew better than to want more, and I did it anyway. I hate that you bring that out in me. That vulnerability. I guess that's my lesson here."

"Cherry—" he tried again, taking a step as he reached for her.

"No. Don't." She held up a hand to stop him from making contact and headed toward the door. "Have a safe trip back. Thank you for your help. I'm sorry for—I'm just sorry."

And she walked out into the night. The sound of his heart breaking sounded a lot like a Jeep Wrangler's tires on gravel pulling down the drive.

WINGED GUARDIANS

CHAPTER 14

CHERRY

"So… you left. And then he left, correct?"

Because of a business trip for her best friend, it was two whole weeks before she could spend time with Pacey. Cherry made up for it by camping out for the weekend. Two nights on her best friend's futon in her guest room measured in pints of ice cream and Netflix baking shows, but the blonde had pretty much hit all the high points. "Yeah, that's about it."

Pacey clicked her tongue as she moved deftly around the kitchen like some kind of manic baking fairy. She was supposed to be baking cupcakes for the FOP Auxiliary Bake Sale but right then it looked like she was practicing straight witchcraft right there at the counter. "And he left the first time because he didn't want to tie you down to life with him before you were ready. He wanted to give you room to learn how to be you."

Cherry leaned against the counter with her arms crossed. This was not the takeaway from the conversation she expected from her best friend. "Ummm...."

"And," she continued mixing up the batter, turning up the speed on the hot pink stand mixer when Cherry attempted to interject. "This time, he came running when you called. With a gunshot wound apparently, and helped you get justice for yourself and those women. And then, afterwards, you shoved him away with both hands."

She winced, cringing slightly at the description. "I wouldn't say—"

With a flick of the wrist, the room fell into stillness as the mixer cut out, leaving them with silence and a silicone spatula between them. "Did you push him away because you don't reciprocate his feelings? Or was it that you were still deeply hurt by him leaving the first time, and seemingly having a life where you didn't even exist, that you wanted to be the one to leave first this time?"

This was quite the change of heart for a woman who threatened to kill Vasily and hide his body not too long ago. "Who are you and what have you done with my best friend?"

"This isn't about me," Pacey replied calmly as she flipped the page in her cookbook. "Let's just say I have a fuller picture at this point and have adjusted my understandings accordingly. Can you say the same?"

She pouted rather than answer the query. Watching as the blonde did her culinary cha-cha with cupcake liners and a measuring scoop for exactly uniform confections. When she put the first couple batches in and started on making the frosting, Cherry retired to the kitchen table with a flounce.

"I want him to choose me, choose us. Is that so hard? It's like he can't get out of his own damn way to be happy." A beater from a hand mixer appeared in her face covered in fluffy white buttercream. "Thank you," she grumbled around the frosting-covered finger in her mouth.

"So, to recap, he's in love with you but terrified about forcing you into a decision so he runs. You're in love with him and you're angry he won't choose to stand and fight and be something to each other. Together. About right?"

She plucked a napkin from the holder on the table and set the now-naked beater on it. "More or less."

"Alright then." Pacey dragged her glittery pink manicured finger through the fluffy sweetness on her beater, smearing it on her tongue like she was savoring it, staring up at the ceiling thoughtfully. "Easy fix. Choose him."

"I'm sorry?"

"Go to Boston, show up on his doorstep. He needs to know that *you're* choosing *him*. For him." She scooped up the beaters and headed over to the sink to wash them off. "You love him, be with him."

"But what about the rest of my life?"

"What? Your job? Online. Your apartment? It's a rental. Your family? You barely see them now, Me? Shit, I'll come out to visit or you'll come here." Taking both of Cherry's hands in hers, she gracefully knelt by her chair. "The only thing stopping you is you. Go and get your man." She rose just in time to catch the dinger on the oven. As an afterthought over her shoulder, she continued, "And get the hell off my futon."

Cherry was caught between a squawk of faux outrage and a laugh, and it sounded like she was deepthroating a grapefruit as she got to her feet. "Really?"

Pacey nodded as she set the pans on cooling racks. "Daniel's sister is coming to visit next week from Seattle, and I need the space." At Cherry's pitiful whine, she looked up with a wink. "I love you very much, but yeah. Go, be grown. Get your shit together. Also, you're gonna need a dress."

Cherry headed out to the room she'd claimed and gathered her stuff into a duffle bag she dug out of her best friend's closet. "The fuck do I need a dress for?" she called down the hallway.

Pace cocked her head to the side, staring at her with an expression that indicated the answer was self-evident. "The royal wedding's in five days."

"What's that got to do with me?"

The baking blonde appeared in the doorway as she hefted her bag onto her shoulder and turned to leave the room. "Just where do you think Vasily is going to be, genius?"

"Oh." She was left blinking as her best friend took her by the arm and steered her toward the front door. "Right now?"

Her very human friend growled in exasperation. "Yes," she confirmed. "Also, you're gonna need an epic hat."

Of all the places in all the world, the last place Cherry expected to end up that day was on the doorstep of Zeke's cabin. She could hear Earl inside, barking his fluffy little fool head off, defending his territory from marauders, invading Huns, and what-have-you, but it only made her more anxious as she waited by the front door.

Was he even there? His pickup was parked out front but that didn't mean anything. He could have taken off on foot or flown out, she had no way of knowing. The strap from the heavy canvas duffle on her back dug into her shoulder as she shifted from foot to foot staring out across the lake. The deep green of the trees faded into darkness of the forest floor, and there were so many competing scents, she couldn't settle down to sort through all the input. This was a bad idea. She shouldn't have presumed. She should have—

"Fancy seeing you here."

Cherry blinked, startled enough she missed Earl settling down and the front door opening behind her. "Zeke!" her voice came out all squeaky and she cleared her throat a couple times to cover her embarrassment. "Um… I'm sorry to just show up unannounced. But I need a favor. A couple of them, actually."

Green eyes traveled from her very proper bun to her Deadpool on a unicorn t-shirt to her jeans and ended at her canary yellow with white daisy banded flipflops. She never traveled without them. He unlocked the door on their trip back up. "I'm sure this'll be entertaining. Come on in."

"We're not killing anyone this time, I swear," she promised as she scooted in the door.

He chuckled warmly as he shut the door behind her. "You say that now."

WINGED GUARDIANS

CHAPTER 15

GWEN

Nights in the French countryside were soft by their very nature. With soft strains of jazz floating in on delicate violet and rose scented breezes, the night air and brightness of a waxing Sugar Moon brought her a soul-deep peace. They made it easy to forget the direness of her situation. Stretched out on a chaise on Dmitri's balcony that overlooked his gorgeous gardens, she luxuriated in the relative quiet of the evening, fur out and wolf form on full display.

Dmitri's purr as he joined her on the porch gave him away, almost at the same time as his scent wafted past her. The lynx strolled by, his tail wrapping lovingly around her muzzle before sliding away to leap nimbly onto the lounge next to her. His tail bridged the gap between the chairs, twining around her back paw affectionately. This time away from her real life had been so fulfilling and restorative, especially in the face of her upcoming challenges.

Stretching with a deep groan, she allowed her fur to recede and felt the moonlight kiss her skin. Gwen reached over and threaded her fingers through his fur, the silky, silvery pelt truly a sensory joy like no other.

"The Equinox is tomorrow. And the wedding is in four days." Its approach had occupied most of her mind since Dmitri had detailed his contingency plan to her. She needed to get back into the US under the radar to marshal her forces, and with the upcoming royal wedding, the Fae had instituted a temporary ceasefire to allow the Summer and Winter Courts to attend the nuptials. That left several less than scrupulous entrepreneurs with a sudden lack of cash.

Their lack is her gain.

With the exception of certain branches of the True Coven, shifter and non-shifter humans were confined to fairly pedestrian modes of travel. Planes, trains, and automobiles meant paperwork, and there was no sneaking around in an airport as a member of the House Lupine. Sure, she could steal one, or more to the point have it stolen, but still, getting in and out of where she needed to be from an international flight was damn near impossible.

Boats, she could stow away on a yacht or a freighter, but again, she was not a heathen. That left more...unconventional, but inordinately faster, means of travel. And those came at a cost.

It wasn't a matter of money. Outside of her royal stipends and accounts, Dmitri had long ensured she had more than enough alternative revenue streams to keep herself in private villas and nameless pool boys for the rest of her life.

The cost for returning to her home turf to mobilize her forces could be anything the Fae deemed of value. The Unseelie were not known for their conventional pricing guidelines. Until she knew what was required, she had no idea how or even if this plan would succeed. A quick glance over her shoulder told her they had but a couple hours to prepare to receive the emissary from the Goblin contingent.

"You'll be home tomorrow," Dima assured her, linking his fingers with hers and squeezing affectionately.

"You could come with me." It was a fanciful gesture, the foolish offerings of a younger, more naive woman who didn't know any better, and yet she felt like giving it anyway. In her heart, she knew his pragmatism wouldn't allow for such fripperies, but it didn't hurt to fantasize, at least a little.

His smile across the darkness was a soft, almost sad, quirk of his lips. "I'll join you when you take the throne." It was more than she expected.

They remained that way, soaking in the encroaching night with their hearts and fingers intertwined for a while longer. At least until the white marble Louis XVI-style clock on the mantel chimed once.

Dmitri lifted her fingers to his lips, his soft kiss brimming with affection. "Shall we?"

With a deep sigh, Gwen nodded and swung her legs over to the side of the lounge to sit up. "Let's."

At precisely two in the morning, a knock sounded at the front door, and they were quickly spirited into a black Rolls Royce Phantom with blackened windows and white leather seats with blackened plum accents. The ride was a circuitous one, designed to obfuscate their actual destination, though the scent of the air when they were ushered from its opulent depths said they were somewhere in Montmartre.

L'Armoise was a club off the beaten path, out of the way from the tourist traps that encircled the hill surrounding Sacre Coeur, with no windows, a metallic emerald green door, and burled wood paneling once you got to the bottom of the stairs. The room itself smelled of licorice and patchouli, though there was a darker, earthier undertone as well that spoke of the clientele.

The walls were paneled, covered in framed reproductions of Mucha paintings behind glass, with the music an intoxicatingly delicate mix of old jazz and samba that sank languorously into the listener's bones like honeyed quicksand. The tables, all enrobed in black tablecloths with white runners under shimmering green tealight candles, were empty save for a single back booth that stood out both for its choice in mahogany wood and red leather accents. No occupant could be seen from the door, but their imposing and heavily armed entourage stood a respectful distance away, looking on intently.

As they neared the table, a being stood, one whose delicate

beauty and perfection transcended mere designations of male or female. He was tall, perhaps even a bit taller than Dmitri's towering height, enviously thin, in a close-cut black silk jacket embroidered with bright red dragons that seemed to move and writhe around one another as they breathed. The embroidery matched his hair, an unnatural ruby that suited his pallor and inquisitive emerald eyes. It was the most unique combination of features Gwen had ever encountered, at once alluring and yet still foreboding.

"Lyncine, Lupine, I am Niemand, of the Unseelie. It is good that we meet," the being opened with a smile that would haunt her nightmares for decades to come. His oddly accented voice was soft and yet just grating enough to set all her fur on edge. It was the first sense she had that perhaps this was not a wise course of action. Of course, to get what she wanted, uncomfortable compromises must occasionally be made.

"Mr. Niemand," Dmitri nodded but did not offer a hand. "It is kind of you to take our audience." With a surreptitious nudge, he directed Gwen to have a seat in the booth, closest to the wall but leaving his left hand free in case they needed a quick exit. Not that they'd get very far, considering their location and the number of Faefolk between them and the door.

The Goblin took their seat as well, a momentary shift of silks and arrangement of unnaturally long limbs. Food was immediately brought to the table, delicious-smelling canapes and tiny petit-fours that looked too pretty to eat. Not that they would be eating, since everyone present knew better than to dine on the Fae's offerings. They did it as a nod to more human customs, and as an amusing trap for the unwary. Neither of those things applied here.

"I am told, Graceful Lupine, that you have a request."

"I do." Everything about this interaction felt like a legal deposition, and she made a point of answering only the question asked and volunteering nothing, Each word between the three of them chosen with the utmost succinctness and care.

"Ask for what you truly want, then, and I shall give you what you truly need."

"For a fee."

His lips twitched into an almost grin. "But of course. Commensurate with the request."

"Naturally." Her own smile unfurled. At its heart, every interaction was a negotiation, and with negotiation came manipulation, and that was where she shined.

"Graceful Lupine, what is it that you desire?"

"Transport, quick, clandestine, and protected."

His eyes twinkled at her exacting turn of phrase. "In exchange for?"

"Money is not an issue."

"What use has a Goblin for money?" he hissed, clearly offended at the offering. "Simply by being here, I am in violation of several treaties, between my people, your people, and numerous others. Money as you know it, while a useful resource in your world, is of very little worth in mine."

Now they were getting somewhere. Having a Goblin at her beck and call could be quite useful in the coming days. "Then what may I offer you in exchange?"

"I seek an alliance, the Unseelie and the kingdom of Therantia united against the Summer Court. Such a thing would bring legitimacy to the grievances of my people."

"And great prestige for yourself as well."

"Naturally."

"And what makes you think that is within my power to give you? Therantia has a new King, and as you can see, I am not there."

"New kings come, and new kings go, do they not?"

She grinned broadly at their tacit implication. Someone had done their homework. "This is true. Ruling a kingdom is a very precarious position indeed."

"And then, of course, there's the matter of collateral."

"Collateral?" Dmitri, who'd been sitting by silently as they navigated the exchange, stiffened noticeably next to her. Niemand's green eyes drifted in his direction before focusing back on her.

"Not that I anticipate failure, of course. Merely the cost of doing business."

"Of course," she agreed with an accompanying nod. "What sort of collateral would please you?"

"Something rare and precious." They sipped their drink, sly smile showing a hint of several unsettlingly sharp teeth as they glanced at her seatmate. "The soul of a loved one, perhaps."

Now they were getting somewhere. "Not his." She placed a hand on a visibly-shaken Dima's knee in an effort to keep the lynx calm. "But I do have a more than suitable substitute."

"Then we understand each other well." They clapped their hands, and a contract appeared on the table between them with a pen materializing in her right hand. "I will transport you, to the destination of your choice, at the time and place. In exchange for an alliance between my people and yours."

Gwen cast an eye over the document, pointedly ignoring Dmitri's looks of concern. She signed with a flourish and slid it back across the table, pocketing the pen. "It's a pleasure doing business with you."

WINGED GUARDIANS

CHAPTER 16

VASILY

I t wasn't that he didn't expect chaos upon his return to the palace. He wasn't woefully naïve enough to think that would be the case. It was more that he did not expect the magnitude of the upheaval at the palace upon his return.

First and foremost, had been the King's autopsy. In terms of terrible first days back on the job, spending the time talking to first Xander and Dev, followed by the most painful conversation he'd ever had with Finn, he'd been wrung out quick, and the two days that followed hadn't been any kinder.

Telling his best friend his father had been the victim of an intentional poisoning had been torturous. There was so much he couldn't answer yet, many rivers to cross to a good answer, and he was left to comfort this man, who was as close as a brother, with the promise that his father didn't die in vain and that the old man would be avenged. It was all he could offer in that moment besides his undying loyalty.

The crushing guilt he felt at failing the King was marginally eased, if only because he knew it wasn't something he could have exactly stopped. It wasn't a bullet, after all, just an insidious conspiracy he somehow missed in his own agency. Fucking hell…

In addition to closed-door briefings with Mos and Marius, there were updates and developments from both Xander and Dev about the Fielding homicide and the rest of the goings-on in his absence. Missing the coronation had been quite the affair, apparently.

There were several members of the extended royal family still in residence, here to maximize their time in the limelight between the coronation and the wedding, some with their own security details and some requiring additional manpower. Not to mention the associated diplomatic dignitaries in and out of the palace gates at any given point in time. Regime change was a prime time to press the flesh and forge new alliances, especially with the incoming King more focused on his upcoming official wedding.

And then, of course, there were the decorators, caterers, florists, and seamstresses, all of whom required the appropriate vetting and investigation. It was a wonder the two Watch Commanders had time to devote to the side case at all, much less help him with his Alaskan adventure.

The paperwork they'd received from an "anonymous source" was extensive, and surprisingly well annotated with possible lines of later inquiry, but one name, helpfully highlighted with an attached biography, was especially interesting. Dmitri Paskarov was a middleman, the guy who knew a guy, and while he'd been on the radar of numerous intelligence agencies for quite some time, none had ever had anything actionable on him until this. And even this was only the most oblique of associations with the Benedicts.

Honestly, his appearance in the investigation would be uniquely unremarkable overall if not for the picture attached to the email. It was in color, at night, the view of the interior of a very nicely appointed vehicle from the vantage point of the rearview mirror. Paskarov in an impeccable suit sitting next to a woman who required no introduction at all.

"What the hell is he doing with the Duchess of Wolffingham?"

he asked. "In Paris, of all places?" Of course, neither of the other two investigators had answers, considering her last known location had been in Lisbon. Members of the immediate royal family going off the grid only to pop up elsewhere unannounced was a red flag that could be seen from space. It was yet another in a long line of moderately-sized fires in need of attention that had greeted him upon his return. And then there was the personal side of things with his family.

In short, Vasily had been back in town, returned to full duty status—after a lengthy joint lecture from Finn, Cora, Xan, and Dev—regarding his not calling them for backup and keeping secrets from them generally, though noticeably, no one had mentioned him coming home solo, beyond the occasional worried looks.

Somehow, despite not involving any gunplay at all, his friends managed to be just as exhausting as taking down a trafficking ring.

Of course, it could also be the pace he was keeping since his return to keep his mind firmly rooted in the present and not at all wandering back to the northwest in search of dark skin, dark eyes, and incomparable beauty. There was a detailed list of the ways he'd managed to fuck himself, but top ten were the ways he came so close to being with her only to set that whole relationship on fire. Probably closer to carpet bombing or nuking it from orbit than simple incineration.

He knew better than to try to rekindle or what-the-fuck-ever his relationship with Cherry. It was impressively stupid on his part, especially since the circumstances that led him to leave in the first place were very much still there. She deserved her own life and her own happiness, and she didn't need to worry about his.

Grumbling, he made his way into his apartment. He could have chosen to sleep in the barracks at the palace, presumably, but he'd been without his bed long enough that he didn't want to worry his mattress was going to file for divorce. He had enough bad breakups in recent memory to last him.

Thankfully, there was a bagel shop on the way home. His fridge was empty except for some butter, a couple bottles of beer, and milk likely potent enough to constitute a bioweapon, so groceries went on his list of "shit to get to eventually,'" but he usually only thought about it when he was deadass tired from a long damn night at work. He slammed the door with an exhausted grunt, leaving his food, keys, and holstered weapon on the breakfast bar as he made his way through the apartment. Throwing off his clothes as he went, Vasi mentally organized his list of shit to do, including shower, maybe start a load of laundry, and think about how ridiculously lame his life was, that this was his excitement for the day.

Vasi got cleaned up in a hurry, foregoing a shirt in favor of some sweatpants, and set about straightening up his apartment before falling into his breakfast bag. Not that it was terribly messy, but he'd jumped right back into work upon getting back he hadn't really unpacked yet, in addition to the other stuff he neglected. Like food. He set an alarm to wake up early and arranged a grocery pickup for later in the day.

The knock on the door was unexpected. He wasn't expecting any deliveries, and at that time of day, the only neighbor home on his floor was Mrs. McNamara, who was normally watching her stories with her nurse attendant, Julio. He cleaned up the crumbs from his stinky garlic bagel with chive cream cheese and lox, giving some thought to just pretending he didn't hear it until the knock sounded again, at which point he picked up his pistol and slid over to the door with probably a more tactical approach than was strictly necessary. With everything he'd been through in the last few weeks, he figured it was warranted.

Nothing at all could have prepared him for what he saw when he peered through the peephole.

"Cherry?"

There she stood, on his doorstep, in rolled-up jeans and an obscure Monty Python shirt on, hair up in these afro-puffs that should not have been nearly that sexy, with a backpack on her back, duffle bag at her feet, and a garment bag over her shoulder. She shifted from foot to foot, a tentative smile on her lips even as she gave in to the urge to chew on the bottom one. "Hi."

"Hi." Her gaze dropped to the pistol hanging loosely in his hand at his side, and he suddenly remembered where he was, standing in his doorway wearing nothing but a pair of sweats, armed for battle.

The way she casually eyeballed him up and down while she licked her lips was not lost on him at all. "Do you always answer the door with a gun?"

"Um…no." He slipped his gun back into the holster on the back of his door quickly, doing his best to look nonchalant and not at all suddenly anxious and more than a little mortified. Stepping back from the doorway, he held out a welcoming hand. "Would you like to come in?"

She nodded, though clearly with hesitation. "Thanks."

Vasi snagged her bag from the hallway and dropped it on the floor in front of the sofa before relieving her of the garment bag to hang in front of his shoulder holster on the back of the door. "You've come a long damn way. You in town for the wedding?"

Cherry blinked like his question startled her. "I'm sorry?"

"I asked what you're doing here, Sweets." He went to the fridge for his sole remaining beer and popped the cap off before handing it to her. "The wedding's in a few days, and you work for a news organization. It's not really a stretch. So, are you chasing another story already?"

She took a long swallow before wiping her mouth off with the back of her hand. "Something like that."

"Oh, yeah?" He smirked because it was expected and not at all to cover the searing pain in his chest at her admission. Leaning back against the breakfast bar, he asked, "What's this one about?"

He admired her elegant shrug as she dropped the heavy blue canvas backpack by her duffle before sauntering over to stand in front of him. "It's the story," she whispered, biting her lip and looking up at him through her lashes, "of the *tâmpit* Romanian who walked out on me. Again."

Vasily flinched in surprise and quickly found himself trapped between her and the counter. His stomach trembled at the brush of her knuckles as she locked a hand around his waistband, holding him to her as her other hand tangled her fingers in the damp hair on the back of his head, and then her lips were on his, and he forgot how to breathe entirely.

He had no idea how they'd ended up in this position, only that she felt perfect in his arms, her body soft and warm with her nails scraping against his scalp as her lips melted under his. One hand on the small of her back, his other hand tilted her chin just so, both sinking deep into the sensations of her tongue tangled with his, their breath mingling. He sampled her lips again and again. Her hand on his face, thumb running across the stubble on his jawline, sent a shift through him that made her smile as she pulled back, panting slightly with her forehead resting against his.

"What is this?" he whispered, strangling hope stealing all but the barest sound from him.

Dark eyes blinked at him, and he watched her square her shoulders like she was prepping for battle. "Okay," she breathed. Taking a couple deep breaths, she met his gaze firmly and raised her chin. "I'm gonna say this once. I love you, Vasily." She bit it out like she dared him to argue about it. "I came here for you. I choose you for you, for us. And if you ever—and I mean literally ever, I swear on my momma—push me away again, I'm yanking out all your feathers and boiling your damn chicken skin and—"

Her words tasted like joy on his tongue as he pulled her back to him, his body locked in the cocoon of singular joy that was having Cherry in his arms, so close she was almost off the ground. He had never expected, or even dared dream he'd have a moment like this, her breathy whimpers on his lips as he pressed her close to him, spreading his legs to cradle her against his body and growing arousal.

"I wasn't done," she murmured against his lips as she gazed up into his eyes mischievously. Her fingers wandered over his flesh from his shoulders down his chest, leaving goosebumps in their wake as his body came to a rolling boil under her attentions.

"Oh." He nuzzled her nose with a quiet chuckle. "Then, by all means," he offered, "please continue."

Of course, when he dropped his arms to release her from his hold, she leaned up and nipped his chin. "Nah. I think we hit all the high points," she murmured before yanking him back down to kiss her again.

In his whole life, he'd never felt more complete than in that moment. Her lips were perfect, tasting like cinnamon and coffee, and so warm and soft against his. Everything about her literally wrecked him, and he could not remember for the life of him why he'd walked out on her in the first place. Clearly, it was a near-fatal case of dumbass.

"I don't deserve this," he muttered between kisses.

Cherry reared back immediately. "I swear to the gods, if you start going on about what you deserve—"

"Let me finish a sentence, huh?" he chided, unable to hide his grin at her quick defense of him. When she puckered her lips so hard her nose wrinkled, he pressed a quick kiss to the tip. "I'm sorry. For all the times I pushed you away, for the times I didn't treat you how you deserved to be treated. Please stay and let me spend the rest of my life making it up to you."

"Why?" her suspicion was written all over her face, but really, he didn't blame her.

"Because I love you." He pulled her closer, touching his forehead to hers. "*Te iubesc, cireşa mea.* I love you; I choose you, and I'm sorry I let my fears dictate our path. And you know what? You don't have to stay." Her blink of shock more than conveyed her thoughts. "Because if you leave, I'm going with you. If you'll have me, I'll never be apart from you again."

Her silence made him nervous, and her stillness in his arms only fed his trepidation as her glittering eyes of black and copper studied him carefully. He had no right to ask anything of her, even less to hope she'd agree, but the warm smile that stole across her beautiful face made his eyes burn.

"I meant what I said, Feathers. I love you. Good luck getting rid of me." Hearing her reiterate it only made it more real, and despite the exhaustion of a long night at work, his whole body seemed to fill with effervescent joy and light. The kind of happiness that had him lifting her over his head and spinning her around in the middle of his damn living room.

When he lowered her back to the ground, Cherry beamed at him, dimples cut deep in her cheeks and her eyes crinkled at the corners.

"Now, I seem to recall you mentioning something about a job."

NICODEMOS

His office had seen quite an uptick in traffic since Vasily's return from the Great White North. That veterinary office had been a treasure trove for several money trails he'd been quietly looking into, and now he had names attached to them. They also opened up several more avenues of inquiry they hadn't had before.

And then there were the connections gleaned from Xander Colgrove's work. With him and Devon Chilton, it was no wonder at all that Brețcu's ship was as tight as it was.

"Tishia," he greeted his father's assistant with a warm smile. The cherub-cheeked older woman had been a member of the staff since before Mos was in college. "Would you hold his calls, please?"

"Of course, Lordship."

Marius was on the phone with the German envoy to the shifter kingdom, a weasel named Gunter with a penchant for vintage champagne and barely legal twinks, according to Mos's intel. His father held up a finger when he saw him and wrapped up his call moments later.

"I wasn't expecting you until tomorrow afternoon."

"Good morning to you, too, Father." His father's sunny smile was startling, given the circumstances. "Are you all right?"

"Of course! Why wouldn't I be? The correct wolf is on the throne and soon to be married, the corrupt wolf is vanquished and still in a coma. We may not have been able to save Niall, but we damn sure took care of the plot against Finn."

His father's ferocious vehemence aside, Mos was definitely

concerned. "I have something you need to see."

Methodically, and in great detail, he expounded on Vasily's findings from the veterinary office. Names, dates, addresses, accounts, everything that had been extrapolated from the info obtained in the rescue. His father digested every fact and figure with the relentless thoroughness that made him both highly esteemed and deeply feared, depending on the circles. He had the kind of brain that could recall Nicodemos's midterm report card. In the third grade.

"And?" His father blinked meaningfully at the packet still in Mos's hands.

He couldn't say why he held on to it instead of handing it over with the first batch, but Mos knew this next step would be the equivalent of crossing the Rubicon. There would be no coming back from this. With his features schooled into placid indifference, he handed over the final packet of folders.

The Marquise had barely cracked the latest folder when he pinned Mos down with an inquisitive smirk. "Paskarov? Buried the lede, yeah?" He slid his glasses up his forehead so he could read unobstructed. He'd been on the radar of numerous intelligence agencies, but somehow nothing ever stuck. Him showing up here was neither a coincidence nor a good sign. "How the hell is he mixed up in all this?"

"It's quite a bit more complicated than that." With exacting sleight of hand, he snagged a picture from the bottom of the pile and dropped it on the top. It was the same one produced by a deep cover operative in Paris and uncovered by Xander.

"This changes things," the old man muttered, pushing back from the desk and moving to the window. It overlooked the flagstone driveway "The Duchess is still in play?"

"And somehow in Paris. With no record as to how she got there."

Since King Niall first began to exhibit symptoms, Marius had taken a keen interest in his best friend's life, and that of his sons. Finn was, of course, pristine as a church altar. In his business dealings, his personal associations, and his friends. Brendan's life was a great deal more colorful. From his friends and acquaintances, to his choice in pastimes, he was the definition of a wastrel. A profligate spendthrift with a gambling and hooker problem. Exactly the type of person who didn't need the added prestige and funds of being the King.

But somehow, while Finn's goodness was front page news, Brendan's bad boy ways remained merely rumors and speculation, proof disappearing like smoke. It became clear early on that Prince Brendan had a benefactor, one with deep pockets and likely a motivation to keep him just clean enough to ascend to the throne without too much fuss. The only person who fit that profile with any amount of regularity was dear Auntie Gwendolyn.

Of course, all of this was merely speculation, until Brendan began to make moves against Finn to consolidate his position and eliminate the competition. Once that all unraveled, though Brendan was thoroughly implicated, the good Duchess was nowhere to be found...at least, until now.

"Does the King know?" the older raven asked his son's reflection.

"Without proof, I saw no need to interrupt his coronation or wedding plans."

The Marquise turned to his son and nodded. "Good. This will keep for another few days, at least." Resuming his seat at the desk, he gathered all the paperwork in an organized pile. "Agent 61 is still engaged?"

Mos's lips twitched, but he otherwise didn't change expressions. "After a fashion." Agent 61, codename Darkwing, was the person contracted by his father out of retirement. She could certainly be considered engaged.

"Good." The old man nodded in satisfaction. "61 hasn't failed me yet."

If he only knew... Nicodemos sighed heavily and retrieved his sheaf of documents. "Indeed."

GWEN

"His poor face," she whispered, her fingers ghosting over the practical basketweave of bandages that covered Brendan's features. The crow slut and the feral mongrel did this, she was sure. She could almost smell their stink seeping from his wounds. Over her shoulder, she offered, "It was really his best feature."

"Good thing I'm not here to check his teeth like a horse." Niemand's smile was polite, but faint. He was here to honor their agreement, starting with a promissory note from Gwen.

"Considering his jaw's wired shut, that could be a problem," she mused, looking over the rest of him. Heavily bandaged, he was on a ventilator, a heart monitor beeping steadily in the background. She wondered how the cacophonous smells of blood, cleaning supplies, and odd sterility didn't drive him to wakefulness all on their own. It was terrible.

Her fingers trailed down to his hands, bandaged and infiltrated with IVs; wrists shackled to the bedrails with soft leather restraints. He looked delicate and frail, two things she would never normally associate with her nephew, but the longer he languished in unconsciousness, the more they became true.

"Do you have a preference?" she asked the Goblin softly as he lurked over her shoulder.

"Left," he replied, his breath smelling vaguely of cinnamon and clove.

With a look at the door, the Guard's silhouette visible through the smoked glass around the sides of the frame, she exhaled and let her claws extend. It was over in an instant, his pinky finger in her hand, the blood and associated trauma healed by the wave of the Fae's hand.

With a flourish, she deposited the disarticulated finger into the Goblin's waiting hand. "A literal pinky swear, Mr. Niemand."

He nodded and took her wrist, the air filling with the scent of the earthy forest floor with an undertone of decay. It was the mark of their magic, the power the Fae used to move between worlds and to Wander this plane unseen and unnoticed. It was exactly what the doctor ordered. "We have a deal, Graceful Lupine. One you would do well to abide."

A Sugar Moon

SHAYLA

"Are you nervous now that the wedding is in less than three weeks?"

"Surprisingly, no," the future Queen replied with a confident smile as she laid a hand over her husband's. "We've been very lucky to have someone as well-versed and competent as Evan and his assistant Shayla in our corners helping to arrange all necessary elements to make this wedding a success."

"This has all been so fast," the King continued. "Normally this would be a year in the making at least, but," the flush on his cheeks would make every woman in the shifter kingdom—and most everywhere else—swoon, "Cora and I very much jumped ahead in terms of expectations."

The reporter's eyes lit up at the opening. "Of course! Congratulations on the baby news! You have a lot to celebrate, Your Majesty. Anything you can share with the viewers on that front? When are you due? What are you having? All kinds of things."

It was an intimate setup in one of the rooms off the ballroom in the palace. Walls lined with inset bookshelves and minimal furniture save for a desk and chair, a two-person settee, and an armchair for the interviewer. It was both posh and understated, much like the couple themselves.

Though they butted heads on more than one occasion, Shayla had come to like Lady Cora. Pregnancy hormones notwithstanding, the Duchess was kind, pragmatic, and appreciative of her attention to detail. She was also smart, decisive, and model-gorgeous, with a taste for adventurous attire and not afraid of anything. She presented as a predator, though that description was more accurate for her fiancé.

The Crown Prince Regent, now King, was a movie-star idol. Unfathomably attractive, smart, generous, incredibly kind, His Majesty King Finn was the kind of guy she'd pin up on her wall as a teenager growing up. It was hard to remember he was a Lupine when in reality, he was such a teddy bear. Together he and his fiancée were the current 'It Couple', and while the demands on their time were many, so far, this was the only exclusive they'd granted.

The interview with Soledad O'Brien had been on her schedule for weeks now, put there by her boss, Evan Antian. There usually wasn't a reason to have a wedding planner onsite for a press junket, but with nineteen days out, there were still questions to be answered about things like seating arrangements and fabric choices.

As the event planning had proceeded, Evan had handed more and more responsibilities off to her, content to rest on his laurels while he made her run her little legs off. This was the event of a lifetime, a literal kingmaker in the event planning industry, and if it came off without a hitch, he would go down in history with a multi-million dollar business venture, and if it failed, in any part, he could pass the blame off on her and she would never work again.

When everything wrapped, Shayla had a few more questions for Cora about her color choices for the napkins, tablecloths, and flatware. They were tiny things, really, but a grand affair was like a mosaic, a fantastic larger picture made up of seemingly inconsequential tiny things. Answers in hand, she headed over to drop off her work at Evan's penthouse. He was home, or so he'd told her on the phone when she'd called en route, and he had a thing about checking her handiwork himself. It was a tight enough rein to chafe at the bridle, but she knew better than to complain. Even if her name didn't get top billing, if this wedding was a success, she could hang out her own shingle and do a damn tidy business all on her own.

The doorman let her into the building with a wave. She was in and out of there so often, it probably looked like she was some ingénue he was banging. It wasn't worth disabusing anyone of the notion, she had more important shit to worry about than her supposed reputation in his high rise. Besides, he owned the building and thus all of them had to answer to him in one way or another, including her.

The 'up' button was lit when she approached his private elevator, which was beneficial to her as she juggled her unwieldy, and well overstuffed event binder and messenger bag. Scraps of fabric were threatening to burst from a new seam in the binder's spine, and that was the last thing she needed, a lobby covered in taffeta and organza squares.

Shayla stopped to attend to the attempted escapees and was blown off her feet by the loudest sound she'd ever heard. Metal on metal screaming from the doors of the elevator, that were now slightly bowed out and gaping apart just far enough for the flickering interior fluorescent lights to reveal something truly horrible—Evan's arm, disarticulated at the shoulder and hanging partially in the lobby, but no sign of the rest of him.

Screaming had been the only course of action her scattered thoughts could agree on.

The next few hours, hell, the next day or so had been a blur as the police and the Guard investigated the horrible elevator accident, but she had no time to really process or mourn, because without Evan, she now bore the sole responsibility of the wedding and thus had shit to *accomplish*.

Of course, the King and Duchess had been more than accommodating to her, even offering to have someone else take over for her to relieve her of the strain, but Shayla was having absolutely none of that. As far as she was concerned, she'd come too damn far to fail now.

Though she lived in an apartment in Brookline, the King and Duchess had insisted, in these last few days running up to the wedding, for her to take a room in the palace. She agreed, because being onsite meant that she could stomp any fires that erupt before they even get off the ground and she was great with that. So, she headed into the office, two days after Evan's horrible demise to collect her and Evan's laptops, his notes on the event itself, and their receptionist Faleena, who, by virtue of her promotion, was now Shayla's assistant.

With her tiny little Chevy Sonic packed to the roof with clothes, gear, and associated wedding paraphernalia, she and Faleena—who had never been to the palace and had only seen it in magazine pictures—pulled up to the Guardhouse by the gate to check in.

"Evening, Miz De La Cruz," the Sergeant-at-Arms greeted her. He'd introduced himself to her as Malik, a kestrel if she recalled correctly, with his college quarterback build and his million-dollar smile. "Lovely to see you as always." He winked at her before turning his attention to Faleena. "Who's your friend?"

"My assistant, Faleena."

Faleena was a delicate little thing, a tiny Myroxine, who looked a great deal younger than she was. A dormouse, she was generally quiet and shy, but nevertheless her fashion sense was truly impressive. She let her clothes do the talking for her. Facing the rapacious gaze of the Guard, her pale cheeks flushed dark pink and she gave him a little finger wave.

"Lovely to make your acquaintance, ma'am." He licked his lips as he looked her up and down.

A part of Shayla felt bad for the girl, who clearly was not all that used to this sort of attention, but the rest of her was just glad to have his eyes off her. Her own romantic fantasies were a little further up the food chain.

"We'll be staying here for the duration, Malik, at least until we get them off on their honeymoon."

His grin broadened and, for a moment, he looked every bit the Bird of Prey. "Excellent. Well, if you'll pull on in, I'll have one of the valets park your car and bring your things to your suite. Will that be acceptable?"

"Yes, Thank you," Shayla answered, ignoring her assistant's startled squeak in the passenger seat. There was no reason at all not to take advantage of the amenities offered to them by staying at the palace as guests of the King. When in Rome, right?

She pulled over the speed bump she passed over every time she entered the grounds, always amazed that as tall as it was, it never scraped her low-slung undercarriage. This time, however, it did beep, and suddenly red lights were flashing all around her.

"Halt!" Malik called and she froze in place with her foot on the brake.

She had no idea what the problem was but suddenly there were several uniformed members of the Palace Guard there and all were toting some pretty serious firepower. "Yes?" she asked as the Sergeant approached her window.

"I need you both to open your doors, *slowly*," he emphasized the word, so she heard it both with an underline and italicized. "Then I need you two to come back to the Guardhouse with me."

No one else spoke or moved, which was unnerving, but she moved very deliberately as she did as he asked. She had no idea what was wrong, but she certainly wasn't going to contribute to it by balking.

Once she and Faleena were at his side, the other Guards descended on her car like a plague of locusts as Malek led them into the Guard house and into some chairs in the lobby. The instant they were seated, he scurried over to the desk phone and punched in a number.

"Commander Brețcu? Yeah, this is Malek at the Front Gate. Miss De La Cruz arrived for His Majesty and Her Grace…right. She's staying in the East Wing. Anyway, as she was driving in, she passed over the speed bump, and the detector went off. According to the readings and a quick view of the undercarriage, it looks like some kind of bomb. Can you come down here? …Thank you."

Shayla wasn't sure she'd ever blink again. All the blood in her body had run out of her fact and was pooling somewhere in the vicinity of her feet, and she had no idea how to process this. "I'm sorry, what? Did you say car bomb?"

Malek whipped around like he had suddenly remembered they were there, big dark eyes rounded with surprise and chagrin. "Um… yeah." In the space of a breath, he recovered himself, composure firmly back in hand. "The Commander will be down to speak with you momentarily. I'm sure this is all a misunderstanding."

She nodded, knowing she had to keep it together for Faleena. Poor kid looked like she was about to shake apart at the seams, which was not the worst idea ever. Damn this was a mistake. Wasn't it?

The third book in the Winged Guardian series, A Sugar Moon featuring Xander and Shayla will be released September 2020. Pre-order your copy on Amazon today.

About the Author

Alexis (Lexie) is a writer with a day job for the last twenty years servicing her community and its everyday heroes.

Born in Tucson her heart still remains there, but she lives, works, and writes in Indy. Her desire to see the whole country is almost complete (seven states left) and as much of the world as she can (7 countries down, 188 to go)!

She collects fountain pens, perfume bottles, rescue animals, and dirty curse words in as many languages as she can. Her list of hobbies is longer than her arms and legs combined (even though she is on the petite side so that isn't hard) including knitting, crocheting, painting, graphic design, and learning to play the piano.

In addition to 'writer', her life has many roles including wife, dog mom, fun aunt, and ghost hunter.

Lexie's goal is to cram as much living into one life as possible and write about it along the way. You can keep up with her internet wanderings by heading over to facebook.com/groups/LexieLyceum and @Dispatchvampire on Twitter.

Works by Alexis D. Craig

Imminent Danger

Undercover Seduction

US Marshals Series

Give Me Shelter
Bulletproof Princess

Behind the Blue Line Series

The Ex File
Dead & Disorderly

Naughty Bedtime Stories-In Three Words (Anthology)

No Such Thing

Shifted Into Love Anthologies

Love Changes Everything
Lust In The Times Of Mardi Gras
Hotel California

The Winged Guardian Series

Book 1: A Killing Moon
Book 2: A Hunter's Moon

Coming Soon

Book 3: A Sugar Moon - September 2020